Tempus Viveve

A Tempus Militibus Novel, Volume 4

A D McCabe

Published by Mizen Publishing, 2025.

TEMPUS VIVEVE

First edition. March 21, 2025.

ISBN: 979-8230772774

Written by A D McCabe.

Also by A D McCabe

A Tempus Militibus Novel
Tempus Militibus
Tempus Fugit
Tempus Venit
Tempus Viveve

Tempus Viveve
Luca
By
A D McCabe

Book 4
A Tempus Militibus Novel

Chapter 1

Rome 79AD

The sun was beating down on the army as they sat around awaiting orders for their return to Brundisium in the south. They had been promised liberty first and the ranks were restless. Vespasian had sent word via a dispatcher that he would be holding a celebration in Rome in their General's honour.

The Princep, Lucian Marius Antonius, second in command to the Primus Pilus, Octavius, was bent over the scroll, that was spread out on the table. The plans for expansion at Brundisium were complete, and the men would have to show great resilience, even though they faced no foe, they would remain alert and ready. The legions were well trained and disciplined and displayed utmost loyalty to their General.

For Lucian was also eager to leave Rome and get back to camp. There was nothing to hold him in Rome, he was bored. He wouldn't mind a skirmish either, with a foe of equal strength. Of course, to admit that one's enemy was equal, openly would have been viewed as treachery, and Lucian was well versed in what that punishment would be: *Death!*

Lucian looked up as the noise outside the tent became louder and the commotion distracted him. He was annoyed now.

The curtain was pulled aside, and a red-faced praetorian hurried in, almost running.

"Praetorian, stop!" Lucian ordered aggressively and glowered at him. "What has you in such a hurry?" The soldier paused and briefly caught his breath before he replied with a little uncertainty and Lucian saw his eyes dart quickly around the tented room.

"Domine, I have come, haste, from the palace," he said, still huffing and puffing. "News of the Emperor." Lucian stood up straight now and looked with a serious expression at the young soldier.

"What news, praetorian?" Lucian demanded forcefully.

"Emperor Vespasian, has died." The soldier said remorsefully, and he hung his head. "The emperor is dead." Lucian stared at him, not quite sure if he had heard him correctly. The emperor was dead. That was impossible.

"Praetorian, how?" Lucian asked. "Has the Emperor been slain?" It was a possibility, the two Caesars could have ordered it, in a bid to hurry up their ascent to power. The soldier shook his head. "Then how?" As far as the Centurion knew, the emperor had been in good health recently, though he had been known to suffer from bouts of diarrhoea, which had incapacitated him from time to time. But otherwise, Vespasian was in fair health.

"I am unsure Domine," the young soldier said, almost panic stricken as he looked at the Princep.

"That's OK," Lucian said, softening his tone a little. "Take refreshment first and then return to the city." The praetorian nodded and left the tent, grateful to be able to depart from the pavilion.

Lucian watched him leave and then let out a long sigh. He would have to inform the Primus Pilus of course and they would then have to ride into the city and receive their orders from the new Emperor. Await to see who the successor would be. It was usually a quick affair, and Lucian knew who he didn't want as his new Emperor.

Naturally, they would all mourn the death of their Emperor Vespasian. He had been a good leader and loved by his subjects. His successor would have to be very tough and somewhat ruthless. Vespasian would be difficult to replace.

Lucian sighed as he walked out of the tent and over to the pavilion where the Primus Pilus resided. The sunshine was glorious and as he glanced up at the deep blue sky, he caught sight of a young hawk, silhouetted against the sky. Momentarily, Lucian was transfixed by the bird soaring in the air. Free.

He walked into the larger tent where the Primus Pilus' quarters were located away from the soldiers. There was laughter and Lucian called out and waited amid the laughter and the catcalls from the occupants inside the inner room.

A few minutes later, a dishevelled man appeared from behind the closed curtain. Lucian could make out the naked body of the courtesan as she lay on the rumpled bed. He suppressed a grin.

"Lucian Marius Antonius, what insolence is this?" the Primus Pilus bellowed while smiling at Lucian, as he came forward. His tall athletic build belied the softer side that he sometimes displayed with his officers.

"Sorry Domine, but I have regretful news." Lucian said as he watched the most important officer of the legion, as he stood in front of the Princep with his hands on his hips.

"Speak, speak, do not keep me in suspense, Lucian." Octavius said smirking as he walked over to the desk and poured generous amounts of wine into two goblets. His generosity with wine was as legendary as his presence on the battlefield.

"Pilus Octavius," Lucian said sombrely. "Emperor Vespasian is dead." Octavius stopped in his tracks. As if unsure that he had heard correctly what his princep had just uttered, so he asked calmly.

"Was he slain?" Octavius handed a goblet to Lucian and raised his own cup to his mouth and took a lengthy gulp.

"No, Pilus, according to the praetorian." Lucian replied as he took the goblet from him. "He died of ill health." Lucian took a sip of wine and watched his commander as he absorbed the devastating news that Emperor Vespasian was deceased.

"To Caesar." Octavius said and raised his glass and Lucian did the same. "We ride to the palace immediately. Have the guards saddle our horses." Lucian nodded and they finished the wine in one gulp, and Lucien left the tent to prepare for their journey to Rome.

It was one journey that Lucian did not want to make, but he had to, it was his obligation as Princep of the legion.

Chapter 2

Lucian travelled with Octavius to the Palatine Hill, on their beautiful white stallions. The horses were the finest breed in the legion and in impeccable condition.

As they rode along the Apian Way in silence. Each of them was lost in their own thoughts. It was a sad time for Rome, for the Empire, they had just lost their Emperor, and the empire was now shrouded in uncertain times.

Vespasian's two sons, Titus and Domitian would now be locked in battle to succeed to the throne. One was benevolent, and the other paranoid. As it usually followed the stronger personality would succeed the throne, while the other bided his time to dethrone the successor.

Before they had left for the Flavian Palace, Octavius told Lucian how, Rome had prospered under the dead Ceasar, he had restored law and order to Rome after the civil war and although he had come from a humble background, he had cleverly used this to his political advantage. Like the great Julius Caesar, Vespasian had been a man of the crowd, and the people loved him. Of course, his military prowess had also been advantageous in winning him his position of emperor.

Lucian had been commissioned by the emperor, but Vespasian had deemed him too young for Primus Pilus, to command his own centurion army, so he only had the honour of serving the emperor for almost five years as Princep.

They were met on the steps of the palace by Flavius Maximus, Vespasian's trusted advisor and head of the Senate.

"Octavius, it is good to see you." Flavius said as he vigorously shook his hand. "But under such circumstances." He rolled his eyes as he eyed Lucian and asked cautiously. "Who is this?" Octavius nodded and replied solemnly.

"Flavius, may I introduce you to Princep Lucian Marius Antonius." Lucian, a little uncertain, held out his hand to the senator, who shook it with a powerful grip, and then he nodded as he turned back to Octavius.

"Corintus Sesmus Antonius' son?" Flavius asked with a raised eyebrow. Lucian nodded. "A fine Primus Pilus," he said with a certain admiration in his voice. "I wonder though, if his son can claim such an accolade?" Lucian looked at him quizzically, aware that like the Caesar, one didn't avert one's eyes from such a powerful man as Flavius Maximus, if you did, it was deemed an insult. An insult which was punishable accordingly.

"Lighten up, Lucian," Octavius said with a smirk on his face now, "Flavius is making fun." Lucian looked from one to the other and nervously smiled. He wasn't sure how to react. The situation was grave and sombre, and certainly not one which called for gaiety.

"The sons are inside, already scrounging for the crown." Flavius said in a sarcastic tone and rolled his eyes. "The bets have been placed and the winner won a resounding victory based clearly on charm alone, he has already been chosen." Just then a slave came over to them and led their horses away.

Lucian, at a distance, followed behind Flavius and Octavius into the Palatine palace, to the state room where the sons of Vespasian were sitting on separate divans, greeting the mourners who paid their respects to their dead father and their beloved emperor.

Flavius strode over to the divan and looked at both Titus and Domitian but addressed Titus first.

"Primus Pilus Octavius and Princep Lucian Marius Antonius, Dominus Noster." Octavius came forward and bowed his head as he put his hand on his heart.

"My condolences, Dominus Noster." He spoke clearly and then he motioned for Lucian to come forward.

"Your loss is felt by all, Dominus Noster." Lucian said and bowed his head. Titus motioned for both officers to look at him, but his gaze was fixed on Lucian. The weight of his stare was heavy, and Lucian tried hard to not look away.

"Princep, and so young," Titus said in an impressed voice. "I am aware of your achievements in battle, Lucian Marius Antonius." The new Emperor said casually. "I remember well, when Vespasian commissioned you." He smiled widely at Lucian, and his smile was warm, and there was a charm about him. An aura of serenity and lure. "You were young, hopeful and yet somewhat distracted, as I recall. I wonder if my father saw it." Another charming smile lit up his face. "Do I have your allegiance as your Emperor, Lucian Marius Antonius?"

"Of course, Emperor Titus, I pledge to defend you as Emperor of Rome and the Empire." Lucian said and bowed his head once more. He felt drawn to the new Emperor, felt his charm, his reign would be a successful one, the empire would be great once more. The house of Flavius would rule supreme.

"Now, Flavius, show our gallant officers' hospitality," Titus said and turned to his brother. "Come Domitian, we must pay our last respects to father." He arose and so did everyone in the room and parted as the new Emperor, Titus passed them.

A glance of distrust from Domitian toward Lucian, though subtle, was not wasted on the Princep.

Lucian wondered just briefly how Domitian would proceed now that his brother was favoured over him as Emperor.

Chapter 3

L ucian was asked to remain in Rome after Titus was officially crowned emperor. He had been invited to dine alone with the new emperor and over the course of the week, Titus made Lucian a Primus Pilus. One of the youngest ever, at thirty years old. Lucian was of course, thrilled to accept the promotion and the honour. It was what he had hoped for, for a long time.

When he had been given liberty for two nights, Emperor Titus had given him a gift of a courtesan, she had been a favourite of the new emperor. He was known to lavish presents to those he preferred, and Lucian was in great standing with the newly crowned emperor.

Lucian had enjoyed the night with the concubine and then he received his orders to join his Centurion legion in Pompeii.

He walked along the path near the small theatre in Pompeii and was humming a tune. Lucian was feeling happy with himself. His men were also in high spirits and were looking forward to the celebrations which were going to follow the games at the amphitheatre. Expectations were high.

As he walked along the street, Lucian admired the goods on display in the stalls. He could hear the distinctive voices of philosophical debate from the academics as they drank wine and lamented their visions and their beliefs. This made Lucian smile as he walked on.

Lucian was making his way back to the barracks, his soldiers were in training, and he was awaiting orders for where they were to be stationed. He didn't think that they would remain in Pompeii, he had a feeling that they would be deployed to the South and to the province of Aegyptus. A posting which wasn't altogether unpleasant to Lucian.

As he walked, Lucian heard from behind him the sound of a twig as it snapped, but as he turned around, he only glimpsed a shadow, he didn't see who it was. He walked on again, but he was alert.

There it was again!

He drew his sword and called out. "Who's there?" Silence. "Show yourself." The sound of laughter and then the tall awkward figure of Partus came into view as he clapped his hands almost mockingly as he approached Lucian.

"Alert, Praetorian." Partus called out, still laughing as he looked Lucian up and down. He wore a callous expression on his face.

"It's Primus Pilus or Domine to you, Partus." Lucian angrily corrected him. He didn't trust, or like this Princep and he couldn't hide it. There was something about him that Lucian couldn't quite figure, an air of treachery perhaps.

"Indeed, so I know." Partus said and gave a snide grin as he encircled Lucian as he tried to intimidate him by his presence. "But do tell me, what favour did you do for the new emperor to be rewarded with such a title so young. Hmmm?" Lucian glared at him, his command and his loyalty was unquestionable and how dare Partus demean it by suggesting otherwise.

"You are a little drunk, Partus. I am willing to overlook it this time." Lucian said after a moment. "Return to base, and I won't reprimand this insubordination." This made the Princep laugh even louder as he paced with a more intensive gimp.

"*You* threaten to not reprimand me, you, a son of a cowardly pilus, who had brought shame when he abandoned his legion." He walked over to him and stood within a foot in front of Lucian. "You can't reprimand me for anything, you upstart. Instead, you should be begging my forgiveness, by the insult you served me." Partus stared at him with a sinister expression on his face.

"Forgiveness for what, Partus?" Lucian stood still and stared back at him. His gaze was as intense as Partus's, neither of them daring to avert their eyes.

"For stealing what was mine." Partus said angrily. "A parvenu, with poor breeding, a commoner promoted over me." He lunged at Lucian, and they scuffled for several minutes, then Lucian felt the teeth sink into his neck as Partus bit deep. He could feel the droplets of blood as it ran down his neck. The Princep was strong, and brutal. Lucian struggled against him but there was no let up. Partus bit harder into Lucian's neck.

Lucian tried hard to push the older man off him but the Princep was stronger and his teeth sunk deeper into his neck, the pain was excruciating. Lucian could feel the teeth pierce the vein. If he didn't get him off him, he would surely die. Lucian felt his limbs were weakening as he lost more blood.

After what seemed like hours, Lucian managed to push Partus off him. He put his hand up to his neck and then looked at it, he was covered in bright red blood. He glared at Partus as he stood, unsteadily on his legs, he could feel the earth moving in a slow motion, a warm sensation began to envelop him, and he felt weakened.

"What have you done to me, Partus?" Lucian shouted at him, but the Princep just laughed as he stood watching Lucian stumble. "You will be court-martialled for this treachery." He fell to his knees, still holding his hand to his neck which was bleeding profusely. He was in a weakened state and his vision was blurred now.

"No, you won't do that, Lucian Marius Antonius." Partus said in a jeering voice as he knelt beside Lucian and bit into his own wrist and then grabbed Lucian by the hair, as his head was pulled back, Partus let the blood from his wrist drip into Lucian's mouth. "From now, soldier, you are like me. Your body is dying agonisingly, soon you will be dead." Partus stood up, he began to laugh now and for a moment, looked at Lucian on the ground, then he kicked him in the scrotum and walked away laughing. All Lucian could do was roll agonisingly on the ground with his hands firmly clasped over his crotch with his eyes rolling back in his head. The pain was excruciating, but it wasn't as intense as the pain he felt from the pierced vein in his neck.

LUCIAN DIDN'T KNOW how long he had lain on the bank near the Odeon, but as he opened his eyes the sunlight blinded him, and it felt hot on his skin. Burning hot, as it seared his skin. Lucian crawled with great effort over to the cover of the wall with its attendant shade, that provided a welcome shelter from the burning sun.

He raised his hand to his neck, the bleeding had stopped, but the puncture wound was still there. Lucian felt weak, he was barely able to stand. He had to get back to the camp. He had to have Partus arrested for this assault. Lucian would make him pay for this attack.

Lucian decided that he would write to Titus and have him imprison Partus, have him tried in a court in Rome. His treachery would not go unpunished. Partus would receive the fustuarium for his insolence.

He groaned loudly and held his stomach as he tried to move, it was such an effort and he was in a debilitated state, he felt he was dying a slow agonising death.

The sun blazed down as he tried to make his way back to camp, his sense of direction was fuzzy. Lucian had travelled this path many times, and yet, here he was, not knowing in which direction he was going, almost as if he was a stranger in this place.

Lucian knew that he would have to return to base, if he didn't, he could be tried for desertion. The emperor would not look kindly on him for deserting his men, his post or the emperor himself. A fustuarium would be his punishment also.

Was that what Partus was hoping for, when he assaulted Lucian? Did he want the emperor to try him and find him guilty and issue the order for the soldiers to cudgel him to death or if Titus was feeling lenient, he would enslave him? Anything was possible behind Partus's reasoning for doing what he did. Lucian didn't know him very well but what he did know of him was that he was dangerous and that he seemed to hold a grudge against Lucian because he was promoted over Partus. Though Lucian had not met Partus before he was made Primus Pilus, therefore it certainly couldn't be personal, how could it?

Why did he feel so hungry? He had unmerciful pains in his gut, hunger he thought. But how, he had eaten and drunk lots, the previous night? Didn't he? It was the previous night, he had eaten, wasn't it?

Lucian didn't know, he had no recollection of time, or where he was. He struggled on and saw the gate. He recognised it, it was Vesuvius gate. His camp was nearby, near the base of the mountain. He needed to pull himself together. Lucian couldn't have his men see him disorientated like this. If the men saw him dazed and confused, or any kind of weakness in their leader, they wouldn't follow his orders. He would lose all deference. A Primus Pilus without the respect of his men was not a leader.

Feeling a little more determined now and with some direction, Lucian struggled on but was weakening further and hurt by the searing heat.

He managed to drag himself out of the gate and with a tremendous effort he made it as far as the field near the camp. He could see the tents and hear the men training. The sound of the steel blades as they clashed against the shafts, the noise was deafening, almost ear-splitting and it hurt his ears.

Why was it so loud?

Lucian couldn't handle the sound any longer as he fell over once more with his hands covering his ears, he closed his eyes and sleep came, an ease to him momentarily.

When he awoke, it was dark. He was ravenous. Lucian had a craving to eat, a craving that needed to be satiated. A hunger for something other than food.

The sound of a soldier walking close by, alerted Lucian and he sat up. He could hear a thick flowing sound like a river, but he was miles from the river. Then he heard the thumping. Was it his heart? Was he fearful? No, of course he wasn't, he was a decorated Roman soldier. Lucian didn't know what fear was.

The warrior came into view, and Lucian could feel his teeth cut through his lip, and a trickle of blood rolled over the soft skin where the tooth had cut into the flesh. He put his finger to his lip and saw the red liquid. It excited him. His heart began to quicken.

He smelt the soldier, he was urinating against a bush, Lucian could smell the water, the salt and the wine that the praetorian had consumed.

How was that possible? What sorcery was this?

Unless the soldier was sick, with a disease. That had to be it. The soldier was dying. That was the only reason Lucian could smell him so distinctly.

Lucian stood up and walked unsteadily over to his soldier who had turned quickly around and let out a sigh of relief which was quickly replaced with terror when he saw his commanding officer. He quickly fixed himself to appear decent.

"Legionary," Lucian called in a voice he didn't recognise as his own, but the soldier stood deathly still. He was paralysed with fear. Lucian moved closer and he looked at him with his head turned sideways as he studied the soldier. "What's the matter?" Lucian demanded but the guardsman just remained fixed to the spot with fright. "Answer me." Lucian shouted at him and then fell to his knees, holding his stomach. The legionary ran to his aid and as he bent down to help Lucian, but Lucien quickly grabbed the soldier and began to struggle with him.

He was taller than the soldier and within a matter of minutes, he had the guard overpowered and Lucian lay on top of him and grinned down at him. He could see the vein in his neck pulsating, he could hear the blood coursing. Not knowing what had come over him, suddenly Lucian sunk his teeth into the soldier's neck and began to drink from the open vein. It was sweet, good, wholesome.

He drank as if he had never tasted water in weeks, but it wasn't water, it was blood, a warrior's blood. Lucian had killed one of his own men, one of his soldiers, in cold blood.

He was an assassin.

Quickly, and with great effort, he managed to run to the undergrowth of the olive bushes and hid. Lucian could hear his own heart beating now, he could feel every beat in his chest, as the blood in his veins began to flow quickly. He felt invincible. He felt strong, stronger than he had ever felt before.

What was happening to him? What magic had overtaken him to make him kill that man? Lucian had no answers, he didn't know what had happened to make him do the abhorrent thing that he had just done. But what was even worse, was how much he had enjoyed it. How good it had felt to drain the man of his blood. To taste the nourishment that the blood filled him with. Lucian craved more. What was wrong with him, that he had this debilitating craving? Had he done something wrong, was that it? No, no it wasn't his fault. No, the legionary had willingly given his life so Lucian could drink, to restore his weakened body. It was like that wasn't it?

Of course it was!

No, he had taken the life of the soldier, one of his own men. The man hadn't willingly given his life for Lucian. He shook his head. What was he becoming? He was no different to Partus. Lucian was inhumane. He was monstrous. A devil!

Lucian knew that he couldn't remain in the bushes any longer, he would have to move and move quickly. When the body of the soldier was found by his men they would search for the perpetrator of the crime, if caught, he would be taken back to camp, he would lose his position for sure and be disgraced for what he had done. But what if his men found him? Would they suspect what he had done? Probably not. But Lucian couldn't take that risk. He had to get out of there. Quickly.

He made his way around the perimeter of the camp, keeping to the shadows. Lucian couldn't just barge in. His mouth and face were covered in the legionary's blood. He was a mess.

Lucian knew that it was cowardly, but he needed to know what illness he had before he turned himself in to his Centurion.

Partus! He would find Partus, Partus would know what was wrong with Lucian. He would be able to help him find a cure, at least he would know if what he had was contagious. If he was a danger to others. But Lucian already knew that he was. The dead soldier was proof of that.

Yes, Lucian thought, he would find Partus, and he would force him to tell Lucian what he had done and persuade him to help restore his old self, before the sickness could spread. He would spare Partus's life if he told him what the cause of his disease was.

It was becoming light, and the sun was almost up, when Lucian opened his eyes. He was awoken by the sound of footsteps on the ground. He carefully looked out from behind the boulder where he had been hiding all night and he glimpsed, Partus walking up the side of the mountain, slowly and with an air of confidence about him. Untroubled.

Stealthily, Lucian followed him, at a distance and under the cover of the vegetation. He could hear the sound of Partus's steady breath, as he climbed the side of the fiery mountain.

Suddenly Partus stopped and without turning around he said in a jeering tone. "Come out, Lucian, I know it's you who is following me." Partus turned slowly around, and Lucian could see the evil grin on his distorted face. It turned Lucian's blood to stone to see that expression.

"What have you done to me, Partus?" Lucian demanded as he walked closer to his nemesis now.

"Ah, I see you have fed already. Good, isn't it?" Partus said as he still wore that vile smirk on his face. "If you could see yourself, Lucian Marius Antonius, tall, beautiful, a fine specimen of true wickedness." Partus laughed loudly as Lucian came and stood before him, just a foot or so from the Princep. His left hand went up to his mouth as he felt the dried crusted blood caked around his lips and down his chin.

"What did you do to me?" Lucian asked again, begging him as he looked him straight in the eye. He hated pleading with this wicked man, pleading for his life, it would seem.

"You are like me now, Lucian." Partus said cruelly as he looked at the handsome Roman General. His eyes were dark, and a flash of red crossed the retina as he half turned his head and glanced at Lucian, taking in the appearance of the elite officer.

"Like you?" Lucian asked Partus questioningly. "What are you?" Partus laughed brutely at the question as he stared at Lucian. *"Answer me!"* Lucian roared as his voice echoed within the cone of the mountain.

"I made you to be like me, to be strong, to be fierce, invincible for when we need you." Partus said proudly, as he stood and studied Lucian. "Your father was a coward. *He* couldn't handle what was before him, Lucian. But now his son will be deemed a slayer but fear not, my handsome protégé, our kind will thrive and grow, our numbers will be far more than this Centurion, that you once commanded." Partus laughed as he put his hand on Lucian's shoulder. "When our kind is needed, you will respond accordingly."

"Our kind?" Lucian asked, confused by what Partus had just said. "What do you mean, *'our kind'*?" He felt the hair on the back of his neck stand up, as a shiver ran down his spine, he glared at Partus. For a sick moment he knew what he had become.

"Vampire," Partus said with a grin. "You are a vampire now, Lucian. Immortality is yours, and I have given you a new life-"

"Noooo!" Lucian screamed as he lunged at Partus, and beat his face with a right fist and then a left hook to his jaw. He pushed the older man so hard, that he fell backwards onto the ground. Lucian fought hard and beat him vigorously in the face. Partus pushed Lucian off of him, and he began to kick him hard, he didn't know where he found the strength to keep punching Partus, but he did. He hated this demon.

Lucian felt winded as he got to his feet. Partus laughed hard as he too, got up. "I see that you are stronger already. It seems I have chosen my protégé wisely." He said and raised his finger to his lip and licked the blood from it. "You will be as strong as the alpha who made you." Lucian glared at him. His body was full of hatred for the man who had turned him into a murderer. A monster. A demon.

"No, I will not be like you, Partus." Lucian said, trying to find his breath. "I will not murder again." He turned to walk away, then Partus laughed out loud and goaded.

"You will have no choice, Lucian Marius Antonius." He jeered. "The hunger will take over, you will kill to feed, to drink the blood of your victims to survive. You will have to."

Lucian stopped for a moment and slowly turned around to face the alpha. "No, I am not a monster, Partus, I am a Roman General." He said deliberately walking back to where

Partus stood. "I will never drink blood, you are the monster here, not I." His speech was controlled but his thirst was beginning to surface again. Lucian stood up to his full height and glared at Partus.

"You can't fight it, Lucian," Partus said. "I made you what you are, you belong to our army now. You are a vampire, and a vampire needs blood." Lucian looked at him for a moment and then lunged at him summoning up all the strength he possessed, as he grabbed Partus he roared and threw the alpha vampire over the edge of Mount Vesuvius. "Ad infernum tecum monstrum." He heard the deafening roar of Partus as his screams echoed in the cone of the fiery mountain.

Lucian stepped backward, and then he heard the rumble. He stopped for a moment to get his bearings. The rumble grew louder and suddenly, the mountain began to shake uncontrollably and to spit fire into the air.

He looked around as ash flew up from inside, quickly Lucian began to run down the mountainside, and he didn't stop even when he reached the base.

Lucian ran as far as he could, he was fast, faster even than he could believe. He moved effortlessly. When he knew he was at a safe distance, only then did he stop and look up at the mountain. Vesuvius was angry, the gods were fuming. The mountain was firing rocks of flames into the sky, when suddenly it began to darken, almost as if it were night. Lucian looked down, and saw that his hands were dirty, he was covered in ash. Everywhere there was ash and pumice rock. The gods were angry, fuming at Lucian, mad at the demon's return to Orcus, and Pluto was being vengeful.

As he looked up once more, he saw with horror, the river of fire tumbling over the cone and racing down the side of the mountain toward him, toward his camp, toward Pompeii.

Fear gripped Lucian, he had to warn them, he had to warn the towns people, but they wouldn't make it in time, they were trapped, they couldn't get out of the way.

What could he do?

He had to do something...But what?

Suddenly there was a loud clap, and day had turned to night, the flicker of light from the lava river lit up the sky, Lucian had to get out of there, the fire was close, closer than he had realised.

"Vulcan please don't be angry!" Lucian cried out helpless and he ran as fast as he could out of the path of the river of fire!

Chapter 4

Word spread quickly about the eruption. Pompeii and Herculaneum were destroyed. Buried under ash and lava. The people in both towns had perished.

Lucian's camp had been in the path of the lava. They never knew what hit them. They would have died valiantly.

He ran until he could run no more and finally after what seemed like months but was in fact only days, Lucian fell down on the ground, exhausted and unable to move. He was overcome with grief. Grief for what he had done by returning the demon to his prison in Orcus. Grief because he had saved himself instead of trying to save the towns of Herculaneum and Pompeii. Lucian knew that his own family had perished in the river of fire. He knew in his heart that they were in Elysium, and it was his fault. Lucian was desolate. He was broken, his men, gone, the two cities, gone. His fault, for not letting them know, but yet, as his heart broke, Lucian knew that there was nothing he could have done. He wouldn't have reached them in time to evacuate.

Lucian stood up and walked on and as he did, he felt the overwhelming pain within him, not just the heartbreak of the annihilation of both towns. No, this pain was hunger. He was ravenous once more. He needed to feed. He needed to kill. He couldn't fight it anymore. He was too weak. The beast which resided within him had won. Lucian was too weak to fight it anymore. He didn't want to live. He despised himself for what he had become, this was punishment for being greedy and wanting more than he should have.

Lucian sat up and looked despairingly around him. The soft grass was blowing in the gentle breeze, it wasn't quite dark, just twilight. He was tired and he was hungry.

"Dear gods, finish me now," Lucian cried out helplessly into the dusk, his voice sounded a little hoarse. But the gods had abandoned him. Everyone had abandoned him. He was a beast.

What was it, Partus had called him, *a vampire! Yes, that was it, a vampire!*

He was a murderous creature that fed on his victim's blood.

Lucian didn't know what a vampire was, but he knew it was bad, he was a creature of Orcus, a child of Pluto, a monster.

Lucian opened his eyes when he heard the snapping of the twig. He jumped to his feet. "Show yourself?" He shouted and drew his sword.

"Greetings, friend." A man wearing a confused expression and a white toga with a brown leather water bottle hung across his body approached. His hair was not styled in the Roman way. Though he greeted, Lucian in Latin, his accent was Greek.

"Who are you?" Lucian roared and stood up straight and pointed his sword at the newcomer.

"My...my name is not important," the man said sheepishly. "I am a friend." He repeated. "I have come to help you. You don't need to fear me." The reassurance only served to annoy Lucian.

"Go away, Greek, you are in danger here." Lucian bent over in pain as his hunger began to take hold of him. "In danger from me." He fell to his knees now, holding his stomach. "Go!"

"Please, let me help you." The Greek begged as he edged closer to Lucian.

"I am not a man... anymore." Lucian said, he was becoming delirious now. "Go away." He shouted as he raised his head to look at the man who dared to show him pity. "Leave me to my hell."

"My name is Demis, take my hand, Lucian Marius Antonius," He held out his hand to Lucian. He wasn't afraid of Lucian. The man showed no fear at all.

"How do you know my name?" Lucian asked him, confused.

"I have been following you since the eruption." Demis said. "Take my hand and let me help you." He held out his hand to Lucian again, as he did, Lucian felt the pain, stronger this time and then as suddenly as the pain began, all he felt was a falling sensation and millions of tiny lights as he fell.

Pluto was taking him back to Orcus, Lucian was going back home.

Chapter 5

Nunc Tempus

The office was dimly lit, with a soft golden hue from the double bulb lamp. The cream concertina shade gave off little rippled patterns on the wall which joined forces with the green art deco reading lamp on the desk to illuminate the room with its subtle hues.

The office was decorated in a dark wood, dating no later than the nineteen twenties. The only two exceptions, which were necessary for the functionality of the occupant, was the electronic wooden venetian blinds and the laptop that sat looking a little lonely by itself, on the dark mahogany desk. The desk had been brought in from Singapore when he had arrived in LA in the late nineteen twenties.

He held the slim ebony coloured pen between his index finger and his pinkie, with his middle and ring finger on top of it covering the gold lettering of his initials: *L.M.A!* A name he hadn't used in a very long time. A name he didn't know anymore. It was a name that he had once been proud of.

Luca was in a pensive mood. He had been sitting with his back pressed into the soft leather swivel chair for the last hour. His mind wasn't focused on the changing ticker on his laptop. It was elsewhere. Another time, another place.

Heedlessly, he reached inside his pocket and took out his cell phone, he looked at the time, it was just gone seven O'clock. Luca had told his Militibus officers that he would meet them at eight. They had been slacking in relation to patrolling recently, particularly since they came back from the Sixth. The truth was, the streets had been relatively quiet since the Jarl had blood eagled the mortal. The dregs were cowering in fear, not of the Jarl, he always had a fearful reputation, and his last escapade had solidified his standing as a Militibus not to be crossed.

Luca smiled wryly at that. He had great respect for Lanny, he would trust him with his life. He would trust all of them, they were exceptional warriors and his best friends. *His only friends.*

With a certain amount of reluctance, Luca stood up and walked over to the coat stand and took down his blazer and put it on, and then he went back over to his desk, leaned over it and shut down the laptop. He smiled again. On the final bell, he had trebled his investment in crypto currency. It had been a profitable day all round. For that at least, Luca was happy. It had been a good day.

He switched off the lights and left his office and he walked over to the lift and waited for the doors to open. In the office at the end of the hall, Luca could hear the cleaners and the light-hearted banter as they vacuumed the floors, and then the laughter between them made him smile.

Luca descended to the lobby and walked confidently to the glass doors and pushed them open and he left the building.

It was a balmy evening, and the night was gearing up to be a lively one for the residents of the vast metropolis. Luca walked with an air of self-assurance over to the bar, he didn't acknowledge the security guard outside as he pushed the door and went inside.

He was a striking figure, as he walked, Luca was tall, at six foot seven, yet he was graceful. His long dark hair was brushed off his face and hung down his back. His clothes were vintage and perfectly cut. Luca enjoyed the finer things that his position afforded him.

In the booth facing the bar and the dance floor, he saw Peo Satimus and the Jarl, they already had a drink in front of them and they were laughing at some joke, one of them had told. Luca smiled as he walked over to where they were sitting, and he sat down.

"I'll have one of those." Luca said to the hostess who had come to the booth.

"You were burning the oil late, General." Lanny said with a wicked grin on his handsome face. Luca grinned as he checked out the dance floor, but he didn't reply.

"That is how you make easy money, Jarl." Peo said in a sarcastic voice and chuckled. "You two, would never get your hands dirty so you play at playing business." Luca turned and looked at him and then laughed loudly as he shook his head.

"You're a dealer of antique weapons, Peo," Luca said sportily. "Not exactly, getting oil on your hands, now, is it?"

"Restoring the classics is what I do best, General." Peo said gaily. "That is art, and it does get oil on your hands."

"Are you telling us, Praetorian," Lanny said with a wide grin, "That you restore those cars for the love of it and not to get rich?" Peo nodded with a smirk. "I call bull, Praetorian." Luca observed his two friends cheerfully teasing each other.

"Bjorn is late." Luca observed as he noted the Berserker was absent from the group and he reached for his glass and took a long sip. He enjoyed fine malt.

"He's on his way." Peo said and looked at him. "You seem tense, Luca, is something wrong?"

"It's been a month since we came back," Luca said with a hint of caution to his tone. "There's been no word from Demis or the council." It worried Luca when everything was too quiet. As it was now in the Fourth. It concerned him because it meant something was up, and he and the Militibus were always last to know about it.

"The old toad is probably fumbling through yet another crisis." Lanny said and laughed loudly, and Peo chuckled too as they hit their glasses together. It was no secret the philosopher was a walking disaster, but he did have his good points too. Though most of the time, they all struggled to see them.

"No doubt, but I don't like it when It's this quiet," Luca confessed. "It's disconcerting."

"I prefer it this way, it means I get more restoration work done on the car." Peo chimed in once more, with a grin on his face.

"When it's this quiet, Peo," Luca reminded with some assertion. "Demis is usually covering up something bad that's about to happen." Bjorn approached their booth and sat down in front of Luca. "You're late, Berserker." Luca said with a deadpan expression as he looked at the handsome Viking.

"I thought that this was a social evening." Bjorn said bemused as he smiled widely at Luca. "Unless the old codger has let loose some hell on the Sixth." Lanny and Peo burst out laughing at this. "What? Did I miss something?" Bjorn asked and looked at them and then back to Luca with a questioning expression.

"Ignore them, Bjorn," Luca said. "They are having fun at the old boy's expense." He put the glass down on the table. "So, any ideas on how to relieve some pent-up stress, Militibus?"

"I have a new DJ starting at the club tonight," Bjorn chimed in. "Promises to be electrifying." He grinned mischievously at Luca. "There is also a private party of very beautiful models who have booked an evening for their personal pleasure."

"Then what are we doing here?" Peo asked with a broad grin, as he downed the contents of his glass and stood up.

LUCA AWOKE WITH A FEELING of being pinned down. He couldn't move. Then he turned his head to his left and smiled widely when he saw the dark-haired mortal, lying naked on her back. He looked at her body for a few minutes. She was pale skinned, unlike a lot of the women that he had been with, with their expensive tans. Her shoulder length black hair was covering the pillow and she still had traces of the deep red lipstick which looked like it had been tattooed onto her voluptuous lips. He couldn't see her eyes, as she was still sleeping. Luca grinned to himself. She had been excellent in bed.

He looked around the strange bedroom. It was minimalist at best, not at all a welcoming room, but then, last night Luca wasn't exactly house hunting, all he had on his mind was what this beautiful creature had given him. Hot, raunchy sex.

Silently, Luca threw off the sheet and got out of the queen-sized bed. He spotted his clothes as they lay strewn across the floor, he smiled as he remembered the rush they had, to continue what had started in the club. Luca had wanted stress relief, and this mortal had provided just that.

He had buttoned the last button on his shirt when the woman opened her eyes and murmured and then she turned onto her side.

"Do you always sneak out and not wake up the woman you gave a fantastic night to?" She asked in a flirtatious voice. Luca turned and smiled across at her, he could ravage her again, if he had time.

"I wasn't sneaking out." Luca said casually as he stuffed his shirt into his trousers. He had enjoyed her, and she had been good company but that wasn't what he remembered most. What he remembered was her mouth on a certain part of his anatomy. Luca grinned now.

"Would you like some coffee?" She asked and swung her legs over the side of the bed and stood up. She stretched like a cat, and he could make out the shape of her ribs underneath her almost translucent skin.

"No, thank you." Luca said carefully. He just wanted to leave and get back to his own place. Luca didn't like these long drawn out 'goodbyes'. He bent down and picked up his jacket and walked with her out of the bedroom, and down the hallway to where the front door was. "Thank you for last night, I enjoyed it." It was such a casual thing that he didn't stop to think about her feelings, nor did he care.

"See you around then." She quickly kissed him on the cheek and then left him standing at the door looking after her as she went into the other room.

This bemused him, how indifferent these 'modern' women were to sex. Luca closed the door behind him and walked down the long corridor to the end and then down the stairs and out of the building.

Chapter 6

It had been late by the time he had gotten to the office. Luca greeted his assistant with a half-smile and as he was about to open the door, she called out to him.

"Mister Meridian, I hope it's ok, but there is a gentleman waiting for you inside your office." Luca nodded and opened the door.

"I'm glad to see you treat your own business as laxly as you do Militibus business."

"Hello to you too, Demis." Luca retorted with a forced smile on his face. "Would you like coffee?" The philosopher shook his head and sat back down on the chair that he had occupied while he waited for Luca to arrive.

"I've been waiting here for almost two hours, Lucian." Demis grumbled as he watched him remove his jacket and hang it up on the coat rack. "Two hours. That's not good enough." Demis tutted now, just to show his irritation.

"I'm here now." Luca said, ignoring the barb. "What's happening?" He asked and looked at the old scholar as he tried to keep his anger in check, which was difficult especially where Demis was concerned.

"Have you seen the papers this morning?" Demis inquired and slid the paper he had had in his hand across the desk to Luca. Luca picked it up and glanced at the headline. Nothing much of interest. "Turn to page seven, last column." Demis encouraged. Luca did so.

'Bodies displayed like noir crime scenes.' Luca read aloud and then looked up at Demis. "And this is what, to us?" Demis sighed loudly as he glared back at Luca.

"You and the Militibus are getting lazy, Lucian." Demis cried out. "Five bodies of well-known theatre directors have been found, all looking like they had been from old gangster movies of this dimension." Luca still looked blankly at him. He just didn't see the connection with the Militibus.

"This is LA, there's lots of crime of this kind." Luca said after a while. "Again, Demis what does this have to do with us?" Demis sighed heavily and stood up. "I don't understand, what you are getting at."

"I'd expect that retort from the Jarl or the Berserker," Demis said cuttingly. "Not from you, Lucian." He rubbed his forehead. "This is a serious crime in any dimension."

"I'm sorry, Demis," Luca said apologetically. "That was unworthy."

"Take a closer look at the article." Demis demanded and Luca reread it.

When he had finished, he still didn't see what Demis was referring to or maybe he just didn't want to see. *Was he becoming lazy?* Perhaps. Or maybe he was just tired of Demis and the condescending way he addressed them.

"Demis, I really can't see how this is for the Militibus?" Luca reiterated much to the annoyance of the old philosopher, who glared back at Luca once more.

"Call a meeting for lunch, Lucian." Demis said frustrated now and he stood up. "I'm going to see what I can find out at the police department." Luca stared at him. The old boy had lost his mind. "Don't worry, they won't see me." He assured and with that he was gone.

Luca let out a long slow sigh. It was going to be a difficult meeting when the others came into the office, especially considering the mood that Demis was in.

IT HAD BEEN A STRUGGLE to get the Militibus to be at his office for lunch but Luca somehow managed to achieve it. Grumpily they each arrived at Luca's office. He half expected them to be angry at the intrusion into their day. He couldn't blame them either.

"Where is he?" Lanny asked as he leaned against the door jamb. It was clear that he would rather be elsewhere.

"He said he'd be here for lunch." Luca reassured all of them and suppressed a sigh.

"The old cad is looking for a free lunch then?" Peo teased and Bjorn burst out laughing as he threw a paper plane across at Peo.

"I am perfectly capable of buying my own lunch, Praetorian." Demis hollered at him as he came into the centre of Luca's office and glared at the Berserker and the Praetorian. "But my money wouldn't be accepted here in this dimension as you are more than aware." Luca suppressed a smile at this. The other vampires got great pleasure out of riling the old philosopher. "Now can we focus here?" Demis continued to glare at them as he walked over to Luca's desk.

"What did you discover, Demis?" Luca asked trying to dampen the flames of three very pissed off Militibus officers.

"As you indicated earlier, Lucian," Demis said as he sat down and glared across at the other three. "There was little information at the police station. So, I went to the newspaper office, and I would have saved myself energy had I gone there first."

"What did you find?" Bjorn asked as he casually put one leg over the other and rested his elbow on the side of the chair.

"Has Lucian, updated you on this?" They all shook their heads. "*Typical!* I have to do everything myself." He glared at Luca this time and began to tut rather loudly.

"I was about to when you came in Demis." Luca corrected in his defence. "There were five bodies discovered over a number of weeks, four directors from the theatre world, murdered and their bodies staged at the scene."

"It's LA, nothing unusual there." Lanny said in a bored tone as he stood up straight, with his back against the wall now.

"For the uneducated, perhaps, Jarl." Demis hurled at him. "What I did discover is the second last body to be found was one of our own." They all looked at him now. "He was known in the Sixth for his dramas, they weren't very good, by the Sixth standard, but they weren't bad either. He was a mix breed, a wannabe director as you would call him, Jarl."

"Mix breed?" Peo questioned. Luca tightened his lips and shook his head as he rolled his eyes. This was going to be a long meeting.

"You really are a lost generation, aren't you, Praetorian?" Demis said in an aggravated tone. "A mix breed is a humanoid, father was a werewolf, mother was a human. Their child was a hybrid."

"Why didn't you just say hybrid then?" Bjorn teased him with a fabulous smile. "So, who is this hybrid?"

"Was," Demis corrected. "He was granted a visa to the Fourth so he could learn his art in more detail, he wanted to be a movie director as all he did in the Sixth was stage. Which were al-"

"Demis, the hybrid, murder..." Peo interrupted the philosopher's rambling, in a raised voice. "Today, please."

"I was getting to that, Praetorian. No need to be rude." Demis said discouraged now. "Well three nights ago his body was found with bite marks on the soles of his feet and his body was drained."

"Bite marks as in wolf marks?" Bjorn asked him now with a raised eyebrow. Demis shook his head. "Vampire?" Again, he shook his head. "Then what?" Luca saw Bjorn shake his head in frustration.

"I think it may be a dakhanavar," Demis said gravely. "It's like a vampire only it sucks the blood from the feet of its victim."

"Kinky!" Lanny said and grinned as Bjorn and Peo erupted in loud laughter, much to the displeasure of Demis.

"Jarl, keep your fetish out of this." Demis called out angrily to him.

"You brought it up, Demis." Lanny retorted but he was still laughing.

"What is a dakhanavar doing here?" Luca asked as he tried to keep a straight face too. "We haven't come across one before."

"Usually, they are loners, they don't have lairs like vampires, and they are extremely shy." Demis said and glanced across at Luca. "They don't enter the city."

"Except to suck on feet." Lanny teased and Luca shot him a look, but he was hardly able to keep a straight face either. "I'm sorry Demis, please continue." The titters filled the office.

"I heard a rumour back in the Sixth that when Greyson had come here, he had failed to contact his agent." Demis said gravely. "I've been here since yesterday trying to locate him, and that is when I discovered the article, found his body and why the Militibus are going to investigate." They all remained silent for a few moments as they glared at Demis, before Luca said to no one in particular.

"What was Greyson working on before he was killed?" Demis walked over to Luca's drinks cabinet and helped himself to a very large glass of single malt whiskey.

"It was something he had written himself." Demis said and came back around to the desk and sat down. He took a sip from the glass.

"You're sure it was a dreg that killed him?" Luca quizzed and Demis nodded. "How?"

"The others that were murdered, had their bodies been drained too?" Peo asked in a serious tone now.

"I didn't look." Demis admitted harshly and Luca glared at him.

"So, you decided that because it was a citizen of the Sixth, that that's the only reason you're here?" Luca demanded and Demis hung his head a little. "Isn't that a bit selfish?" Luca added. "Even for you?"

"Maybe it is," Demis said. "But I want you to investigate this. Now, I'll be back in a few days." He stood up and looked at Luca before he walked over to the door and then he was gone.

Luca leaned back in the chair and let out a long low sigh. Lanny laughed and walked casually over to the chair that Demis had been sitting on just moments earlier.

"We are basically doing a favour for the old toad, here." Lanny said sarcastically as he grinned. "He has some nerve to expect us to devote time to this." Luca looked at him. The Jarl was right, but Luca couldn't say so verbally any way.

"Technically, this Greyson was a citizen of the Sixth and slain here in the Fourth," Luca said half smiling. "We have an obligation to investigate." Lanny groaned loudly and brushed his blond hair back off his face.

"What do we do, round up the usual suspects?" Bjorn asked and grinned across at Lanny. Luca nodded and both Bjorn and Lanny stood up and left Luca's office.

"Peo, can you hold on a moment?" Luca asked and Peo hung back.

After Bjorn and Lanny had gone, Luca stood up and came round and slapped his fellow Roman on the arm. "A whiskey?" Peo grinned and he nodded as he sat back down on the chair.

"What's troubling you, Luca?" Peo asked as he took the glass from him.

"You think something is troubling me?" Luca queried with a half-smile, and Peo nodded and then took a sip. Then Luca laughed. "My friend you have always been very perceptive."

"So, what is it?" Peo pressed.

"I didn't want to say anything in front of the Jarl or Bjorn," Luca said in a low tone, as though someone might be listening. "It almost seems like I am betraying him even as we are talking here." Peo leaned forward in his seat now, his elbow rested on his thigh.

"The Jarl?" Peo asked but Luca smiled and shook his head. "Not Bjorn?"

"No, not the Vikings," Luca said and took a deep breath. "Demis."

"Demis?" Peo asked and almost huffed as he grinned at Luca. "What about him?" Demis never endeared himself to anyone. Now was no exception.

"Like I said, I feel as if I'm betraying him." Luca uttered. "I have wondered about him, and his state of mind since Lanny told him he had the book, and the old boy hasn't asked for it. The longer the Jarl has it, the longer it will take to close the Tenth." Peo agreed but he looked as though he were pondering about something else.

"Luca, we still have been unable to find the physical key." Peo said momentarily. "Without that, the book is useless anyway. You are right though, he seems muddled and I don't think Demis realises how close he is coming to being exiled." Luca agreed but the hardest part for Luca was, he didn't believe that Demis cared any more. He didn't know how to voice his opinion without sounding callous, either.

"This case, he wants us on," Luca said after a moment and then shrugged his broad shoulders, "I think it's a smoke screen, to hide yet another blunder he's made." Peo looked at him intently for a moment.

"What do you want us to do, Luca?" Peo asked seriously. "You know, we'll follow your orders." Luca nodded. His men were loyal and trustworthy.

"Just keep this with the Militibus for now. Let's not involve the council for the moment." Luca said and then smiled at his friend. "I'll check out this killing, see what I can come up with, OK." Peo nodded, stood up and as he walked over to the door, he turned to him and said seriously.

"You need to get out and have some fun tonight." Peo grinned at Luca and added before he left the office. "This could be a long case."

Peo had a point, he didn't get out much lately, and his social life was suffering badly because of it.

Chapter 7

The theatre was dark and there was a distinctive smell of stale beer and old musk. It assaulted his nose immediately as he entered the auditorium. The carpet seemed threadbare, and the furniture scattered around in the lobby bar had seen better days.

Luca walked over to the bottom of the stage and glanced up at it. In its heyday it probably was an impressive place to be, but today, all it served was a few amateur dramatists and their actors who dreamed of a life in the theatre. Of making it big someday.

The stage lights were dimmed and as he glanced up, Luca saw the painted ceiling, it depicted a rather coarse version of the familiar scene of the Sistine Chapel. This made him smile as the cherub looked a little more obese than it should, and its hair was more reminiscent of a bad home perm than an angelic mop of curls. Though despite the archetypal scene, it was charming. Theatrical.

He walked over to the side of the stage and walked up the four wooden steps. Luca moved over purposefully to the centre of the stage and looked around him. There was a time, when he was a small boy, that he enjoyed listening to some of the actors rehearse their lines for some plays that were hosted at the amphitheatre in his hometown of Surrentum. Luca briefly closed his eyes. He hadn't thought of that for a long time. In fact, he had thought that he had wiped his past from his mind completely. *Unsuccessfully now, it seemed.*

"It's impressive from up there, isn't it?" A man's voice called out from the centre of the auditorium. Luca looked out into the darkness and then sniffed the air, and he could smell the man. He smelt his pride.

"It is, have you performed up here?" Luca asked in a friendly tone to draw his companion out more in conversation.

"No, oh dear no but I saw some of the greats perform up there." The man said and came forward. Luca saw him, as he was hunched over with a sweeping brush in his hand. He looked about seventy, but he could have been younger or older. He had a fine mop of wavy hair tinged with a selection of dark grey and almost white hairs. His eyes were a bright blue but lacked the lustre of the here and now. Luca looked at him, he appeared lost in thought.

"You did?" Luca asked and smiled at the man. "Who performed here?" He watched the man as he walked with an effort, up the steps, which Luca had used minutes before.

"Let me see, there was the great Amelia Fortune, my but she had a great voice, soprano, she was, and she was quite the looker too. Then there was Clifford Miller, though that wasn't really his name you know." The man chuckled loudly now, and Luca saw his whole body shake with the hilarity as he remembered the old days.

"Wasn't it?" Luca asked with a broad grin on his face. "What was his real name?"

"No, his name was Dusty Mullpeter," The man said still chuckling. "That wouldn't have got him nowhere in Tinsel town, so he changed it." Luca smiled warmly at him. "You can smile, young man but in them days it was all in a name, you know. If you didn't have a good crowd pullin name, then you didn't get the opportunity to show what you could a done up here." He nodded wilfully at Luca now, who was well and truly scolded.

"No Sir, I meant no disrespect," Luca apologised. "I like to hear the stories about theatres and who played them." This pleased the old guy, and his demeanour relaxed once more.

"You know who played here for two weeks afore the great war?" Luca shook his head. "The legendary BJ Sympson and his orchestra. Man, those were the days." He scratched his head now. "All the greats wanted a piece of the tinsel town dream."

"Really?" Luca replied, he knew BJ Sympson from his acquaintance with Bjorn. "He played here?"

"You heard a him, young man?" Luca nodded. "Course I don't remember him. My father hadn't met my mother yet." He chuckled again, and his body shook jovially. "But my pop saw him here with his pop, that was in... let me see... nineteen thirteen. Poor bastard died of the influenza when he came back from the war." Luca raised an eyebrow. He wondered who he had referred to, his father, or to BJ. As if sensing Luca's confusion, the old guy said to him. "BJ Sympson, of course. My pop met my mother in forty-one, I was born in forty-two." He chuckled again. Luca nodded. The old man was friendly, and he seemed very trusting.

"How long have you been at the theatre, Sir?" Luca asked him. The old boy scratched his head for a moment. Again, he appeared lost in thought.

"I been here since I was thirteen years old, young man." He said proudly.

"Frankie, stop pestering this man," A stern voice said coming from behind them. "The johns need cleaning. Go." The new arrival's voice was harsh and full of disdain for the old man.

"I'll see you again." Frankie said to Luca, and he shuffled off behind the curtains.

"Can I help you?" The newcomer asked abruptly, and he eyed Luca with suspicion.

"I was told that I'd find the manager here." Luca replied, he had taken an instant dislike to this guy. He was slimy. Luca could smell his vice immediately.

"That's me." He spoke. "George Willis, what can I do for you...Mister?"

"Meridian, Luca Meridian." Luca said and held out his hand to him. "I heard from a colleague that you facilitate new directors here in the theatre." Willis smiled wily at him now, and he looked Luca up and down. He was clearly trying to gauge if Luca had money or not.

"We've been known to help some of the students from the college put on plays and the like, from time to time." He replied and his eyes narrowed a little as he looked at Luca, undoubtedly calculating how much he must have paid for his suit.

"I'm not with the college." Luca quickly corrected him. "I have some...let's say I have an interest in directing...So it is you that I see about hiring the theatre to have my play shown?" Luca chose his words carefully, and he judged from the change in his pheromones that his greed was coming to the forefront of his mind as he imagined making some easy money off Luca.

Foolish mortal! Luca thought to himself.

"Well, as you know it's expensive to stage a play these days," Willis informed and then smiled in a condescending manner at Luca. "Lots of upfront costs and then there's staff..."

"Come now, Mister Willis," Luca said with a forced smile. "Do I look like I can't afford to put on a play?" He saw the manager's face redden slightly and then he quickly regained his professionalism.

"I didn't mean to imply, Mister Meridian," he said grovelling. "The fee of course would be based on the production and the costumes and so on, but I am sure we can come to a suitable arrangement."

"I'm glad to hear it," Luca said and smiled equally as fake as Willis had. "Your theatre came highly recommended by a colleague." He saw his face light up at this, as he had done before, to some poor dreamer that he had ripped off in the past.

"Who would that be, Mister Meridian?" His vanity had now overtaken his greed as he waited to be flattered by the recommendation.

"Greyson, William Greyson." Luca studied Willis's expression, he sniffed for any change in his pheromones, some kind of change, but there was little. His greed reeked from every pore.

"I'm afraid, I don't know the name." Willis said and Luca smirked at him. He knew he had just lied, and Luca wondered what he was hiding. "We get so many hopefuls wanting to use our little theatre."

"Perhaps you have just forgotten his name." Luca persisted and then crossed over to where Willis stood, and studied him for a moment. Then he held out his hand to him and shook it briefly. The manager's grip was limp, as Luca expected it to be. "I shall be in touch soon." Luca walked over to the steps and descended them quickly and walked out of the theatre and into the evening air. He didn't have to think too much about the encounter with the manager, he was a shady individual, and Luca knew without a shadow of a doubt that he knew Greyson, but not only that, he knew that Willis had ripped off the hybrid too.

Chapter 8

Rome 73 AD

He smashed the blade against his opponent and sent the sword flying through the air and both soldiers watched as it lodged in the ground and stood to attention. Both the Romans laughed, and Lucian held out his hand to his friend Aeneus.

"That was a trick of the gods." Lucian said with a wicked grin on his face.

"You are just peeved because I am the better swordsman." Aeneus chuckled loudly as Lucian pulled his blade from the ground. Lucian stood up straight and put his sword back in its scabbard.

Lucian looked around at the other soldiers as they went through their paces during training. He loved the army. He loved the training, and he knew that he was ready to command a legion or two.

It was bred deep in his blood, this life as a Centurian officer. But what Lucian wanted was to be sent somewhere where he would be able to prove himself and his worth quickly. He was ready for somewhere like Gallia, though that was controlled. Although he would probably prefer to command a large legion which was on their way to Masada.

"You are lost in thought, Lucian Marius Antonius." Aeneus shouted to him as they began to walk back to their tent.

"Am I?" Lucian queried but he just grinned. It was no secret that he was ambitious, but it would do no good to have it common knowledge exactly how ambitious he really was and what that ambition held for him, was to become the youngest ever legate of the Roman Empire.

"Shall we drink, or shall we go to the bathhouse?" Aeneus quipped but Lucian just laughed.

"Why not just admit, Aeneus," Lucian replied jovially. "That the slave girls at the bathhouse are worth a Centurian officer's wage for a month." They both laughed loudly.

"What if it is true, are you joining me?" Aeneus insisted but Lucian just grinned and shook his head. "Why not? It is not like you to shirk away from the hands of a concubine." Lucian laughed loudly now and slapped his friend on the back.

"Another time, Aeneus," Lucian said as they stopped outside their tent. "My father has requested my company." He looked at his friend now. "He has made a special trip to Rome. Another time." He went into the tent and threw off his scabbard and walked over to his bed and began to remove his armour and then his tunic.

LUCIAN WAS IN A GOOD mood as he walked along the street on his way to the villa where his father was staying for the duration of his visit to Rome. Brutus Caius had been an old family friend of his father when he lived in Surrentum, but he had decided that such a small place had no appeal when compared to the allure of Rome. He moved his family from Surrentum to Rome and made a career for himself in politics.

Lucian was shown into the large room where his father and members of the senate were gathered for a feast, given in Lucian's father's honour. Corintus Sesmus Antonius was legate to one of the legions in Gallia Belgica in the Gaul Roman Empire. In the year 70 AD, Corintus Sesmus Antonius had commanded a legion along with the legion of Quintus Pettillius Cerialis and they defeated the Batavi tribes but not before the uprising caused the Roman armies a certain number of humiliating defeats. It was following this battle that the Batavi conceded and was once more under Roman rule. Corintus Sesmus Antonius received a handsome gift from the emperor and the offer of a political position in Rome.

He waved at his father and was then greeted by Brutus with a bear hug. The man was as Lucian had remembered, big and full of the corruption that was Rome.

Lucian was seated next to his father, and they feasted on a banquet of pig, pheasant and chicken. The wine flowed freely, and the conversation was merry. Lucian listened with interest as politics was discussed and then the fate of the zealots in Masada. There were many takes on the outcome of the war, but everyone at the table knew that the empire would be victorious.

"Come, Lucian, walk with me." His father said as they stood up from the table and made their way out into the vast garden.

They walked in a contented quietness for a while, neither broke the silence until they were well out of earshot from the villa.

"How is mother?" Lucian asked finally making conversation. His father grinned and looked up at his son. Lucian was tall, six foot seven and he dwarfed his father who stood at six feet.

"Disappointed you haven't been home, my son." Corintus Sesmus Antonius said with a broad smile on his weathered face.

"I have been occupied with training." Lucian defended and his father just chuckled. "It is true. There is much to train for now, particularly with Masada." He watched as his father picked at a leaf from the bay tree and rubbed it between his fingers until it crumpled and then he threw it on the ground.

"It is of Masada, I wish to speak with you, Lucian." Corintus said in a low tone. Lucian's ears perked up now as he stopped in front of his father. "For a young Centurian as yourself, Masada would be a great skirmish to prove your worth with the emperor." Lucian nodded enthusiastically in agreement with his father. "But do not be hasty in finishing training quickly. Keep to your programme, for you will not be promoted during this campaign, Lucian." His father's eyes were glassed for a moment as he glanced over Lucian's shoulder back in the direction of the villa. His expression was grim, and his whole demeanour was cautious.

"What do you mean, father?" Lucian asked, his curiosity building as he looked at his pater, tall, proud and yet he carried himself at that moment with the poise of someone who had vital information, information that could prove detrimental for anyone he would tell.

"Just trust me when I say that you will not have your just promotion, my son." Corintus uttered in a low tone. "There are certain people who hold the confidence of the emperor, that do not have the best interest of the empire at heart."

"Who?" Lucian pressed but it seemed that his father had regretted what he had said, and he just looked at his son and placed a fatherly hand on his shoulder.

"If I were to burden you with names, Lucian, it would compromise your position in the army." Corintus said almost in a whisper. "I am returning to Surrentum the day after tomorrow. I am Legate to one of the finest legions in the Roman army, my men are loyal but upon my return to Surrentum, you will hear rumour that I have chosen cowardice. I haven't, Lucian, I promise you." Lucian stared at his father now, almost incredulous. "I leave with the blessing of the emperor and a fine sum in my pocket. I am no coward Lucian, no coward." They stood looking at each other for a few moments before Corintus smiled and took his hand from his son's shoulder. "I have said too much already, perhaps overwhelmed you with cryptic detail. The emperor knows what I have told him, and I believe he will honour our pact but Lucian," Corintus fell silent once more just briefly. Lucian looked at his father now. He wore a pained frown. It was clear that he held a weighty conundrum, and he couldn't share it, not even with his son.

"What is it father?" Lucian asked him as his father stood up straight.

"There are things which surround us, things that even the gods cannot protect us from." Corintus said almost morbidly. "I hope you never witness what I did in Noviomagus."

"What did you witness father?" Lucian begged, concerned now that there was something more than what his father was relaying to him.

"If you encounter a tall dark stranger, do not trust him. He is not Roman nor a soldier." Corintus Sesmus Antonius uttered now as his hand rested on Lucian's arm. "This man is not a man. He is straight from Orcus. Be wary of him, my son." He gave a quick smile to Lucian and then he walked briskly across the path toward the villa, leaving Lucian staring after him.

Chapter 9

Nunc Tempus

Luca took his drink over to the leather armchair and sat down. He was enjoying the notes from the piano as the classical piece filled the room. This time of the evening was the time that he enjoyed the most. When he was finished working for himself, and he had also finished Militibus business. This time was his to enjoy. To relax. To Think.

He had learned to play the piano from Frederic, he had been a tough teacher and didn't take too kindly to foolish mistakes made by Luca. In turn, Luca had been Frederic's guinea pig, he had been forced to listen to his creations. Luca grinned at that. Frederic was fierce when it came to his teaching and he had chastised Luca for silly mistakes when playing, but he had also valued Luca's input when he himself played his latest composition, before it was played publicly for the first time. Or just affirmation that he was a worthy composer.

The arrangement had suited both of them, but as the teacher and student became friends, then the arrangement lost its formality and dissolved into a mutual respect for each other's playing. Although Frederic had been a child prodigy and needed no guidance, least of all from Luca, their friendship became a reciprocal admiration.

Luca let out a contented sigh. These memories were good ones, these memories he enjoyed, but he missed his friend too, and that couldn't be helped. Luca had asked Demis, rather naïvely, once, why all the artists and composers couldn't come and live in the Sixth, but Demis was too critical and short in manner when he told Luca that it was only those who had been turned and who had had a special gift or talent that found a home in the dimensions. Though the answer had been sufficient for Demis, the reply, had never truly sufficed for Luca and his question had remained unanswered. Satisfactorily anyway. Luca sighed now.

The record skipped and Luca glanced over to the gramophone and momentarily, it hadn't registered with him that the record was skipping.

Then he got up and walked over to it and lifted the needle and turned it off. Luca finished his drink in a single gulp and placed the leaded crystal glass on the cabinet beside the record player.

He wondered about going out to Bjorn's club. It had been almost a week since he had been out, and he was getting cabin fever, staying in trying to work out who or what had killed the hybrid.

The buzzer sounded and he walked over to the door and lifted the handpiece. "General," it was Lanny.

"Come on up." Luca opened the door and retreated back into the lounge. Several minutes later Lanny had closed the door behind him. "Do you want one of these Jarl?" Luca asked him, but without waiting for a reply Luca poured two large glasses of whiskey. He walked back over to where Lanny stood and handed him a glass. Luca noticed that he was dressed for patrolling, and just for a second, Luca wondered if he had told the Jarl that he would go out with him that night.

"Are you going on patrol or coming from a patrol?" Luca asked casually, trying to disguise his forgetfulness but Lanny just laughed as he raised the glass in a toasting gesture.

"I'm finished." Lanny said with a smirk. "None of the dregs I spoke with earlier even heard of this hybrid, Greyson, let alone the dakhanavar." Luca nodded earnestly. "What about you, have you come up with anything?"

"I went to check out some theatres, earlier." Luca said and sat down, and he motioned for Lanny to sit down too. "The first four I checked were dead ends but the last one I went to, the manager reeked of corruption." Lanny looked at him. "He denied that he had heard of Greyson, but he had lied."

"You sure?" Lanny asked. "None of the dregs that I questioned knew of anyone coming here from the Sixth recently." Luca took a long sip of his drink as he listened to the Jarl. "Seems a little too elaborate, even for Demis." Luca thought about what the Jarl had said. It was conceivable that it was yet another coverup.

"That manager, he knew him alright," Luca said now with a smile. "Probably because he took all his money, just to put on this play of his." They both laughed.

"Well, if this Greyson is a friend of Demis, then he has to be as doddery as the old fool." Lanny said jovially as he played with the glass in his hand by turning it to and from the light. "What makes you so sure that he was ripped off by the manager?" Luca took another sip of the whiskey.

"His pheromones were highly aroused, and he was fearful at first." Luca said and grinned. "I don't believe he suspected I was a vampire, but you never know." They both laughed. In a perverse way, all of them loved to play with unsuspecting mortals who showed fear, though they never revealed that they were vampires, it was just a torment.

"What are you going to do?" Lanny asked him in a half serious tone. "Are you going to go back, interrogate him?" Luca looked at the Viking and then he chuckled, he knew what Lanny meant by *'interrogate'*, and it wasn't pleasant.

"You know, Jarl, in Surrentum where I grew up," Luca said grinning at him. "I was enthralled by the actors at the amphitheatre when they rehearsed. I wondered what it would be like to perform in public for the crowd." He took a sip from his glass. He remembered the wonderment of the amphitheatre, the crowds it attracted. "I've decided to hire the theatre and put on a play."

"Are you going to act, General?" Lanny asked in an amused voice, hardly able to conceal his smile as they looked at each other. Luca grinned for a moment before he replied.

"I've been acting for almost two millennia, Lanny." Luca said quite seriously, his voice reflective of their affliction. "No, I'm going to go undercover, to direct a play and see what I can find out." Lanny stared at him as if he had gone mad, but he was perfectly serious. Luca wanted to do this.

"You do know that theatre people are closed," the Jarl said bemused. "They are even more secretive than vampires." It was Luca's turn to laugh now. He beamed at his friend.

"Don't you think I can do it, Jarl?" Luca chuckled. "Direct a play?" But Lanny just shook his head and smirked at him as he raised the glass to his mouth.

"What play?" curiosity had gotten the better of the Jarl now. "The Scottish play?" Then Lanny laughed and looked closely at Luca. They both enjoyed the easiness of their friendship. When they first met, Luca had thought that the Jarl was superior and obnoxious but when he got to know him, he discovered a different side to Lanny, and it didn't take long for them to become good friends.

"What would a Roman General put on for the masses?" Luca asked mischievously as he played with the glass in his hand. "I'm going to direct the Greek tragedy, Medea." He looked smug as he glanced across at Lanny, who was looking at him as if he had gone mad. Luca could see that he was unable to conceal his grin.

"General, I hope you will have concession tickets for your loyal officers." Lanny teased. "Or perhaps you should ban us from the theatre to save your reputation." Luca stood up and chortled.

"Shut up, Jarl, you philistine." Luca uttered and laughed loudly. "Have another drink and let's go out tonight." Lanny snickered vociferously and handed him his empty glass. "I feel like celebrating in advance."

Chapter 10

Luca sat back in his black leather swivel chair, although his gaze was directed at the laptop screen, he wasn't taking any notice of the graph which indicated the stock price or the performance of the stock in question. No, Luca was preoccupied, his mind and thoughts were elsewhere.

He just couldn't shake off the feeling that the theatre manager, Willis was hiding something. His demeanour was evasive at best, and Luca didn't trust him.

Luca knew that if he were to get any lead, he would have to talk to Frankie, the old janitor. He would have to get him alone, away from Willis and the theatre. He didn't think that it would be too difficult, he thought that Frankie would be only too willing to talk, especially if there was a drink in it for him. Not that he thought for a moment that he was an alcoholic. Luca didn't know, nor was it any of his business.

He sighed loudly now as he turned the chair around and glanced out of the window. The other Militibus were not as concerned about the murder of this Greyson, unlike Demis, who had been rattled by the crime. Demis hadn't been put out by the previous crimes they had encountered, but with Greyson, it had shaken him to the point where he was even more muddled than usual. It was completely unlike the old academic to be this concerned about someone from the Sixth losing their life. His concern was usually non-existent except when it came to an important member of the Sixth.

There was a knock on the door and Luca just said, 'Come in'. He didn't turn around. "Yes." He said still looking out the window.

"Sir, there is a Mister Demis, to see you." His personal assistant said a little nervously. Her uncertainty was wearing on Luca.

"Send him in." Luca replied and before the secretary left, he added. "Mister Demis is always allowed in, with or without an appointment." He was clearly irritated by the mistakes that the new clerk was continually making, despite being given specific instruction, unlike his old assistant who had been great and aware of Luca's eccentricities and habits. This new girl seemed very unsure of herself, and she seemed almost afraid of Luca. This amused him somewhat. As if she sensed he was a vampire and something to be feared.

"Lucian," Demis said to him as Luca turned around and stood up. Luca smiled widely when he saw the old scholar standing in front of him and he looked particularly harried.

"Demis, I wasn't expecting you until the end of the week." Luca said casually. "What news do you have?" Demis walked over to the window and stood beside Luca, and glanced out at the expansive vista of Downtown LA. He appeared mesmerised by the view.

"I never really liked this dimension, but I never tire of this view either." Demis said without looking at Luca. "Not so much the city, but beyond the limits, its beauty, its solitude." Luca looked carefully at him. He had known Demis a long time and, in that time, he never ceased to amaze him. "It has a certain something about it. Unlike the Sixth, with its spuriousness, the Fourth is alive with wonder."

"I never believed that I would find a city I would like." Luca said, almost to himself as he stood next to the philosopher. "I never believed that there would be another city like Rome, with its wonders, its sights." Demis glanced sideways at him. "Then I came here, and I marvel at it, all the time." Luca gave a quick titter.

"You find this city better than Rome?" Demis asked incredulously, as if the notion was absurd. Then he let out a sound which was an attempt at a laugh.

"Rome had its day, Demis." Luca said almost regretfully now. "With the empire at its peak, there was no place to equal it." He was remembering the city where he had lived for a while, as he trained to become a Centurion soldier. The city where he had been in love. "As with all empires at their peak, they are magnificent, a marvel to behold before the inevitable collapse." They both grinned now. "This one too, will fall to ruin." Luca said feeling rather sage now.

"You are becoming quite the philosopher, Lucian Marius Antonius." Demis declared with a grin, one of the few times that he certainly felt jovial. Luca smirked. It had been a long time since his full name had been used. It felt strange to hear his name used in the twenty first century as it had been in the first century.

"Perhaps I am just getting old, Demis." Luca laughed and walked over to the drink's cabinet. "Will you have a whiskey with me?" Demis nodded and went to sit down in front of the large desk.

"Where are the other Militibus?" Demis asked and his tone changed back to being grumpy again as he settled himself in the armchair and held out his hand to take the glass from Luca.

"Bjorn is conducting some final business of his own, in San Francisco, Peo and Lanny are working at their individual businesses today." Luca said and sat down behind his desk. "I will call a meeting with Peo and Lanny this evening." Demis nodded and took a large gulp from the glass. Luca observed the satisfied look on the scholar's face as he sipped the whiskey, evidently, he enjoyed the fine malt, as they all did.

"Have you discovered any news regarding Greyson?" He asked but Luca shook his head. "I hate this business. Especially when it is one of our own." Demis said pensively. Luca watched him intently. *What was he hiding?* Luca wondered.

"I did have a conversation with the theatre manager, where Greyson was to put on his play." Luca informed him. Demis sat up now, alert. "He's concealing something, so I informed him I will be hiring the theatre to stage a production of my own." Luca knew that this would perk up the old codger.

"Your own production?" Demis replied after a moment or so, the surprise was written all over his face. "Of what? You're not a producer or an actor, Lucian. Have you written something?" Curiosity was written all over him now.

"No, but I can direct a play." Luca said with a lobsided smile at the philosopher. "I have watched some of the greats perform in Rome and Pompeii." His smile was wide now, as Demis huffed at him and this made Luca chuckle loudly. He rarely saw Demis so loose.

"My dear Lucian," Demis cried hopelessly. "That was over two thousand years ago." Luca laughed heartily at the preciseness of the man. "The times have changed. These people only want sex and gore. What are you going to direct?" Luca chuckled loudly as he glimpsed the older man's discomfort at the word 'sex'. They all got great pleasure in riling the old academic.

"By infiltrating the theatre, Demis," Luca said in a serious tone again. "I will be able to ask questions without drawing unwanted attention to myself." He studied the expression on his friend's face. "Now, are you going to tell me what brings you back to the Fourth or is it top secret?" His mouth curled as he tried to supress his gorgeous smile.

"No, I was hoping you had some updates by now, but," he drained his glass and placed it on the desk in front of him. "If the others are not investigating, then I assume you have nothing." He sounded downbeat once more.

"That's unfair, Demis," Luca defended his officers now. "They are giving their best as they always do." He wasn't going to allow anyone to slag off his men. They were exceptional warriors.

"Well, I shall leave it for you to oversee the investigation," he stood up and so did Luca. "I'll be back soon." He turned on his heel and left the office. Demis had slipped into yet another of his moods, and this time Luca was glad to see the back of him.

Chapter 11

The manager's office was dark, bijou and smelt of stale whiskey and cigarettes. There were photos adorning the dark beige walls of past performers, which were discoloured by the smoke, some were recognisable, at least the plays that they had acted in were known. Other photos were barely visible because of age and the film of grime that covered the glass.

There were two larger posters depicting musicals that had been popular in the fifties. Another smaller one, was of a play that Luca wasn't familiar with. It must have been an obscure or an unpopular play because it was half covered by a signed publicity photo of a silent movie star from nineteen twenty.

"In its day," Willis said when he realised that Luca wasn't listening to him. "This place attracted all the stars before they made it into the movies. As you can see, Lettice Warboise played here, as Cleopatra in January nineteen twenty." Luca forced himself to listen to what he said. "She had such star quality." Willis went on, his voice full of smarmy admiration.

"Indeed. I gather from, Frankie," Luca said seriously. "That some big names acted and played music here." He was gauging the manager's reaction to his words.

"Unfortunately, Frankie, is a drunk and he's old. He imagines things you know." Willis said abruptly, barely containing his anger toward the old man. "I wouldn't pay too much heed to what he says." Luca could hear the man's heart pounding. He was obviously nervous and was on edge sitting across from Luca. "I thought about what you said the other day." Luca raised an eyebrow. "I remember your friend...Greyson."

"Is that so, Willis?" Luca asked and flashed him a brilliant smile now. Willis nodded.

"Yes, from what I remember of him he was... how shall I say this delicately." George Willis looked at Luca with a toadying expression. "Not a very nice man. Rather shifty." Luca gave him a smile. So, Greyson wasn't exactly lily white then.

"Well, as I said before he was only an acquaintance." Luca responded as charmingly as he could muster with Willis. "I choose my friends rather carefully." They looked at each other for a few moments before Willis announced.

"I'm sure your time is very valuable, Mister Meridian," Willis said now as he lowered his eyes from Luca's gaze, and he changed the subject quickly, it was clear that he didn't like or trust Luca. "Let's discuss the play you intend to stage."

"Medea," Luca replied steadily, and without batting an eyelid. Willis gaped at him for a long time, but Luca just remained reticent and unflinching. "It's a classic play, Mister Willis." Luca added as if to suggest that the theatre manager was ignorant to the classics. He loved the shocked look on his face.

"I...I am aware of it." Willis replied dryly. "A production of that kind would be rather expensive." He replied now in a shocked voice and quickly recovered his composure. "Especially for a theatre of this size." His voice was highly aroused suddenly as he glanced across at Luca, who had sat back in the chair and crossed one leg over the other. He brushed a piece of dust from his muscular thigh.

"Are you saying you can't accommodate such a play?" Luca pressed him directly as he listened to managers heart rate while Willis tried to think up an excuse, though Luca knew from experience that greed invariably got in the way and this mortal would be no different. He flashed Willis a brilliant smile.

"No, no, not at all Mister Meridian," Willis grovelled again as he regained some of his greedy countenance. "All I am saying is it would be expensive...for you." He smirked at Luca and Luca could smell the unscrupulousness in his pheromones. Willis was a detestable man in every way.

"No need for you to worry about that, Willis," Luca said charmingly. One thing he realised very quickly about the twenty first century, within the Fourth dimension, was that money talked. "I am willing to pay whatever it costs to stage this play." He flashed him another radiant smile. "As you have indicated before, time is precious to me, so why not run some figures into that computer of yours and get back to me as soon as possible." Luca stood up and held out his hand to the manager, they shook hands briefly and then Luca turned on his heel and left the office.

Chapter 12

It took only an hour for Willis to contact Luca regarding his production of Medea. Willis was apologetic that he couldn't lower the price, but he had assured him, it was a rock bottom price as it was. This made Luca smirk, and his estimation of the theatre manager plummeted even further than it already was. He was sleazy and he couldn't hide it.

"The estimated costs, for theatre hire, actors' wages, costumes etcetera, etcetera," Willis said in a highly excitable voice and Luca could almost see him rubbing his hands together as he had the phone on loudspeaker. "You wouldn't have any change from 115K." He paused as he waited for Luca to absorb and respond to the figure he had given. Luca wasn't sure if Willis had quoted the sum to discourage him and to have him walk away from the production or if he was just so greedy, he plucked the first number out of his head, based purely on how Luca presented himself to him at the theatre. Either way, Luca had no other option but to agree to the fee.

"That's all the overheads?" Luca asked him. Willis muttered something but Luca didn't understand. "Great, so I will front this production. When can I have the theatre?" Luca knew that it would be next to impossible for him to oversee everything, but he had to put his faith in this man, so he could expose and bring to justice the murder of Greyson.

"As of when I receive the down payment," Willis said, again Luca could almost see him grin. "I will make sure the theatre is not hired by anyone else. When would you be in a position to...um to pay the deposit, Mister Meridian?" Luca heard him cough. He despised everything about this crooked man. He knew that he was dirty in every way. It really wouldn't take a whole lot to expose him for what he was.

"Email me your bank details and I'll transfer the funds immediately." Luca replied and hung up.

He stared at the phone for a moment or so and then sat back in his chair and let out a slow contented sigh. It would be difficult for him to work with Willis but, Luca had worked harder cases before with more difficult dregs. Besides, he was looking forward to directing the play. It was a dream he had harboured for such a long time.

Luca called Lanny and waited for the Jarl to answer. "Hello," his sleepy voice uttered, and Luca smiled. He hadn't seen much of the Jarl in the last few days, but he knew that he had been out patrolling with Peo. They had been working relentlessly on the case.

"Did I disturb you, Jarl?" Luca asked grinning.

"Of course not, General." Lanny replied sleepily. "What's up?"

"Bjorn is still in San Francisco," Luca said in a curt businesslike manner. "So, I am calling a meeting with you and Peo, my office, in an hour."

"Very well, General." Lanny replied and hung up. Luca looked at his phone for a moment and then called Peo.

An hour and a half later, Luca looked up as his personal assistant came in and announced that Lanny and Peo were waiting to see him. He sighed audibly and bellowed at her to send them in.

"You have us announced now?" Lanny said grumpily as he sauntered into the office and stood with his legs apart and his hands on his hips, Peo joined him, both wore an unamused expression.

"It's my new assistant," Luca said equally unimpressed. "She's not in tune with certain visitors." He forced himself to smile at them.

"Why the meeting here, and not the Militibus office?" Peo asked, both the Militibus vampires remained standing.

"It still needs to be cleaned," Luca said a little gruffly. He didn't like being questioned by his underlings. "Until I am certain it is clear, I will not discuss anything there or the warehouse." He stared hard at Peo now.

"Why the meeting?" Lanny asked wearily and then he sat down on the leather chair in front of Luca's desk, and he rubbed his eyes.

"I have secured the theatre for my production." Luca said smugly as he glanced at Lanny who grinned back at him. "The manager is a suspect for now, and I think he knows a little more than he has revealed to me in the few meetings I have had with him."

"Is he a dreg?" Peo asked casually as he too, sat down. The tension in the office seemed to have evaporated now between all of them.

"I don't know." Luca admitted to him. "I believe he is a mortal, because I can smell his pheromones, and I can hear the blood and heart motions."

"But?" Lanny interjected.

"I think he may have dreg connections." Luca said and leaned back in the chair, slightly rocking backward and forward on it. Enjoying the motion as he pondered.

"Why do you think that?" Lanny asked, as he shifted in his seat.

"There's a janitor there, who is a talker, and he has revealed quite a lot," Luca smiled at both of them. "Willis doesn't want me talking to him. I don't like it when someone tells me I can't talk to a mortal."

"Do you want one of us to talk to him, General?" Peo asked and glanced casually over at Lanny, who smiled back at him.

"No, Peo," Luca said instantly. "I'll see what I can find out from Frankie, myself. What I want from you and the Jarl is to keep Willis under surveillance. See who he knows, hangs around with." They both nodded. "I want to know what he gets up to outside of the theatre."

"So, when are the auditions taking place?" Lanny asked roguishly. Luca and Peo laughed as they looked across at the Jarl. "Need any help choosing the leading lady?"

"You will have to wait until opening night to see the stars, Jarl." Luca said laughing. "I got off the phone over an hour ago, so I assume Willis is still there, at the theatre. If you feel like checking him out and reporting back when you have found something." It was clear to both Lanny and Peo that Luca had finished the meeting.

"This is your classy way of dismissing us, Luca." Peo chuckled. "For a moment, I thought the old codger was here." Lanny laughed heavily.

"Where is the toad?" Lanny asked.

"Worried sick and back in the Sixth." Luca said and stood up, indicating they were free to go. Lanny paused at the door and turned to look at Luca.

"I still think something is off." Lanny said and shrugged. "About this case. It has all the signs of a Demis coverup." Luca watched as the Jarl left his office. Though he knew that there was an ever-present distrust with Lanny regarding Demis, Luca also felt that there was something not quite right about the case, and especially the manner in which Demis had informed them of the murder of Greyson. His concern for the dreg who had been murdered was unlike Demis, who usually didn't put in such an intense time or effort into something that he deemed was a waste of time, and in normal circumstances, the academic would have deemed this case a waste of time.

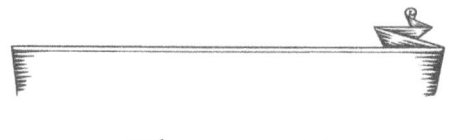

Chapter 13

The front row seats in the auditorium were empty and Luca decided that it would be less intimidating for the actors if he were to sit in the third row. He had the clipboard on his lap, and he had carefully laid his jacket over the seat beside him. The atmosphere in the theatre was full of anticipation. Luca could hear the actors backstage as they warmed up, and some rehearsed their lines. He smiled to himself, so far, he was enjoying the buzz.

The three stagehands that he had asked to help him set up the scene in which, Medea is meeting with Jason, had just left the stage. It was a pivotal scene in the play and Luca had seen its production many times over the centuries and many times it had had a profound effect on him. He had enjoyed all Euripides plays, but it was Medea that he had found the most intriguing in all its tragic splendour.

"Can the first actor please come on stage and read the passage." The other man who was sitting a few seats away from Luca called out in an authoritative voice.

A tall, dark-haired woman in her late twenties came onto the stage. She wore a pair of black leggings, which clung to her thighs and emphasised her shapely legs. She wore a white tank top, and a red checked shirt tied around her waist. If he had passed her on the street, Luca would not have guessed her to be an actor.

"What do you want me to read?" She called out to them, and Luca could see her squint as the stage lights blinded her. He half smirked at her boldness.

"The scene in which Medea requests Jason to come into the room where she is waiting to speak with him." The man said, quite irritated. This woman clearly didn't have a clue about what she was auditioning for.

"Oh, right." She said and cleared her throat, then she began in a loud voice. "*So be it! Whatever you say now is wasted-*"

"Read the script as it is," the man interrupted her. "No improvising, please. Again."

Luca observed the woman on the stage. He wasn't sure if she had deliberately improvised or if she just wanted the audition over as quickly as possible because she assumed she wouldn't get the part. Or perhaps she was just cocky. Either way, he liked her style.

[i] "*So be it! Anything you say now is wasted.*" A pause. "*Come! Go fetch Jason here-*"

"Thank you. We'll be in touch. Next." The man called out and the young woman just stood where she was. Disbelief written all over her face.

"That's it?" She demanded in an astonished tone. With her left hand on her hip and the script down her right side.

"Yes, thank you for coming. Next." He called out again. The woman swore as she pounded off the stage.

Luca looked on in amusement and then stood up. "I'll be back, in a moment, Amos." Luca left the row where he was sitting and went backstage.

In the semi darkness, he didn't have to search hard for the young woman. He heard her ranting at no one in particular or at whoever was listening. Luca stood up straight and smiled as he listened to the diatribe. She was passionate about the role, and very indignant about the abrupt dismissal. So typical of an actor, he thought.

She turned around and glared at him standing there, interrupting her tirade.

"What are you staring at?" She demanded. *"Asshole!"* She muttered under her breath, and he just smiled at her. "Who are you?" Luca stepped forward and held out his hand to her. She didn't take it, she just glared at him for his interruption.

"I'm Luca and you are?" Luca asked her casually.

"None of your damn business." She retorted and turned her back to him. At that moment a stagehand came up to him and said, almost in a breathless voice.

"They are almost ready for your decision on who to call back on stage, Mister Meridian." The young man said and glanced uncertainly at the actor and then back to Luca.

"Thank you, I'll be there in a moment." Luca replied and gave a final glance at the young woman and as he was about to walk away the performer turned back to face him, she was blushing hard now.

"What, you're the director?" She inquired, shamefaced. He nodded as he suppressed a smile, and he looked at her. "Look I am not usually rude, but that guy back there just pushed all the wrong buttons today." She looked at Luca.

"Now, I've blown it. Haven't I? Just my luck!" She was about to walk away when he said to her.

"I'm looking for a strong female lead." She stopped and turned to look at him. "I haven't made the final decision yet, but I would like to discuss the role with you." A slow smile swept across her face, and she lowered her eyes and then looked up at him again.

"Sure." She said and bit her lower lip and rocked her body from side to side.

"Great. After I finish with the casting director," Luca said with a broad smile. "How about a coffee?" She nodded. "I'll meet you outside the theatre in twenty minutes." He turned and walked back onto the stage.

Luca glanced at his watch several times as he listened to Amos and his ideas. He didn't want to appear bored, and besides he needed his expertise, as this was all new to Luca.

"There are three from the ten who read today." Amos said briefly. "We'll call them back for tomorrow, if you like." Luca nodded and scribbled on his clipboard.

"Sure, that girl, you know the one who improvised the lines, earlier." Luca said with a smile. "Add her to the list." He looked at the disbelief on his casting director's face as he shook his head and muttered.

"Of course." Amos said in a discouraged tone. "Anything else?" Luca shook his head and stood up and slapped Amos on the shoulder then he walked out of the theatre.

Luca stopped for a moment as he watched from behind the theatre door. She paced up and down outside. Her demeanour suggested a fight or flight disposition.

He opened the glass door and walked casually over to her. "Ready?" She looked up at him and nodded and he walked a little ahead of her, so she had to sprint almost to keep up with him.

Luca held the door of the bistro open for her and let her in ahead of him. They were seated at the window table, and they ordered two coffees from the server.

"A name would be helpful." Luca said after a moment and when they were alone.

"Thea." She replied and fiddled with the sugar sachet in her hand. Thea appeared to be nervous. "You said your name is Luca, right?" Luca nodded and sat back and observed her. He could hear that her breathing was a little rapid, her blood was running fast. Adrenalin! He thought.

"That's right, Luca Meridian." He held out his hand to her once more and this time she shook it. "Tell me, Thea, what experience have you?" She raised a perfectly shaped brow. "As an actor." He clarified but he was grinning at her.

"Professionally, just community theatre." She stated a little shyly.

"In other words," Luca retorted in a serious tone. "You are an amateur, with no real experience, correct?" He looked at her intently now. The server brought their coffees and placed them in front of them on the table.

"Well, it's hard to get a role with dicks like that guy." Thea said aggressively. This made Luca smile. She was feisty. He liked her spirit.

"Amos is the consummate professional." Luca countered with a grin. "Tell me Thea, why did you read for the role of Medea and not one of the lesser roles?" He watched as she played with the spoon in her coffee cup. "If you have no experience a lesser role would have been better." She looked up into his eyes. She was stunningly beautiful. "Less demanding for an actress with little to no experience." He was being gentle but yet it came out condescending.

"You know, I am good. I probably know the play better than the ones who are auditioning anyway." Thea said defiantly and put the spoon down on the table. The dark brown line flowed effortlessly onto the linen cloth causing the stain to widen in the shape of the spoon head.

"I am sure you are," Luca said gently. "Though what we specifically specified in the advert was for an actor with experience. The female lead is very demanding."

"And so, you decided to let me down by buying me a coffee." Thea stood up and glared at him. "Thanks for nothing." She made to leave but he quickly said.

"That's not why I asked you to come for coffee." She stood beside the table for a moment, fidgeting with her fingers, but she didn't dare to look at him, she just hung her head. "I want to hear your interpretation of the role." Thea looked up at him suddenly, with wide eyes.

"You want me to tell you what the role involves?" Luca smiled momentarily as he looked at her now and then he shook his head. "Then what?" She asked as she reluctantly sat back down at the table.

"Back there, on stage," Luca reminded. "You read the lines with an improvisation. That intrigued me. I have never heard Medea read like that before."

"The classics are great, but they only reach a few because most people see them as elitist," Thea said with a huge grin now. "I see them as interpretive, you know, open to whatever it means to you personally." She seemed very excited as she explained this to him. "That way, you see anyone who goes to the theatre can enjoy them without them being too academic." Luca wore an amused expression on his face. He certainly didn't think of it like that. This way of thinking about the classics was new to him. "You know what I mean?"

"That's a new way of looking at it." Luca said after a moment. "Classics for the masses." Thea giggled as she picked up the spoon again. "You've convinced me, Thea, come by the theatre tomorrow. The same time." He said and stood up and put some money on the table and walked over to the door and left. This actor had impressed him.

Chapter 14

All the hopefuls had arrived an hour earlier, and they were standing in the centre of the stage chatting nervously to each other and giggling every now and then.

Luca had arrived a few minutes prior to the casting director, and he chose to sit in the centre seat in the second row. He was glancing up at the Medea hopefuls and every now and then he would look at the clipboard on his knee. Just for something to do. He wasn't feeling nervous, but he was feeling an excitement, something that he hadn't felt before, not like this anyway. He felt alive, almost human.

He wondered if he had made the right decision to put on this particular play but as he glanced up at the stage once more, he smiled and knew that he had. It would be a wonderful opportunity to stage this classic Greek tragedy.

"Sorry I'm late." Amos said almost in a whisper as he sat down and handed Luca a cardboard takeaway cup of coffee.

"Thanks." Luca said and took the cup from him. "I'd like Thea to read first and then this girl, I think she may be perfect in the role of the nurse." Amos stared at him for a moment as if he had gone mad.

"Mister Meridian, I know you are putting on the production but that girl Thea," Amos first looked across to the stage and then at Luca with a serious expression. "She has no experience in acting in a lead role, or even a supporting role." Luca had to agree with him, as he was a seasoned professional. Though it was true that Thea had no formal acting experience, but what experience did Luca have? None whatsoever. A smile crossed his handsome face. That's what was so good about this idea of his, not just that he needed to find a murderer, but he was looking forward to putting on this play. "Plus, she has an attitude problem, that I think could be problematic to the show." Amos gave a long hard look at Luca but seeing Luca's steadfast expression, he knew it was hopeless to try to dissuade him from his decision.

"That's true but let's just see how she performs, OK?" Luca said determined to see if Thea would do justice to the role. He believed that she would, because she was so determined, and that was what was needed in his cast. "Now, let's get started, shall we?" He flashed Amos a fantastic smile and turned his attention to the ladies on the stage.

"Can I have your attention, please." Amos called from the second row and everyone on the stage turned to look at him. "I want to hear, Thea, Maggie, and Solei, I want you to read from the script, you'll find it there on the table behind you." Amos indicated to the table at the back of the stage. "Each piece is different, so relax and up first," He looked down as if he were reading from the clipboard. "Solei, when you are ready." Amos sat back down beside Luca, and they smiled at each other as Solei came forward and with the script in her hand, she began to read the passage in a flat yet formal voice.

It took just over two hours to hear all the potential Medea's', read the script. By which time, Luca was beginning to bore of the different interpretations. None of which impressed him as being powerful enough to carry off such a demanding and complicated character like Medea. He wanted a strong lead, and he wanted to hear it as close to the way Euripides had intended it to sound. As it had done, when he heard it performed in Pompeii and then later in Rome.

"Thank you, ladies," Luca said and stood up. "Your understanding of the role is interesting. Now, I will be calling just two of you back to re-read and then by the end of the week, we will have cast our Medea, and you will all know the roles you have been chosen for." He looked up at the stage and smiled warmly at all of the actors as they walked single file off the stage, discussing and giggling amongst themselves.

Luca sat down once more and let out a long sigh of relief. The hard part was now beginning, but he knew who he wanted as Medea.

"It really isn't a difficult choice here." Amos said from the seat beside him, and Luca half turned his head to look at him. "I believe that Maggie will make a great Medea and Solei a great nurse." Luca laughed but he shook his head and Amos stared at him incredulously.

"I would like to see Thea as Medea, and Maggie as the nurse." Luca said dismissively and then stood up. "The rest of the casting, I leave up to you, Amos." He left the second row and walked out of the auditorium and into the street. Luca began to hum a tune to himself. It was his decision after all who he wanted to play Medea.

It was a controversial decision that he had made, and he knew that Amos was perplexed as to why Luca would give someone without any kind of experience a lead role, but Luca liked how Thea's spirit came through in how she saw Medea. He didn't know how he could convince Amos that she was right for the role. Only time would tell, but he knew that she would prove herself during rehearsals.

Chapter 15

Luca saw Lanny sitting on the panigale as he came into the street. The Viking vampire was ready for that night's patrol and Luca knew afterwards that the Jarl would probably want to go for a drink. He himself didn't mind it usually, but tonight, all Luca wanted was to go back to his penthouse and relax. It had been a long, but exciting day.

"You are late, General." Lanny said with a smirk and began to put on his helmet. "Where do you want to cruise?" Luca laughed and started his bike. The Jarl was keen to patrol, it seemed. This truly was a first!

"Let's go by the theatre." Luca advised and put on his own helmet. Lanny rode out ahead of Luca and the two Militibus vampires cruised the streets, keeping a keen eye out for unusual activity that might be happening.

They slowed down almost to a crawl as they passed by alleys. Luca glanced down one of them and saw a tall dreg fighting with another. He pulled up beside Lanny and motioned down the alley. Lanny stopped his bike and glanced down. He nodded and they pulled over the bikes and parked up onto the sidewalk. They both removed their helmets and walked purposefully down the alleyway side by side. They were impressive figures.

"What's the problem?" Luca called out, both the dregs, who had stopped fighting now turned to look at the Militibus. Luca looked at Lanny and grinned. Wolves!

"Nothing that concerns you." One of the wolves replied gruffly.

"It is when you are fighting in my city." Luca grinned back as he walked in front of the wolf. "What's the problem?" The tall dark-haired wolf snorted. There wasn't a full moon for another few weeks, and there really wasn't any reason why these two werewolves should be fighting.

"It's a turf war, nothing for the Militibus to interfere with." The second wolf spat, and Luca turned to Lanny who had just joined him, in front of the fighting wolves.

"What's the fight about?" The Jarl asked and removed his sword from inside his scabbard. The silver blade glistened in the dim light from the building at the end of the alley.

"This douche has decided to move in on my turf." The silver-haired wolf said angrily. "We had a deal, no one but the silvers work this end of the city. Nothing for you to intrude on, Militibus."

"Fighting inside the city limits amongst the dregs is our business." Luca said as he too removed his sword. "Why are the Malas moving in?" the malawolf laughed at the question and then he sniffed the air.

"We have every right to be here," he said angrily. "Not just the silvers."

Luca looked at Lanny and then he looked back to the mala. "Answer a few of our questions," Luca said with a broad grin. "We may just turn a blind eye to this misdemeanour."

Lanny turned away for a moment and then he chuckled and nodded.

"What do you want to know." The silver wolf asked, he was mistrustful of the Militibus. He stood up straight, and though he was tall, he was dwarfed in front of the two vampires.

"Have you seen anything going down here recently?" Lanny asked and the two wolves looked at each other, they seemed confused by the question. "Specifically, bodies with their blood sucked dry?" Luca smiled to himself. Lanny wasn't one for subtlety, that was for sure.

"Only the Militibus." The malawolf said and laughed loudly.

"Answer the question," Lanny held out the blade of his sword to his throat and stepped forward. He had no sense of humour with dregs and particularly when he was asking questions about a case they were working on.

"You mean the theatre guys, don't you?" The silver asked. Luca looked at him now.

"What have you heard?" Luca prodded.

"There's been rumours that there's a navar recently moved here from the East." The silver said in an earnest voice and looked at both the vampires and then shrugged.

"Not from the Seventh?" Lanny asked and the silver wolf just shook his head.

"I only heard talk down by the docks." He replied quickly. The docks were a favoured spot for the dregs who moved from other parts of the world to the West Coast. They usually hid in the cargo hold, or some would be hired as deck hands. It depended on how they wanted to enter the city, they would either feed on vermin or sometimes a crew member. There were times when a dreg would pay a trafficker to bring them in but that route was slowly being closed and it was harder now to find someone willing to transport them in, no matter how much the dreg was willing to pay.

"What talk?" Luca asked him. He was interested to find out what the dregs knew and just exactly what the talk on the street was.

"A guy there, was paid twenty grand to take a navar from Mexico to LA." The silver said. "Look, it's only a rumour, I don't know anyone who would be that stupid to let a sucker like that in, it's too dangerous."

"When did the navar come in?" Lanny asked. "How long ago?"

"Five, maybe six weeks ago." The malawolf said. "Look, I didn't see it, but I heard it, any dreg hanging out down there heard it, I'm sure of it. But it wasn't none of my business, OK." Luca looked at Lanny and then back to the wolf. "I don't interfere with it, it don't interfere with me. Just how I like life. Capice?"

"Did you see the hybrid who was sucked dry?" Luca asked as he put his sword back into his scabbard.

"Yeah, I saw him." The malawolf said. "Ignorant little prick, thought he was too good to share the same air as us." The silver wolf chuckled but he nodded in agreement with the malawolf.

"When did you see him?" Lanny asked them.

"A couple of hours before I heard the navar." The malawolf said, and Luca could sense that he was nervous.

"If you hear anything, let us know." Luca said and handed him a Militibus card.

"Why? What will you do, spare us, is that it?" The silver wolf asked sarcastically.

"We might just save your worthless lives." Lanny said and stepped a little closer. "Call us if you hear anything." He reiterated, with his voice full of cautious warning.

Luca turned and retreated back down the alley, followed by Lanny.

When they reached their bikes, Luca leaned against his and looked at Lanny with a serious expression.

"What is it, General?" Lanny asked as he threw a long leg over the saddle and sat on the sleek black panigale.

"That's not the first time, that I've heard that this Greyson was not a nice guy." Luca said as he glanced down the street. It always worried him when a so-called victim had a reputation for being a prick. He wanted to know what he was dealing with.

"You think the wolves are right?" Lanny asked him almost in a cavalier voice.

"Willis, the theatre manager said Greyson was not what you call a decent guy." Luca said and shook his head. "I'm beginning to suspect, someone had it in for him." Lanny grinned. "Maybe he crossed someone that he shouldn't have."

"Like a dreg?" But Luca just shook his head. "Then who? I seriously doubt he knew anyone here in the Fourth." Lanny said in a serious voice. "If you believe Demis, that is."

"We know virtually nothing about him, yet the wolves and a mortal, all say the same thing." Luca pondered. "Demis has told us nothing about this Greyson either."

"The old toad tells us practically nothing anyway, Luca." Lanny grumbled. "We have to find out from other sources besides Demis." Luca looked at him. "That's why the old codger has the council on his case all the time."

Luca knew that Lanny was right, but he also was aware that Demis came through for them when they needed him. Especially for Luca. Was that enough of a reason for him to defend Demis all the time? It certainly wasn't enough for the other Militibus. But then Luca knew Demis better than the others did. He knew him longer.

As Luca casually glanced around, he thought about how the Militibus were always taking the micky out of Demis, it seemed to Luca that the Jarl never missed an opportunity to make a barb against Demis, and it was apparent to Luca, that Lanny was pushing the boundaries further and further in disrespect. As the superior officer, Luca wondered if he should pull the Jarl up on his defiance regarding his tone toward Demis? Insubordination and the Jarl went hand in glove. But Luca couldn't do that to his officer, if he did, he was no different than Demis.

Even as he thought about it, Luca knew that Lanny was right, and to call him out on it, it would only rile Lanny even further. Get his back up. The Jarl was a good officer, and warrior, Luca knew if he charged Lanny with being disrespectful, he would lose the respect of the Berserker and the Praetorian, and Luca's authority would be lost for all time.

"Let's just do what we need to do here." Luca replied after a moment, and he put on his helmet and got on the panigale.

It was going to be a long night, Luca thought to himself. *A long night indeed!*

Chapter 16

He sat through the rehearsals for the first act. Luca had been right in casting Thea in the lead. She knew the part well. However, Luca wasn't as convinced of the lead actor, that Amos had chosen to play Jason. The actor seemed unsure of how he should push the character and if he should be a little remote from Medea.

Amos was certain that the actor would loosen up and that he would grow into the role. To Luca, he seemed completely wrong for the role.

"OK, from the beginning once more." Amos bellowed and then Luca read the opening act. The actors gathered around, and Luca looked up from where he stood in the third row, and saw Thea shake her arms and her head, as if wakening up her body. This amused him as he watched her.

He listened and watched closely as Medea, and the nurse conversed. Medea's voice was carried out into the auditorium. It was powerful and authoritative, as she was caught up in the scene. Thea had become Medea.

This impressed Luca. Thea was as he remembered the play when he first saw it performed in Pompeii. He had been a small boy of ten years then, and his father had been home on leave, Emperor Nero had just promoted him to

Primus Pilus, and he had taken Luca to the magnificent amphitheatre in Pompeii.

Even then, Medea had caused a sensation amongst the audience with its scandal. But to a young Luca, it had made a lasting impression, one that he never forgot.

He stood up and walked over to the steps and climbed onto the stage.

"Gather round." Luca commanded and smiled warmly at all of them. His voice was deep with just the slightest hint of an accent. "This is a very good start." He said encouragingly to them as he spoke. "Medea is a powerful woman, but she is also a very angry lady. Her husband has left her and married another. I don't know about you, but if it were me, I'd be downright furious." They all laughed, and some shook their hands by their sides. Luca turned to Thea and smiled amiably at her. "Thea your voice is strong, but I want feeling from you, you don't trust the nurse, and you now have a bad feeling toward your children, a feeling of hate is beginning to surface because of what their father has done to you. Show me that angst. Show me your pain!" He looked at her intently and saw the anger flash in her eyes as if the criticism were personal.

"Mister Meridian, do I start from the beginning again?" Thea asked sharply and there was no mistaking the fury in her voice as she flashed him an acidic look.

"Of course," Luca retorted equally as sharp, but he wore a smile and then turned on his heel and left the stage. He sat down beside Amos and looked up at the stage. Luca knew that Thea's anger would spill over to Medea, and he would get the best from her now. She was determined to prove to him that she was the perfect actor to play the tragic Medea.

"Again." Amos called out and the actors took their places and Luca sat back and watched with interest. He was grinning from ear to ear. This was a victory for him.

IT WAS DARK OUTSIDE when Luca was leaving the theatre. He walked over to the door and then he heard footsteps behind him. He was alert, as always.

"Mister Meridian, I hope you don't mind," a man's voice said eagerly from behind Luca, and Luca turned around. It was George Willis, the theatre manager. "I snuck in to have a look at rehearsals earlier." Luca forced himself to smile at him. He didn't like this sleaze bag, but he had to tolerate him. For now, at least.

"What did you think?" Luca asked but he didn't care what Willis thought.

"Exceptional choice for the female lead." Willis said with a smarmy smile. "Beautiful and talented." He added, as he made a snorting sound, which Luca assumed was a laugh. "A rare quality these days."

"Indeed." Luca said and reached for the door.

"Of course," Willis said again, and Luca let the door go and it closed with a bang. "I haven't seen the entire rehearsal, but I wonder if she won't suppress her leading man. He seems rather unsure of himself, and she is powerful." Luca turned and looked at him. He sniffed the air, and he could smell his arrogance but there was something else too, Luca wasn't sure, but he could smell it. A change in his pheromones. "That's just my opinion, of course, based on the briefest of observation."

"Allow me to invite you to sit in on the full rehearsal in the morning." Luca flashed Willis a brilliant smile. He needed to remain somewhat cordial to him though he certainly didn't feel like it.

"I wasn't looking for an invite to see what you're doing," Willis replied in mock protest and looked slightly embarrassed now. Luca smiled at him again.

"It would be my pleasure to have you there, Willis," Luca's responded in a friendly tone. "To give some valuable input to the production." Luca chose that moment as Willis mulled over what he had said, to escape.

Out on the street he saw Thea, she was talking to two of the actors. Luca smiled and strolled along casually. He had no major plans for the evening. The Jarl and the other Militibus were going out on the town, but Luca didn't feel like clubbing. Not that night any way.

Chapter 17

"**M**ister Meridian," Luca turned around when he heard his name called. It was Thea. He smiled warmly at her. "You walk very fast." Thea commented, she was almost out of breath trying to keep up with him.

"Hello, Thea." Luca said and grinned at her.

"About earlier," Thea said, almost embarrassed by the incident. "Was I really that terrible?" He looked into her eyes, and he could see a little sadness there. A lack of confidence. It always surprised Luca how shy people chose to go into acting when they could hardly hold a conversation with a stranger without turning several shades of red.

"You weren't terrible, Thea." Luca said reassuringly. "I wanted you to embrace the role, feel what Medea feels." She lowered her eyes from his. This amused him.

"I thought that I was." Thea replied wistfully. "I guess that you have a different idea of what anger is, than I do." She was clearly insulted and then she turned to walk away, and Luca stood there for a moment and then he called out to her.

"Thea." She stopped and turned around and looked at him. "Do you want to go for a drink?" Luca asked and as he listened, he heard her heart, it had an unusual rhythm. She looked at him for a moment.

"OK." Thea replied, almost shyly.

They walked for a block or so and then stopped outside a trendy bar. Luca held the door open for her and they went inside.

After they had ordered their drinks, they walked over to a table near the bar and sat down. Luca undid the button of his jacket and sat back in the seat. Neither of them spoke, not until after the server had brought them their drinks.

"Thank you." Thea said and picked up her glass of red wine. Luca watched her carefully. She was very beautiful and yet she seemed so vulnerable and very unsure of herself. This added to her attractiveness. He felt an overwhelming urge to protect her, from what he didn't know, but he just wanted to.

"I didn't mean to suggest that you didn't interpret Medea's anger correctly." Luca said after a moment.

"It's not you, Mister Meridian." Thea said and blushed a bright pink. "I'm just far too sensitive."

"Please, call me Luca." He insisted now and smiled warmly at her. "Sensitivity is part of your profession." She looked at him and giggled.

"I guess it is." Thea admitted and raised the glass to her mouth and took a sip. Luca watched her, as she ran the tip of her tongue over her lower lip, and the red of her lipstick glistened. It was a very erotic scene, even though she was totally oblivious to it. But Luca hadn't been. It certainly wasn't lost on him.

Thea giggled and Luca stared at her with a confused look on his face. "I asked if you were from LA?" He grinned at her, as now it was his turn to be embarrassed. Luca had been too busy watching her voluptuous mouth, just wondering what it would be like to kiss her, that he hadn't heard her.

"Yes, I've lived here for a long time." Replied Luca, as he regained his composure, and reached for his own glass.

"You don't have an LA accent." Thea persisted and looked at him intently. Luca chuckled at that. He still had traces of his Roman accent even though these days it was only slight, and usually stronger when he spoke Latin.

"I grew up near Sorrento." He said and put his glass down on the table. It was the first time he had referred to the modern name of the city of his birth.

"You're Italian?" Thea exclaimed and Luca grinned at her and nodded. "But your name isn't very Italian sounding." She glanced at him, a little puzzled and Luca laughed at this now.

"It's not just actors who change their name for their profession." Luca said almost mysteriously and then changed the questioning away from him and back to her. He didn't like personal questions. "What about you, Thea, where are you from?" Luca noticed the change in her eyes.

"I'm East Coast bred." Thea said after a moment, and it was clear from her tone that she wasn't going to reveal anything else.

"Have you always been an actress?" Luca asked her and she nodded. "To acting." He said and raised his glass to hers.

"Have you always been a director?" Luca held the glass between his thumb and index finger and moved it from side to side, as the light from the downlighters caught the reflection on the thin glass, then raised it to his mouth and took a sip before he put the glass down on the table. Did he really want to answer these probing questions? Weren't questions asked when one was on a date? Not on the ones he had been on though. Luca thought to himself and smiled wryly.

"In a way, I have." Luca replied, distantly. Suddenly he felt uncomfortable with personal questions, and he knew why. They usually became probing about his background, and that was when the lies started, because Luca could never reveal that he was a vampire, a Tempus Militibus vampire from the Sixth dimension.

"You're a very handsome man." Thea said and then he saw her bite her lower lip, almost regretting having said it. He grinned at her now.

"Thank you, Thea." Luca said. He was flattered and he was very attracted to her. "You are incredibly beautiful too." Luca saw her lower her eyes at the compliment and again, her shyness became a little too obvious.

"Some of the other girls in the show, were saying how hunky you are." Luca stared at her and then he laughed out loud. This wasn't new to him. Women always found him attractive, but this forwardness made him smile. He liked it. He was flattered by it.

"Should you be telling me this?" Luca teased her and she giggled. "The tales from the locker room."

"I think I might be getting drunk." Thea admitted with a giggle. "I'm not used to drinking alcohol on an empty stomach."

"Would you like to have dinner with me?" Luca asked her and she nodded. He stood up and held out his hand to her.

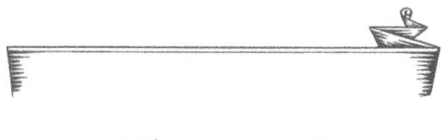

Chapter 18

The restaurant was dimly lit, and they were seated next to the window. Luca ordered a blue fillet steak and Thea just opted for the chicken salad.

In the light from the flickering candle, Luca gazed into her beautiful expressive eyes. He wanted to kiss her, and he had wanted to do so since he first met her. He had to force himself to stop looking at her like that. She was his leading lady and not a romantic interest. But Luca couldn't help it, he was horny, and he couldn't hide it.

"You are a very intense man." Thea said after a while. As Luca looked at her, he sensed that she was feeling like he was.

"Am I?" He asked her in a teasing tone, and she nodded. "Maybe it's because I am enthralled by you." Luca knew he was threading on dangerous ground by flirting with the actress the way that he was, but he couldn't help himself, she was stunning.

"Really?" Thea asked in a flirtatious voice too. Luca grinned at her. "*You're* enthralled by *me?*"

"I don't see why you are incredulous by that, Thea." Luca said in a light-hearted tone. "You are a very desirable woman." Their eyes met briefly now before Thea lowered her head once more. This amused Luca, because she was so introverted.

"Talk like that could get you in trouble, Luca." Thea said in a teasing tone as she caressed the stem of the glass with her thumb and index finger. Luca laughed at that. At that moment he just didn't care if it landed him in trouble. He enjoyed their playful teasing.

"As long as it doesn't with you." Luca flirted back with her, and she giggled as she turned her head to the side and looked at him. Momentarily they just glanced into each other's eyes, both feeling the tension that had just enveloped them. The side of Luca's mouth turned up as he reached out and touched his own glass with his index finger and knowingly caressed it as if it were Thea's hand. He saw her shiver as she watched his finger slide up and down on the glass.

"Not at all." Thea replied after she inhaled deeply and gave Luca a knowing look. "I hope it leads to a different kind of trouble." She licked her lips seductively now, and he groaned loudly as he leaned forward and covered her hand with his. Her hand was surprisingly cold. Luca looked at her as he caressed the back of her hand with his thumb. "What?" Thea asked coquettishly as she looked away from the weight of his eyes on hers.

"I think you know what I want to happen after dinner." Luca said in a low tone, his gaze as intense as the atmosphere that was between them.

"I want it too." Thea replied with a flirtatious smile and Luca grinned at her. "My apartment is nearby." She added and he could smell the excitement from her body.

"Let's go then." Luca said and called the server for the bill. Neither of them wanting to wait any longer to be in each other's arms.

THEA OPENED THE DOOR to the small bungalow, and holding his hand loosely in hers, she led Luca inside. Her apartment was bijou. There was a couch which doubled as a bed and along the back wall, where the second window was located, was the kitchen area. There was a door off to the right where the tiny bathroom was located.

She looked longingly at Luca, and she walked over to where he stood. Thea reached out to touch his chest with her hand, he smiled down at her and just looked at her as she began to open the buttons of his linen shirt.

"You are such a beautiful man." Thea whispered huskily as her cold hand caressed his bare chest. He closed his eyes as her fingers lingered on the waistband of his pants. Luca inhaled deeply. He was getting harder.

Luca pulled her into his arms and kissed her passionately as his hand caressed her shapely ass. He felt her arms go around his neck as she stood up on her toes as their kiss deepened.

He wanted her so badly as his tongue probed her hot mouth. Luca could hear Thea's heart pounding in her chest as she pressed herself against him, each movement making him harder.

Luca groaned as he felt her hand slip inside his trousers, and she began to move her hand up and down on his impressive cock.

Luca's fangs began to descend the more aroused he became. Thea got on her knees and hurriedly began to open his belt and then the button. She slid his pants over his hips and with her long fingernails, she scraped the skin of his cock and then she took him deep in her mouth. Luca closed his eyes as he put his head back, the groans from his throat were almost a growl as she expertly wrapped her lips around his hardness. His fangs were fully descended now as he pumped her mouth rhythmically, and her fingernails scraped his balls as she caressed them.

He could feel himself explode inside her hot mouth as her tongue went into hyper drive on the head of his cock. Luca began to shudder hard.

Slowly he opened his eyes and held out his hand to her and she smiled up at him as she took his hand.

Thea looked into his dark eyes and smiled as she pushed his shirt off his shoulders and soon, they were lying down on the sofa, naked. Luca closed his eyes as he kissed her breasts and Thea moved slowly on him as they made love.

He rolled her off him and covered her hands with his as she pressed them flat against the back of the sofa. Luca entered her forcefully from behind. His vampiric body had taken over now as he pumped her hard, Thea's moans were equal to Luca's, loud and primal. Unsatiated.

With his eyes closed and his body in a heightened state of arousal, Luca pushed harder and then he felt his orgasm, powerful and feral, and just the release that he wanted.

LUCA AWOKE WITH A START. There was something sticking into his back. He moved and as he did, Thea stirred too.

"What's wrong?" She asked sleepily as she turned onto her back. Luca laughed as he picked up a stiletto shoe which had been sticking into his lower back. He held it out to her.

"I believe this is yours." Luca said with a smirk on his face. Thea opened her eyes fully now and giggled as she took it from him.

"Where did you find it?" She asked and then she reached out to touch his muscular arm.

"In my lower back." Luca teased and sat up, with his back resting against the sofa.

"I've been looking for that everywhere." She giggled and supported herself on her elbow. Luca threw off the sheet and stood up. He was naked. "Do you have to leave?" Thea asked him as he picked up his clothes and began to dress.

"I do." Luca replied as he buckled his belt. "I am sorry." Thea sat up in the bed and covered herself with the sheet. "I won't be at rehearsals until Friday." He said it, almost regretfully, as he sat back down on the sofa bed and reached out to touch her face with his hand. She looked disappointed and he smiled at her. "It can't be helped, Thea." She reached out and covered his hand with hers and held his gaze for a moment longer.

"I can't wait to see you then." Thea whispered and Luca stood up and put on his shirt and buttoned it. He glanced at his watch. It was gone three. He was running late for the patrol. But then a night off from time to time was sometimes needed too. Besides he was the General, the commander of the group, surely, he was entitled to play hooky occasionally? He didn't do it very often either.

Luca picked up his jacket and looked over longingly to where Thea lay. She sat up on the sofa, looking seductively at him with her 'come to bed eyes.' He wanted to get back into bed with her. Luca smiled and said as he walked over to the door. "I'll see you Friday." He opened the door and left the small bungalow.

Chapter 19

Luca took out his phone and called Lanny. He had missed the patrol, and a wry smile crossed his handsome face.

"General, what's up?" Lanny asked casually and Luca grinned now.

"Just checking in." Luca said and he could hear Peo talking to someone in the background. "Everything good?"

"All quiet here." Lanny informed. "We are just finishing up. None of the dregs know anything. At least that is what they tell us." Luca glanced around him. Something felt off, as he sniffed the air. He could smell something wasn't right. But he couldn't say what. "General?" Lanny's voice called out to him.

"I'm...I'm here." Luca said and walked on. "I just thought...nothing...It doesn't matter. See you tomorrow at my office. Goodnight Jarl."

"Goodnight, General." Then Luca hung up.

He walked over to his car and opened the door and got in. This was strange, his senses were acute...*normally*.

The drive back to his own penthouse took him less than half an hour. He parked the car and walked over to the elevator. He glanced around again. The place was deserted. There was nothing unusual going on.

Luca stepped into the elevator and the doors closed and he let out a long sigh. He couldn't believe how the evening had turned out. He grinned as he slicked back his dark hair. It hadn't been planned, but then, some of his best evenings had been unplanned.

Luca threw his keys into the vintage art deco bowl on the console table and removed his jacket and threw it over the back of the sofa. He wore a self-satisfied grin, and he walked over to his drinks cabinet and fixed himself a single malt whiskey.

He knew that he had wanted to go to bed with Thea the moment he had seen her at the auditions. Even though he gave in to temptations, a lot, Luca knew that this would now complicate the play, but he didn't care. He had wanted her, and he hadn't been disappointed either. Thea was good in bed, and she had fulfilled him for now at least.

Luca downed the contents of his glass and walked into his bedroom. Quickly he removed his clothes and walked naked into the ensuite bathroom and stepped under the shower. Luca closed his eyes, and the warm water cascaded over his muscular body, and he gave a quick laugh as he recalled the sex that he had had earlier with Thea.

Luca turned off the faucet and wrapped the fluffy white towel around his waist and brushed his long, wet hair from his face and returned to the bedroom. He had enjoyed the night, and now he was tired. He would be at his office first thing. Demis was due to pay them a visit and he wasn't looking forward to it.

"CAN I GET YOU ANYTHING, Mister Meridian?" The soft voice of his PA asked a little more confidently than she had in previous times. She also seemed less nervous these days and Luca wondered if it was because he wasn't in the office as often as he normally would be, if he wasn't working at the theatre.

"No, thank you." Luca said and smiled at her. "When my friends arrive, just send them in." She smiled and retreated outside to her own space, where he no doubt knew she felt completely at ease.

He didn't have to wait long before the Militibus arrived at his office.

"Good morning, General." The happy voice of his friend Peo said as he closed the door behind him. Luca looked up at him. He knew that they had gone out, probably to Bjorn's nightclub, the previous night, but Peo looked refreshed. "You're an early bird." Peo teased and Luca just laughed, and half shook his head. It was true that he liked the early morning, usually it was quiet, and he had time to himself before he had to bark orders.

"Anything unusual last night?" Luca asked as he looked up and saw Lanny as he walked in casually. Not in any hurry, as usual. Ever the arrogant Jarl.

"Nothing out of the ordinary." Peo replied and then high fived Lanny and Bjorn. "Seems we are chasing our tails here, General." Luca nodded and sat back in his chair. He felt he needed a little more sleep, but it would have to wait.

"We always are when the old codger sends us off on a wild goose chase." Lanny said sarcastically and then laughed. Luca did understand his frustration, he felt it too, but he didn't like the way the Jarl constantly made sniping retorts about the philosopher. As always, Luca decided to ignore it.

"When did you get back, Bjorn?" Luca asked, avoiding the subject of Demis for as long as possible.

"Two nights ago." Bjorn said and grinned. "So, what's going on with this navar?" He asked and Luca groaned silently, though his expression gave his feeling on the subject away.

"It would appear that the dreg who killed Greyson was a navar." Luca said gravely. "According to the wolves, it came in on a passage from Mexico."

"Only we've spoken to other wolves, suckers and shees," Peo said deflated. "No one has seen anything." Lanny nodded in agreement.

"Are we sure it's even here? Right now, it seems that it's just speculation." Bjorn asked and then the door opened, and Demis came in, he looked perplexed. "No one seems to have seen it, General."

"Any news, Militibus?" Demis asked urgently as he looked around the office, as if he had lost something.

"Good morning to you too, Demis." Lanny said curtly and Peo supressed a laugh.

"What?" Demis asked and then nodded in Lanny's direction. "Oh, good morning, Jarl."

"You have an update for us, Demis?" Luca asked when Demis finally stopped pacing around.

"Update?" He queried and then nodded. "The council wants to postpone the inquiry until after we solve this case." They all stared at him.

"Demis, do you have any updates on *this case?*" Lanny asked exasperated, and it was clear he was losing patience with Demis.

"No, I thought that you might." Demis responded and then sat down and sighed.

"Is something bothering you, Demis?" Luca asked as they all looked at the scholar. He certainly was a lot more preoccupied than usual. "Why have you summoned the meeting?" Luca asked as he tried not to sound irritated.

"Lucian, what do you know about the dakhanavar?" Demis asked, almost as if he had just remembered where he was.

"Not a lot, except what you told us." Luca replied earnestly. "We've been asking questions, but no one seems to know anything." Demis looked over at him blankly. There was something about the way that the academic looked, which alerted Luca to the fact that he was holding something back.

"What's your connection to this Greyson?" Lanny asked him straight out, not mincing words, in true Jarl style.

"My...what?" Demis asked, sounding confused, as if he wasn't grasping the question.

"Connection, what is Greyson to you?" Lanny persisted in a steady voice.

"Nothing." Demis said dismissively but Luca could see that he was struggling.

"Demis, unless you are honest with us," Luca said, carefully choosing his words. "We can't fully investigate his murder." He seemed to be always defending the philosopher.

"Unless you are honest with us," Peo interjected. "I, for one, refuse to investigate this case any further." They all looked at Peo, he had just said what they were all thinking but afraid to say aloud. "It's wasting our time."

"I wish you didn't feel that way, Peo." Demis said, defeated. Sensing that he had something to say but was faltering, Luca looked at Demis and said in a softer tone than he would normally use.

"My office is clean." Luca looked at Demis. "There are no listening devices here, just us." The academic seemed to perk up a little at this. "Talk to us, Demis." Luca urged.

"You are right, Lucian," Demis said, and he looked at all of them. "I know I have been a little more than vague with you all, and for that I apologise most sincerely." The relief was evident on his face now, as if a tremendous burden had been lifted. "It's been very difficult, you know."

"Are you going to tell us what's going on?" Bjorn asked him. He tried to get him to focus on the matter in question, he was very distracted.

"You're right, Jarl, as always." Demis said and gave a half smile across at Lanny. "Greyson is...was my nephew." They all stared at him now. "My sister was his...his mother, she had a brief liaison with his father and..." He broke off and looked sympathetically across at Lanny. "He was forbidden to have relations with a human woman." Demis shifted uneasily in the chair, as if talking about it was going to make him sick. "Of course, I took Grey under my wing and put it to the council, about his request to come to the Fourth. He was a gifted playwright, you see."

"You used your influence you mean." Lanny said argumentatively. "Nepotism, Demis, not a good quality in the council, is it?" Luca saw the Jarl's jaw tighten as he clenched and unclenched his fist as he tried hard to control his anger.

"No...no it isn't Jarl." Demis agreed with Lanny, but grudgingly. "You see when they banished both of Greyson's parents, I was all he had left in the Sixth, and I blame myself for insisting on the visa for him to come here."

"Not only did you go out of your way to set your nephew up in luxury, here in the Fourth," Lanny continued angrily as he argued with him. "You also decided to use the elite Militibus to bring his killer to justice. Everything that the council preaches against." Lanny stood up straight and glared at Demis, then he walked over to the filing cabinet and leaned his back against it. "Typical...one set of rules and all of that." The Jarl continued angrily, as Luca watched his second in command as he tried to keep his temper in check. He couldn't blame him for being furious.

"I understand your anger, Jarl," Demis defended his position now. "But what am I to do? He's my kin, my family." Luca looked at Demis and then back to where Lanny stood. He understood perfectly Lanny's bitterness. Demis had had him brought before the disciplinary board for no reason other than to punish him for having feelings for a mortal woman.

"You are a hypocrite, you old toad, you know that?" Lanny barked at Demis. "You break rules when it suits you, but you forbid us, who *you* depend on, to not react in a way that is natural."

"Lanny, this can be discussed another time." Luca interrupted. He knew where the argument would lead to, and he didn't want it to go there. "I take it, the council is not aware of any of this?" Luca asked Demis, who ashamedly nodded. "Well, apart from, Greyson, there have been four other murders, all from the theatre community. As Militibus officers," Luca said in a serious tone, and looked at each of the Militibus in turn. "We are duty bound to investigate, as it is a dreg from one of our dimensions that is involved in these crimes." Luca glared at Lanny as he grunted something, but Bjorn and Peo agreed with Luca.

"Lanny, are you with us on this?" Luca demanded firmly from the Jarl.

"Yes, of course." Lanny said reluctantly and Luca knew that despite his petulance, he was dependable and would pull out all the stops to find the killer.

"OK, Demis, we will continue the investigation." Luca warned him. "When we find the murderer, you will have to tell the council about this, we are not taking any blame on this for you, do you understand?" Even Luca had a limit as to how much he could take from Demis, and right now, the old scholar was threading on thin ice as far as Luca's limits were concerned. He certainly wouldn't have any of his men face disciplinary charges for investigating a crime because Demis was incompetent.

"Of...of course, Lucian." Demis muttered, a little incoherently. "You have my word."

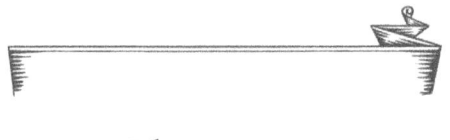

Chapter 20

The side door to the auditorium opened, noiselessly but to Luca's acute hearing, it distracted him from what was happening onstage. He glanced backwards to the door, and he groaned silently when he saw that Willis had slipped in and sat down on a seat in the middle row. Willis wore a smug but expectant expression on his face as he absorbed what was going on.

So far that day, the rehearsals were not going as well as Luca would have liked, which left Luca feeling irritated. Jason was still a little uncertain about his lines, and he was completely overwhelmed by Medea.

"Let's take five," Luca called out and stood up. The last thing he wanted was for Willis to critique the play when he had no idea what was going on.

Luca was walking over to the stairs when he saw Thea come over to the edge of the stage. She wore a huge grin on her face. Luca didn't want the others to know that he and Thea had slept together, even though it didn't matter to him who knew that they had, but he felt it would be more sensitive to her feelings if it remained just between them. Luca was being discreet, even though Thea wasn't, and he wished that she would.

"Do you want to go for something to eat later?" Thea asked in a low tone, but there was no mistaking what she was referring to. He shook his head.

"I can't Thea," Luca said regretfully, and he joined her on the stage, he was aware that they were being scrutinised not only by the cast but also by Willis. "I'm meeting some friends later." She lowered her eyes, she couldn't hide her disappointment, and he could also see the hurt look on her face. It couldn't be helped. Besides, Luca hadn't promised her, that their sleeping together would be a regular thing anyway. "Maybe, tomorrow." He replied in a short tone. Luca didn't look at her as he walked to the centre of the stage.

Quickly, the cast all formed a circle around him, and he smiled warmly at them. "Making sure I am trapped here?" Luca remarked jokingly. They all laughed except for Thea. "First of all, you are doing great. Jason, I know you are feeling a little unsure about how to deal with Medea. Go with your feeling. She's an angry woman, and she has just killed your children, so you are feeling bereft that she won't allow you to oversee the burial. Go with your despair, show us that awful lament. Make us *feel* it." Luca encouraged but Jason just looked at him, not quite understanding Luca's advice. Luca just sighed inwardly now. "Make us feel what you feel toward her." He almost pleaded with his leading man.

"Medea, come here," Luca called out to Thea. "You are telling me it's my fault you killed my children. Take it from there." Luca stepped backwards and looked intently at Thea as she got into character.

'No, it was your lustful heart and that new marriage of yours' Medea shouted.

'You decided to kill them...because I loved another...' Jason retorted.

'...This minor annoyance to a woman?' Medea shrieked!

'....But to you it is all that is evil..'

'...Hate me!...'

'...I welcome the moment of our parting...'

Luca smiled warmly at Thea. "That was great, Thea." He said and then he turned to Jason. "You hate her for what she has put you through...Give us that hatred, show us that angst." He looked across to Thea and smiled once more but she didn't return his smile, he could see the anger flash in her eyes. "Let's take a break for an hour, water our throats so to speak." The cast laughed and Luca grinned as he walked off the stage and went over to where Willis was sitting. "Have you enjoyed our rehearsal?" Luca asked him as he tried to sound jovial.

"Well, it certainly is a heart pounding play, isn't it?" Willis said with a false grin on his face as he looked up at Luca. Then the side door opened, and Luca saw old Frankie slip in. He smiled and said to Willis.

"Excuse me," Luca didn't wait for a reply he walked over to where Frankie was standing with his elbows resting on the brush handle.

"I missed it!" Frankie exclaimed and gave a little laugh and shook his head as he leaned on the handle of the brush. "I thought I was early too." Luca chuckled.

"Have you enjoyed it so far, Frankie?" Luca asked him with a broad smile and Frankie laughed and nodded. "Come, I have a break, I'd like to buy you a drink." Luca heralded the janitor out of the door, he wanted to talk to him alone, about Willis.

In the bar near the theatre, where he had first taken Thea, Luca ordered two whiskies and took them over to the table to where the janitor was now sitting, looking out the window. He looked unsure of himself. Afraid almost to take the glass from Luca.

"Thank you, Mister Meridian." Frankie said with a trembling voice and then he raised the glass, a little shakily to his mouth. "Thank you very much."

"Call me Luca," Luca said and grinned at him. "I'm glad we had time to talk today, Frankie." The old man took another sip and then put the glass down. His hands juddered a little.

"Willis told me not to be bothering you." Frankie said cautiously and then he asked. "I ain't a bother, am I Luca?" Luca smiled at him and shook his head. He liked the old man. He belonged to a bygone era, just like Luca.

"Not at all, Sir." Luca replied respectfully. "Tell me, Frankie, did the other directors allow you in to watch them rehearse?" He watched as the old janitor reached for the glass once more and take a sip, his hand shook a little uncontrollably as he held it in his left hand.

"Some did." Frankie replied with a grin. "Some thought they were so good you had to pay to see them take a piss." Frankie shook his head from side to side as he laughed to himself, and Luca chuckled as he glanced at him.

"What about Greyson?" Luca asked him as he reached for his own glass. "Did he let anyone in to see rehearsals?" He was careful not to upset the old guy. Luca was sensitive to the questions he could ask that would garner a response from this old man.

"He was one of them you had to pay to see the shit show." Frankie muttered and Luca laughed. He enjoyed Frankie's attitude to life and his forthrightness. He liked his no-nonsense opinion. His mannerisms belonged to another time.

"Did he let Willis in?" The old man took another sip. Luca suspected that it wasn't the first drink he had had that day, though he knew that he shouldn't judge. But he didn't say anything.

"You know BJ Sympson played on that same stage you are on now, Luca?" Frankie asked as he put down the glass and looked at Luca with a twinkle in his eyes. "He was a class act, knew how to play. They did in them days. You know he died of the influenza?" Frankie began to cough now, and his hand trembled uncontrollably. Luca could see the tell-tale signs that old age was invading fast, and the old man was almost resigned to stop fighting it. He was giving in to his age, it seemed.

"Yes, I know, Frankie, you told me." Luca said gently. "Can you tell me about Greyson?" He gently brought the conversation back to the hybrid.

"I didn't like him," Frankie admitted now. "No one did. Something not right with that fella." Luca looked at him quickly. Did the old man know what Greyson was? It was unlikely, Luca thought but he couldn't be certain.

"What do you mean, not right?" Luca asked him. Frankie lifted the glass again and took a long sip of the whiskey. His eyes seemed to glaze over, as if he had an addiction to the alcohol and it was only just being satisfied. Or maybe it was something else, Luca didn't know.

"He had mean eyes, couldn't look you in the eyes when he talked to ya." Frankie said when he put the glass back on the table. "He had a wolf's eyes, always watching and observing. Waiting. Dark." This made Luca smile at how observant the old man was regarding Greyson. "Never trust a man who can't look you in the eyes. Something not right with a guy who can't look at you." He motioned between his own two eyes and nodded. "If he can't look you, then the prick is hiding something."

"He was mean?" Luca encouraged the janitor. "Did you ever see him talk to anyone in a heated argument or anything like that?" He wondered if he was overwhelming the old man with his line of questioning. Luca was a lot gentler than he usually would be. He had to know, and the old guy had a loose tongue thanks to the whiskey, as Luca had suspected he would have.

"I know that he didn't get on with Willis." Frankie said outright and he began to chuckle. "No one gets on with Willis. Ignorant fuck." Luca looked at him intently. "Mean as they come. No class." He had a faraway look in his eyes again and Luca knew that this was as much as he would get out of the old man. "Likes to show 'em who's boss. You know the type, Luca?" Luca nodded, Frankie's lucidity was waning again.

"Frankie, do you want another whiskey?" The janitor perked up with an impish smile. Luca called over the bartender and ordered another whiskey and paid for it. Then he turned to Frankie and smiled. "I have to get back to the theatre. Stay here and enjoy your drink, Frankie." Luca stood up. He would like to stay and talk some more. He knew that Frankie knew a lot more and he needed just a little encouragement, but Luca was also needed back at the theatre.

"You know that prick with the wolf eyes, he did have an argument with a woman, she was angry, and she was moving fast." Frankie said, Luca stopped in his tracks, and he turned around and looked at him.

"What woman?" Luca asked him hurriedly now.

"Willis don't know I know, either," Frankie said and chuckled to himself. "He don't know I know. I keep an eye on him, see." He repeated. "I know lots a things. Cause I watch, see. I knows what goes on there, see." The old janitor began to chuckle to himself now as he took another gulp.

"Know what, Frankie?" Luca asked him again, but it was clear that his clarity of the moment was fading once more.

"Thanks for the drinks, Luca, you're a gentleman." He raised the glass and took a sip. "A real gentleman. Not a prick like wolf eyes." Frankie put the glass down again. "I seen em, I seen em together. They don't know I seen em." His voice trailed off now. Luca nodded and walked out of the bar, leaving Frankie alone talking to himself.

Chapter 21

Luca and Peo were patrolling around the arts district. Unlike most areas where they rode, they both liked the arts district with its bijou living quarters and trendy streets where the buildings were fronted with quaint restaurants.

There were a few well to do wolves who lived there, but the area had not been home to suckers for almost five years. Luca had contemplated moving to the arts district, but he also liked the comfort of his spacious penthouse too much and he preferred not to move into something smaller. Besides, he didn't relish being the only vampire living amongst wolves and shees. Or maybe there was just a small element of snobbery in his ultimate decision not to move there.

He chuckled as he thought how much like the Jarl he had become. They all jeered Lanny for choosing to stay in an exclusive part of the city. Luca could understand Lanny's decision to stay in the select apartment block where he lived, but he understood the appeal of the arts district also.

"General, over there." Peo indicated with his hand. Luca glanced across to where Peo was pointing, and he saw two shees who appeared as if they were lookouts.

"Let's check it out." Luca said and both vampires turned their bikes in the direction of the shees.

They put their bikes on the stands and removed their helmets. Luca and Peo walked side by side and they noticed the two shees smile at them as they approached.

"Sexy vampires," one of the shees said coarsely and the other one giggled. "I'll take the tallest one." She added with a broad smile as she eyed Luca up and down.

"Now, now, no need to fight, ladies." Luca said and grinned broadly at them. "What are you two doing out here?" The two shees giggled and glanced at each other with a knowing expression.

"Waiting for you to come along, sexy." The second shee said and giggled loudly.

"Well, we're here now, so you can tell us what you are doing in this side of town?" Peo said sternly and with a dead pan expression. The two shees stopped their playful banter and became serious.

"You're Militibus?" The first one asked and Peo nodded with a wide grin. "We're just playing, man."

"With whom?" Luca asked them. But neither would answer. He looked at Peo.

"You know soliciting a Militibus officer carries a hefty sentence?" Peo said harshly. The two shees just stared at each other.

"But we didn't do anything." They protested together.

"How long have you been out here?" Luca asked the first shee and he saw the second one look nervously over her shoulder. "What's down there?" He demanded and reached for his sword.

"It's...nothing." The shee said quickly. "Look, we're running low on food, we thought there'd be something in here."

"You sound like the sluaghs." Peo said angrily. "Lying scum, ripping off unsuspecting mortals." The two shees looked at him and then at each other and without warning ran off down the side street, Luca and Peo ran after them.

They caught them before they slipped into a steel doorway. Peo grabbed one of the shees by the arm and roughly pushed her against the door.

"I am not in the mood for lies tonight." Peo said gruffly. "Now answer our questions or I will send you to the Eighth." The shee looked scared and nodded at him.

"How long have you been coming into this district?" Luca demanded of both of them.

"About a month." The first shee answered. "We began to run low on food and our nest was hungry."

"How many are there in your nest?" Peo asked.

"There was ten." The second shee replied and Luca saw her look at the other one.

"Look at me." Luca demanded. The shee looked scared now. "How many now?"

"There's four of us left." The shee said warily.

"What happened the others?" Peo asked as he let go of the first shee and stood up straight.

"They got scared." Luca knew they were lying.

"Shees don't get scared." Peo jeered. "What happened?" He repeated, getting angry again.

"There's talk of a sucker taking us," the shee said in a low tone. "Not just shees but any dreg that's out on their own.

We're all scared. Two from our nest went missing five days ago. That's when the others upped and left."

"Why didn't you report it to the guardians?" Luca asked. The two shees sneered contemptuously.

"We don't know who to trust." The shee said mournfully. "It's not like the Militibus or the guardians welcome us dregs into the city, is it?"

"You have your areas where you are free to mingle." Luca said in an understanding voice. "You said two from your nest went missing, were they found, or did they just flee?"

"Sure, they were found," the second shee said sarcastically. "Frizzled up and drained. I recognised Lyra but not Kiree."

"A sucker drained them?" Peo asked, they both nodded. "You are sure it was a vampire?" they both nodded in agreement.

"Suckers usually only feed on mortals." Luca said as he glanced at Peo.

"Look, don't believe us then, we're only dregs." The first shee said angrily. "That ain't no ordinary sucker, and it ain't special like the Militibus. It drained Lyra and Kiree, and most of us are frightened, but we should know better than to expect anything from the Militibus. You only look after the toffs." She glared at Luca. "Come on, Laie, let's go." The shee dragged her friend by her arm and pushed past Luca and Peo.

When they were out of earshot, Luca turned to Peo and asked in a grave tone.

"Do you think it's the Navar?" Peo was still looking after the two shees as they turned the corner out of sight.

"I don't know, Luca," he answered. "But I don't think that those two were telling us a fanciful tale. I think we need to have a talk with the guardians. Have them patrol the streets until this navar is caught." Luca stared at him. This was the first time he had ever seen Peo so riled up.

"I agree," Luca said as they began to walk back to their bikes. "But we should wait until we have more evidence that it is a navar."

"You don't think it is the navar?" Peo asked incredulously and looked at Luca and shook his head.

"We don't have enough intel to go on," Luca said cautiously. "If we go head on deploying guardians on the street to protect dregs, the council will start asking questions about what we are investigating and why we haven't informed them, especially when it is such a dangerous dreg like a navar." Luca didn't want to act before he had solid evidence and then they would tackle the navar with all that they had gathered. "We could land ourselves in trouble. I don't want to do that...not until we have hard evidence."

"Whatever you think is best, General." Peo said almost deflated. Luca laughed and said with a grin.

"Hey, how about a drink?" This brought a smile back to Peo's face.

"Some mortals?" Peo asked in a mischievous tone and Luca laughed loudly and agreed.

They got onto the bikes and started them and then drove back to the Downtown area.

Luca knew that the dregs were running scared now and that he would have to call the guardians in to patrol the areas of the city where the dregs lived but when he did, Luca didn't relish having to explain to the council of Elders why he was doing it and why they didn't inform the council sooner. There was trouble ahead, for sure.

Damn Demis and his fumbling!

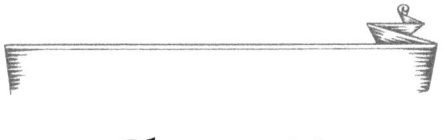

Chapter 22

The raised voices of the traders were at fever pitch as Lucian passed the stalls. He glanced casually from stall to stall but showed little interest in their wares. Nor did he show much attention to the scurrying of the thieves and beggars as they scuttled past him in a blind fury to get away from their retinue.

As he walked his hand was resting on the hilt of his sword, ready for any eventuality. The sky above him was blue, not a cloud in sight and the sun was searing down. His armour was pressing into his skin, and it irritated him, and he wanted to scratch his chest.

The man beside him grinned and gave a chuckle as he glanced at Lucian.

"The city heat not suiting you today, Lucian?" Aeneas who was his best friend queried, Lucian laughed as he shook his head.

"It is not the sun which afflicts me today." He gave a knowing look as he stopped in front of the fountain. "But the merriment of last night, Aeneas." He slapped him on the arm.

"Or perhaps not so much the merriment but with whom you had made merry," Aeneas chuckled and bent his head to drink from the fountain. Lucian looked around him. There were some soldiers across the piazza, but they were not interested in him or his friend. Lucian had to be discreet. He was already compromised because of his budding relationship with the courtesan, Porcia. A centurion officer and a concubine weren't unusual but when that paramour was the mistress to the emperor, it became dangerous. A courtesan in Roman life generally only had one patron, even though Vespasian already had a mistress in Caenis, he had fallen for the allure of the young concubine Porcia. He had taken her on several important engagements. It was on his conference as a Princep that Lucian met Porcia.

He had needed to relieve himself and had made use of the oleander trees when the young woman came walking along the path and had seen Lucian with his penis in his hand pissing against the old tree. Porcia had stopped and had looked at Lucian's penis and he had seen the glint in her eye as she stared at it and then after a moment or so she looked up at the handsome officer and smiled at him.

"Infigo penis sed es ut infigo?" She concealed a smile as Lucian shook the last of the urine from it and stood up straight and looked at her. She was an incredible beauty with hair as black as soot, cascading over her shoulders in curls. Her dark eyes teased as they looked out from under long lashes. Her mouth so voluptuous that it screamed to be kissed. Her breasts could give sustenance to a grown man by just sucking on the ripened nipples.

"Cur non virgo tibi est sed virgo non es dea ?" Lucian said with a grin as he stepped closer to her. He towered over her, and he gazed, mesmerised into her eyes. Without warning he pulled her into his arms and kissed her hard on the mouth.

He groaned when he felt her hand slip under his tunic and she stroked his penis as she kissed him.

"I want to taste you." She whispered as she got on her knees and raised his tunic and took him fully in her mouth. Lucian groaned as her tongue expertly licked the tip of his head. He felt like he would burst from the insanity that he had slipped into while her mouth took his penis deeper until his thrusts were hitting the back of her throat. He couldn't help himself as he exploded with pleasure in her hot mouth.

Lucian groaned as he convulsed and suddenly, she stood up and smiled at him as she wiped the sides of her mouth.

"You taste as good as you look, Centurion." She whispered as she stood up on her toes and kissed him on the cheek. "I hope we meet again." Her smile was flirtatious as she stepped back onto the path and continued to walk up to the impressive palace.

"Wait." Lucian called after her, but she just kept walking. "What's your name?" He asked but his words fell on deaf ears for she didn't reply, nor did she give a backward glance.

Lucian stood with his hands on his hips for several minutes as he looked at her fading silhouette go up the steps into the palace. He didn't know who she was, but he knew that he had to see her again. He had never had a woman tease him or pleasure him as this beauty had just done so unashamedly against the oleander tree.

He fixed his tunic and his sword by his side and then he walked in the direction of the palace. As he approached the steps he saw his friend, Aeneas in the marbled hallway he was talking to a senator. He looked across at Lucian as he approached.

"Ah Lucian," Senator Amulius said as Lucian approached the two men. "I was beginning to wonder if the dinner would be served before you arrived." The three men laughed but Lucian gave a quick glance around to see if he could see the young woman. But she was nowhere to be seen. "Shall we go, before our esteemed emperor arrives?" Amulius motioned the two officers into the great dining room.

Lucian was seated next to Aeneas and beside the other stoic philosopher, Caius. He listened to the small talk as he glanced around the large dining table. Which was laid out with intense greenery and displayed on solid gold platters were bunches of grapes, apples and fruits of an exotic nature brought back from afar to Rome, by returning legion generals.

Suddenly everyone in the room stood up, as the emperor Vespasian entered. Holding on to his left arm was a darked haired woman wearing a beautiful white tunic with a lilac cloak. She nodded and smiled at those closest to them as they walked.

Lucian groaned inside when he recognised her. In the candlelight of the large dining room, she was even more beautiful than she had been in the moonlight.

Vespasian sat down and motioned to those in attendance to sit. The servants were quickly beside the emperor, filling his goblet with wine and they quickly made their way along the table to serve the other guests.

Lucian turned to the philosopher Caius and asked him in a low tone, so as he wouldn't be overheard.

"Who is the woman with the emperor?" Caius lifted the golden goblet and took a sip of the red wine and then with his napkin he dabbed the side of his mouth which also served to cover his lips in case anyone was reading them.

"She is his latest courtesan." Caius said. "She is a younger version of her aunt. It would seem they both like to fuck the emperor." Lucian looked at Caius and then across to where the woman sat, smiling and listening to whatever Vespasian was whispering in her ear.

"What's her name?" Lucian inquired not taking his eyes off the courtesan. Her flirtatious smile and her seductive mouth pouted, and he could still feel those lips around his penis.

"Porcia, niece to Caenis, the emperor's contubernium," Caius said and smirked. "Or as the heirs prefer, their father's whore." He gave a laugh and reached for the leg of the foul that had been placed on the table in front of him.

"Has she been a courtesan long?" Lucian asked, unable to hide his fascination for this beautiful creature, even though he knew it was dangerous. Caius turned and looked at him and lowered the chicken leg in his hand, on to his plate and then he leaned close to Lucian.

"The emperor's concubine is suum et suum solum." The warning was heeded as Lucian flashed the stoic a brilliant smile. He understood the caution and the meaning behind it.

"But of course." Lucian said in a low tone. "Emperor Vespasian has impeccable taste. For this spread he has put before us, shall march us on to victory. Iubentium." He nodded his head and turned his attention to the other men gathered near him.

FOR SEVERAL DAYS THE banquet continued, and the orgies were as legendary as the men who attended them.

Unable to drink anymore wine, Lucian managed to leave the great hall. The men and women were engaged in various carnal acts, and some were still drinking excessively. The more argumentative of the men argued politics, and philosophy while next to them on the various divans, some senators engaged in bawdy sexual acts with the prostitutes within the halls.

Lucian made his way along the shaded avenue of the cypresses, their shadow cast welcome shade from the heat of the sun. His head hurt from the overindulgence, but he smiled. From midday the next day, he would be making his way to join his legion, outside of Rome, before they were to be sent to the coast to join the other legions in Lycia.

As he walked, he heard a light giggle, and he turned and saw Porcia running on the other path, parallel to where he was walking, which led to the bathhouse. Lucian stopped walking and so did Porcia. She removed a curl from her cheek and lowered her eyes from his and then took off in a giddy trot. Lucian smiled and then ran after her.

When he caught up to her, he grabbed her arm and pulled her to him. She giggled as she rested her hand on his broad chest. They looked intently at each other for a moment.

"Why are you teasing me?" Lucian asked her in a serious voice, and she touched his face softly.

"Am I teasing you?" Porcia asked in an innocent tone as she sucked in her lower lip.

"You know damn well you are." Lucian said and he tried hard to suppress a grin as he held her in his arms and smiled down at her. "What you did to me the other night, you need to repeat it right now." He desperately needed to feel her mouth on him again. She giggled and stood up on her toes and he bent his head and kissed her hard on the mouth. She tasted good and he could feel himself get hard as they kissed.

"Maybe I will." Porcia said in a teasing mood. "Then again...maybe I will punish you for not coming to my room last night instead of that woman you took in the hall." Lucian pulled away from her and laughed.

"Weren't you in the emperor's bed last night?" Lucian probed in a serious tone. Porcia's expression changed and she lowered her head. "Porcia?" She looked up at him, and her eyes had a sadness to them now.

"How do you know my name?" She asked with a smile.

"I asked around." Lucian admitted, just for a moment he saw a look of panic set in. "Don't worry, I was discreet." Lucian reassured her and then reached for her hand, and they walked toward the bathhouse.

They stopped when they reached the bathhouse door, and he held her hand close to his chest and looked at her.

She was an intoxicating creature. He was obsessed with her, even though he knew that he shouldn't be. She was a slave girl, and she wasn't free to make any decisions for herself.

"After dinner tonight," Porcia said almost in a whisper. "Come to my room, we can be alone then." Lucian smiled at her, and she reached up and kissed him on the cheek and then she turned, and ran off in the direction of the villa.

Lucian heard voices in the bathhouse, and he opened the door and went inside.

Vespasian held a dinner to celebrate the promotion of his closest friends and loyal officers in his legions, for their duty and devotion to him and the empire. There had been talk that Lucian was in line for Primus Pilus, an honour of the highest level and rank, particularly since he had only turned twenty-five.

The dining room was filled once more with the elite of Roman life, and Lucian was grinning from ear to ear as he greeted those he met. He was hoping that the legion he would command in Lycia would be a large one. Lucian was hungry to prove himself.

He glanced across to the doorway and saw Porcia come in, she was walking with her aunt Caenis, Vespasian's mistress. A few minutes later the emperor himself graced the great hall with his presence. There was a hushed silence now in the room as Vespasian made his way over to the throne and sat down and motioned for those around him to come closer and ply him with praise.

Lucian stood patiently, waiting for when the announcement was made, and his promotion had been proclaimed.

"Friends, advisors, it is my honour this evening," Vespasian said to those gathered in the room. "To announce five promotions to the loyal legions of the empire in Lycia, Lusitania, and Baetica." He smiled at those present and there was a loud applause from those gathered. Lucian inhaled deeply, hardly able to contain his excitement. He wanted to go to Lycia. It would be fresh, and new, to him at least. He had spent too long in Masada, and he needed this promotion. He needed the change of scenery. "First it is my pleasure to promote to optio, in the Baetica legion I congratulate Aeneas. Optio to Lusitania legion, Quirinus. Finally, Octavius I promote you to Primus Pilus of Lycia and Pamphylia with Lucian Marius Antonius as your tribune, Princep." There was a loud cheer from those present as the newly promoted officers stepped forward and waited to receive their congratulations from the emperor.

Everyone was excited. Everyone except Lucian. He was livid, and he could hardly hide it. It had been a slap in the face, particularly for one as ambitious as Lucian.

As he waited in line for the emperor to come and personally congratulate him, Lucian stared straight ahead of him, and then he saw Porcia discreetly leave the great hall and slip away to her room, Lucian thought.

"Congratulations, Lucian Marius Antonius." Vespasian held out his hand to Lucian. "I had the honour of serving with your father. When Nero passed, your father was instrumental in making me emperor." Lucian looked at his emperor. He had to conceal his disappointment. "You seem none too happy not to be primus pilus legate."

"No, Dominus Noster." Lucian lied as he looked at the emperor, who still held his hand. "I am honoured you think so highly of me." Vespasian smiled and covered Lucian's hand with his.

"Youth is a good thing given to you by the gods, but it is also a curse inflicted on you by the gods. You are young Lucian Marius Antonius. That is why I cannot give you full legate, you will thank me when you gain experience, as I thanked your father." He smiled at Lucian and then turned his back to his newly promoted officers and returned to his throne.

Lucian didn't think that he would ever be thankful for being passed over for Primus Pilus but to save face he had to pretend to be happy with his promotion in rank.

Chapter 23

For two nights Lucian and Porcia didn't leave her aunt's villa. They remained there out of sight, and he was close to being charged as a deserter. But Lucian didn't care. He wanted to take something for him. Something that was dear to the emperor. Something that the emperor had stolen from him. In Lucian's mind, what he was doing with Porcia was justified in his disappointment in not being fully promoted.

He turned onto his back and sighed. Porcia kissed his hardened stomach, and her hand slipped under the light sheet and found his hardness.

"You are so distant, and yet you are here, Lucian." Her hand began to move on him. He didn't look at her. He had no idea what to say to her about his moroseness. "Lucian, I have to go to the palace this evening." He still didn't look at her. She stopped her movements and sat up and looked at him. "Don't you care?" Porcia raised her voice as she glared at him. Lucian forced himself to look at her. She was exquisite, a goddess both in the bedroom and on the eye.

"You are the emperor's whore, Porcia," Lucian said after a while. "Why should I care? You leave my bed full of my semen and you go to his to be treated as a concubine." The sting was instantaneous, and he grabbed her hand and glared at her. Then he lashed out hard as he slapped her across her beautiful face. His handprint almost tattooed to her cheek "Don't you ever hit me again." She jumped off the bed and ran from the room, followed by Lucian. He had instantly regretted the act.

He grabbed her arm and swung her around to face him. He could see the redness on her cheek and the tears as they fell down her face. Lucian pulled her into his arms and tried to soothe her sobs. But she just shook in his arms.

"Lucian," Porcia sobbed as she wrapped her arms around his broad back, and they held on to each other tightly. "I don't love him. I hate it every time his old fat hands touch me." Lucian held her close to him and he could feel the wetness of her tears as they rolled onto his bare skin. "I am born to this life, but it is not what I choose. I will always choose you, my love."

"I'm sorry Porcia." Lucian whispered and then kissed her on the temple. "Forgive me." Her slender body heaved with the weight of her sorrow. "Don't go to the palace again, Porcia." Lucian pleaded in a low tone.

"Lucian, I have to." Porcia said in alarm now as she looked up at him. "I am a slave, a courtesan. He owns me." The tears rolled freely down her beautiful face as her dark eyes looked up at him again. Pleading with him to understand her predicament. But Lucian didn't want to understand. "Until you return from Lycia, I must do what Vespasian asks of me. Till he tires of me." Lucian bent his head and kissed her hard on the mouth. When he released her, he cupped her face in both his hands.

"When I return from Lycia, I will buy your freedom." Lucian said as he looked at her. "Then you will never have to leave my bed to go to another's." He kissed her passionately again and then he led her back to the bedroom, and they made love for the remainder of the afternoon.

Chapter 24

Nunc Tempus

Luca was sitting at the bar. He was waiting for Lanny to join him. The Jarl had called him earlier when Luca was just leaving the theatre and ready to return to his office. He motioned to the barman to bring him a whiskey.

Luca looked up as the door opened and he saw the Jarl stroll in, he looked like a movie star incognito with his dark designer shades and his perfectly cut designer suit.

"Hey there." Luca said as Lanny pulled out the bar stool and sat down. "Whiskey?" The Jarl nodded and grinned at him.

"How's life as a hotshot director?" Lanny asked and Luca laughed at this as he looked across at the barman.

"It's interesting, to say the least." Luca replied and then ordered a whiskey for Lanny. "Why the clandestine meeting?" The bar tender left the glass on the counter in front of Lanny.

"Shall we sit over there?" The Jarl motioned to a vacant booth and Luca nodded as they both stood up and walked over to the table.

"Are you going to tell me or am I going to have to interrogate you, Jarl?" Luca teased him and Lanny just chuckled at this.

"Bjorn and I checked out what the shees told you and Peo the other night." Lanny said in a low tone. "The nest has diminished substantially. There was a lot more than they said though. Two of their nestmates disappeared and were found dead." Lanny said and he glanced over at the bar. "However, last night, we were discreetly following the nest leader, Mercelle, she met up with a mercenary hix." Luca stared at him, and Lanny nodded. The hix were known for being ruthless soul eaters, not unlike the banshees but he wondered why the shees would engage a rival to help them. It wasn't like the banshees to be so trusting.

"Did you and Bjorn confront them?" Luca asked him. The Jarl smiled slowly as he played with the glass on the table.

"Bjorn followed the hix and I spoke with Mercelle." Lanny said. "As we were talking, we heard a scuffle but before we reached the place where we heard the fracas, we found the drained body of another shee from Mercelle's nest." Luca gaped incredulously at him, and Lanny just nodded. "There was no one there, I checked everywhere. Nothing." This worried Luca. The navar, it seemed, was getting bolder, surely it sensed a Tempus Militibus officer was in the area? "What is it General?" Lanny asked him, after seeing the expression change on Luca's face.

"Why is it going for dregs as well as mortals?" Luca asked him. "Dreg blood has no value whatsoever." Luca mused to himself. Nothing about the circumstances of this case made sense to Luca.

"Unless it requires it for recovery." Lanny said after a moment. "When we battled, if our food sources were low or we needed to recover but had nothing to eat, our men would raid farms and steel eggs and fruit, it would sustain us until we could eat meat." Lanny stated. "This navar might be in a state of recovery." It was conceivable, Luca thought.

"If that's so, then the navar is not working alone." Luca confirmed in a grave tone. Damn, they needed a break. Why the hell didn't Demis furnish them with more reliable intel?

"A human perhaps?" Lanny questioned but Luca shrugged. He didn't know. They knew so little about the dakhanavar, and they could not even broach the investigation with the council for fear of getting Demis into more trouble with them. The whole farce was hopeless. Luca felt helpless.

"We'll step up patrols in the areas where the shees are located." Luca said after a moment. "But we can't warn the dregs to be vigilant as they would see it as us ceding the streets to the navar." Luca frowned. "We need to have a meeting with Demis." Lanny laughed now and shook his head and Luca watched him as he glanced out the window.

"It's because of him, we can't do anything." Lanny said. "The old codger has compromised us not just here in the Fourth dimension but back in the Sixth as well." Luca had to agree, it seemed as if their situation was dire and there didn't appear to be anything that the Militibus could do to stop it. They were stymied every way that they turned. Once the council of Elders discovered they were doing a little private investigation for Demis, then they would certainly be disciplined, and the old coot wouldn't defend them either.

"It's not all his fault, Lanny." Luca said hopelessly as he looked at the Jarl.

"When are you going to stop defending him, Luca?" Lanny asked in an aroused voice. "The old guy needs to retire. He's caused so many disasters that he has become more of a liability than usual." Luca couldn't disagree with the Jarl, but he also felt a loyalty to Demis. He may have been careless in the past, but this current situation wasn't caused by him. "Who knows what disaster he'll cause next."

"I agree, Lanny, that he is disastrous, but he isn't responsible for this incident." Luca said defensively. "I know you have a deep grievance with Demis, and you are right to feel aggrieved, but you need to put that aside or we will lose sight of what we are doing here." He watched as his friend sat back in the seat and glanced out the window again. Luca knew he was paying a high price for giving his oath to the council and staying away from the nun. Luca didn't know if he could ever feel that much for someone. It hadn't happened to him, yet, not even with... *Porcia*. He doubted it ever would.

"Of course, General." Lanny replied and let out a long sigh. "My loyalty to the Tempus Militibus comes first, even if I don't always agree with what the council rules in favour of."

"I'm not your General now, Lanny." Luca said in a temperate tone. "I am your friend." He nodded and then his expression changed, and the Jarl smiled at him.

"How close are you to opening night?" Luca grinned now and shook his head.

Opening night. It had a nice ring to it. He had to admit.

"I sometimes wonder if I did the right thing taking on that challenge." Luca said casually and picked up the glass of whiskey. "Sic nocte foramen primum amplectamur." Lanny laughed and raised his glass too.

"Prima nocte successu." Lanny said with a wide smile, and they hit their glasses together.

Chapter 25

Although he was in the theatre observing the rehearsals, Luca's mind was elsewhere. He was perturbed by what Lanny had reported to him in relation to the shees and the other undesirables. Without better intel about the navar though, they were at the mercy of what they could discover from the dregs. Which wasn't a whole lot.

So far, there had been no other mortal murders. That at least made the case less complicated. No crimes against humans meant that the Militibus didn't have to liaise with the mortal police.

Luca continued to observe the stage, but he wasn't taking in much of what was going on. The Militibus had increased their patrols from nine in the evening until five in the morning. Still, they had nothing solid to go on. They really needed to bring the guardians in to cover more areas, but Luca knew that if he ordered that, he would be called back to the Sixth to brief the council of Elders and he had no answers for any of their questions. Not just yet, anyway.

"That's a wrap until after lunch." Luca said and put down the clipboard that he had been holding. Amos, who was sitting beside him looked at him a little confused now and Luca returned his gaze questioningly.

"It's only eleven, Luca." Amos said quizzically and Luca smiled disarmingly at him, disguising the fact that he was also confused as to why he had called a break in rehearsal.

"I know what time it is, Amos." Luca said casually, if a little curt. "We have wardrobe coming in to fit the costumes." *Thank goodness for memos*. He thought to himself and gave a quick smile.

"I had forgotten." Amos said but Luca also knew that Amos had lied to him just to save face for Luca.

"I'll be out until Monday, Amos." Luca said as he stood up. He stretched his long legs and moved his head from side to side. Luca had seen the actors use the actions often enough and surprisingly it worked. It also made him feel somewhat *human*. "Any problems you know where to find me."

As he was walking out into the lobby, he heard his name called. He turned around and saw Willis coming toward him. Luca sighed audibly. He really didn't want this conversation.

"Good morning." Luca said and forced a smile as Willis approached him.

"Leaving so early, Mister Meridian?" Willis enquired with a smarmy smile on his plump face. He really was a disagreeable man in so many ways.

"I leave the show in very capable hands, as you no doubt are aware." Luca replied. If he had been a street vampire and not a Tempus Militibus, he would bite Willis in the neck, just to put him and everyone else out of the misery of having to breathe the same air as the sleaze ball.

"I'm sure you are." Willis said erroneously. "Amos is one of the best underlings in the theatre world." Luca just looked at him. "I enjoy working with him, whenever I can. He calls me when he feels overwhelmed, you know."

"What can I do for you, Willis?" Luca asked irritated, and clearly wanting to get away but Willis was not taking the hint.

"I understand, you took Frankie out drinking a few weeks ago." Willis said in a serious tone and then smiled falsely at Luca. Luca rolled his eyes.

"What of it?" Luca retorted, as he tried hard not to show his anger. "He's his own man."

"How do I put this delicately, Mister Meridian." Willis said in a condescending voice now, while he smirked and wrung his hands together. It was clear to Luca that he loved what he was about to divulge. "Frankie has a problem with the demon drink. He gets confused about things." Luca read his body language. He could tell that he was hiding something. "He makes things up, you see." Luca stared at him, waiting for the punchline, but he didn't continue.

"So?" Luca asked in an aggravated voice. "What has that to do with you...or me for that matter?" He glared at Willis now, making him unnerved.

"It's like this, Mister Meridian, when Frankie goes on a bender, as he frequently does. The theatre suffers, by not being cleaned. I can't have that, now, can I?" Willis said and forced yet another smile. "I'd appreciate it if you didn't encourage him to drink. I know you think that you are being his friend but trust me, you aren't." Luca glared at him emotionless. *Just once*, he thought, *one bite and he'd be history, no one would have to suffer him anymore.*

"Don't you think Frankie is old enough to make his own decisions?" Luca asked, exasperated now and was about to walk away.

"Excuse me, Mister Meridian, I don't think you grasp the seriousness of the situation." Willis said with another fake smile. "The theatre will suffer, and if it isn't cleaned, the punters won't want come to an untidy place." Luca turned around slowly and scowled at him, and it was clear from his stance that he disliked Willis. "You do get my meaning, I'm sure."

"Frankie is old, he shouldn't even be working at his age." Luca almost spat the words. "If you are so concerned about the theatre, hire professional cleaners, not an old man with the onset of dementia and crippling arthritis."

"Your concern for old Frankie is touching, Mister Meridian," Willis said, and Luca could see that he was trying hard to remain composed. "But long after you and your fun diminutive show is gone from here, our little theatre will still be the centre of this community. Preferably, with our tired old janitor at the core." Willis smiled smarmily at him once more. "At least, do me the service of taking my request seriously. I am saying this out of concern for Frankie, that's all." Willis turned on his heel and walked back in the direction he had come from, leaving Luca feeling very frustrated but well and truly scolded as was his original intention.

Luca strolled back to his car and as he sat in, his mood still hadn't improved. Luca liked old Frankie, but he didn't like the way that Willis treated the old guy. From his every expression, Luca knew that Willis was hiding something, and his concern for the janitor was a coverup for something else. Willis had only concern for himself, his own interests and what Frankie might reveal with the aid of a drink.

As he started the car, Luca began to wonder what it was that Frankie knew about Willis and just what did Willis have against the old man? Something just didn't quite add up.

He drove over to his office. Luca hadn't been in, in almost a week. With his old assistant, he didn't have to worry that his affairs would not be taken care of, but he didn't have the same faith with the new personal assistant, although she was improving. For Luca it was a slow and testing course though, with his patience running thin.

As he walked down the hall and opened the door to his office, he called out. "I'm expecting some friends just send them in." Luca said but didn't give her a chance to reply.

Luca closed the door behind him and was surprised when he saw the Militibus were already waiting for him.

"Tough morning, General?" Peo asked him with a devilish grin on his handsome face as Luca walked over to the desk and sat down. Luca let out a long sigh.

"I hope you have some good news to report, Militibus." Luca said now and sat back in the leather swivel chair and briefly closed his eyes.

"Nothing to report here, General." Bjorn said. "The sluaghs have reported one of their nestmates has gone missing but there's no body to report." Luca nodded, opened his eyes and then looked across at Peo.

"Same, no one knows anything." Peo said and shrugged as he looked at him carefully.

"Jarl, anything new?" Lanny shook his head also.

"Mercelle, has engaged the hix but she has heard nothing back from him." Lanny said. "I advised her to call him off and we'd look into it for her."

"What did she say?" Luca asked him with a serious expression, but Bjorn laughed out loud as Luca stared over at him. "What's funny Berserker?"

"The shee was very forward in what she wanted from the Jarl." Bjorn replied still laughing loudly and so did Lanny.

"So, you are saying we still have nothing to go on," Luca sighed. "Just a bunch of mercenaries about to run riot in the city of Angels." He didn't know how they were going to contain this navar. Without an actual visual on the scum, they were chasing nothing but a phantom.

"Where's Demis?" Peo asked in a casual tone as he glanced around.

"He was supposed to be here." Luca said, stressed now. "He's late." As if on cue, the door opened, and Demis walked in. He seemed a little chirpier than usual and this amused them all.

"I'm sorry I was held up." Demis said as he looked at their questioning expressions.

"What do you have for us?" Luca asked him, his stress was beginning to surface again, and his temper was short with everyone, and he couldn't hide it.

"I thought that you might have a report for me." Demis said, puzzled as he looked indignantly at Luca.

"There's a lot happening here, dregs are being murdered, and we don't know what we are dealing with." Lanny said irately to Demis. "Some intel about what this navar is, would be helpful, if it isn't too much of an imposition into your time, Demis." This time, Luca chose to let Lanny have his say, because he too, was tired of the chaotic way Demis was handling it.

"I told you what the dakhanavar were," Demis said in a slightly raised voice as he watched the Jarl carefully. "They are vampire-like creatures, it should be easy to find. How many vampires are within the city limits?" Lanny stood up and walked over to where Demis stood. He was much taller than the old philosopher, towering over him.

"This isn't just a vampire, though, is it?" Lanny said heatedly. "The dregs don't see it, it creeps up on them and before they can react, it paralyses the victim and then it drains them. Now I don't know about you, Demis, but that is not an easy dreg to locate." Lanny stared coldly at the philosopher.

"No...no it isn't." Demis admitted. "I'm sorry I am not much help." He said and as Luca watched him, he couldn't help but feel sorry for him for being at the mercy of Lanny's temper. Demis had that effect on them, mostly.

"There's something else," Peo said, as he too stood up. "The banshees are scared, so scared they have hired a mercenary hix, to find the navar." Demis stared at them, and then Luca saw the colour drain from his face.

"We can't allow mercenary hix loose in this dimension." Demis said, "Can't you get the guardians out to protect the district where the banshees are? This is your job to make these decisions, Lucian. I can't do everything for you." He glared over at Luca now, with an expression that besieged Luca to take command and do his job.

"If we send the guardians out, we will have to answer to the council as to why we are protecting dregs in this way." Luca said in a controlled voice, almost biting his tongue. He felt that they had to show reason here, as Demis was too deep in this coverup of his, and Luca had allowed himself and his men to be dragged into it. "So that is a no-go, for now."

"I see," Demis said sorrowfully, it appeared that the gravity of the situation was finally getting through to him. "What can we do then?" He asked of no one in particular. "To protect the dregs."

"Did the navar escape from the Seventh or was it hiding somewhere, waiting for the portal to open?" Bjorn asked him. "It can't have been here in the Fourth, all this time, dormant, can it?" Luca looked at him for a moment. It was possible for the navar to have been subdued, sleeping and then awoken, wasn't it?

"No, I haven't heard of any escapes from the wasteland colony, nor a breach of any of the portals." Demis said and removed his glasses and began to clean the left lens with a handkerchief that he had taken from his jacket.

"Would you have even noticed if it came from the Sixth, Demis?" Lanny asked sarcastically.

"I'm not a complete fool, Jarl." Demis said dismissively and glared coldly at Lanny for a moment. "We have no use for navars in the Sixth." He shivered as if it had suddenly gone cold.

"This bickering isn't getting us anywhere." Peo said but he was grinning at Lanny. "Is it possible, they hibernate until something urges them awake?" Demis shook his head. It was clear to Luca that he didn't know anything about navars, and he was unable to pass on any intelligence to the Militibus.

"Great," Luca said and stood up. "We'll patrol again, all night, see what we can come up with." He felt defeated now as he looked at his men. Like them, he didn't know what to do. Until they got a sighting as to what the navar looked like, it was hopeless. Luca felt desperate. He didn't like it.

"Thank you, Lucian." Demis said. "I'll be in touch." He walked over to the door and left.

"Well, that was very enlightening." Lanny said cynically and Bjorn laughed and shook his head. "Do you get the feeling he's hiding something from us?" Luca looked at him. He did pick up on a change within the academic, but he couldn't pinpoint it.

"Like what, Lanny?" Bjorn asked, he still wore a smirk on his face.

"He knows something more than he is letting on, or..." Lanny looked across at Luca, "or he is covering up yet another mess that he has made."

"What kind of mess?" Luca asked as he ran his fingers through his hair, not wanting to hear the Jarl's response.

"Maybe he inadvertently let the navar out through the portal," Lanny said seriously. "And is now, trying to cover the whole thing up, before the council discovers it." Luca watched as Lanny walked over to the door and before he opened it, he added. "Peo, you and I will check on the shees tonight." Peo nodded and Lanny waved and left the office.

Luca glanced over at Bjorn and grinned at him. "You and I take the theatre district, Bjorn." He nodded and stood up and waved his hand as he too left Luca's office.

"You seem stressed, Luca." Peo said after Bjorn had left the office. "Is there something other than this navar business on your mind?" Luca poured a drink for both of them and handed the glass to Peo.

"Iubentium." Luca said in Latin.

"Iubentium." Peo said as he raised the glass.

"I will be glad when this case is over, Peo." Luca stated and took a long sip of his drink. "I shall take a long vacation and enjoy the delights of a female." They both laughed. "Or two." Luca grinned at him and then took another generous sip.

Chapter 26

Lycia 76 AD

Lucian was standing watching the soldiers as they trained. They were moving out of the barracks the next day, and back to Rome. Octavius was in his tent 'entertaining'. This brought a smile to Lucian's face. In the two years since they were sent to the territory of Lycia, he had taken over more and more duties from Octavius, while Octavius felt his duties were better suited for less strenuous activities, so he entertained the local chieftains and other dignitaries in a more political way rather than militarily. Particularly the daughters and the concubines.

For his part, Lucian had remained as faithful as he had wanted to, to Porcia. He had taken a mistress, as was befitting his status and he had her stay with him in his tent, but now that he was returning to Rome, Lucian was going to have Sabina, the courtesan return with him.

"Soon we will be back in Rome, Lucian Marius Antonius." The cheerful voice of his commander said from behind him. This made Lucian grin. "Will you be glad to be back in the arms of our beloved city?" Octavius asked as he stood proud with his legs apart as he too glanced out at the soldiers as they went through their paces in the searing sun.

"It is not the city I long to see." Lucian said with a broad grin, without turning to glance at Octavius.

"Something else," Octavius jeered. "Or perhaps someone?" Both Romans laughed.

"That would be telling." Lucian said still grinning.

"I have had news from Vespasian." Octavius said in a more serious tone. "We are to report to the palace upon our return."

"Wasn't that the original plan, Octavius?" Lucian asked, not understanding why, his commander would be so solemn at this time.

"I fear there is more to report than our emperor wishes to reveal in his letter." Octavius said, almost cryptically as he turned and smiled at Lucian. "We leave first thing." He turned and left and went back inside. No doubt to say goodbye to the concubine.

In the early light of the morning, Lucian saddled his horse and quickly mounted and as he rode along, he glanced around at the camp which had been his home for the last two years. He had enjoyed the posting. Lycia had been relatively peaceful. Lucian had quashed a few rebellious factions which thought they could beat the might of the Roman army, but they weren't serious attempts against the empire. But it had been good practice for Lucian.

"General, when we get to Rome," Lucian asked with a wicked grin. "Will the emperor put on a welcome home feast for us?" Octavius burst out laughing.

"You see yourself as par with Julius Caesar, Lucian?" Both men laughed heartily as they rode.

"Don't you, Octavius?" Lucian quipped and rode ahead of his commander.

They pitched their camp for the night and the soldiers saw that the horses were fed and watered.

Lucian lay on the bed and closed his eyes as his lover massaged his muscles and set to relaxing him. But his mind was on Porcia. He hadn't heard from her, not for several months. Not that she could write very well, she couldn't but she had always made an effort to communicate with him. He wondered why she had stopped. Had Vespasian discovered their secret affair? Or had Porcia found herself a new lover? Lucian couldn't guess. All he knew was something wasn't right.

Sabina smiled up at him and then as she was about to take him in her mouth, Lucian waved his hand and dismissed her. He stood up and fixed his tunic and left his quarters.

Outside, the moon was shining brightly, and he looked up at it, and wondered what Porcia was doing. He closed his eyes. Lucian didn't want to think of his woman with the emperor. He loved her, and it galled him that he had to share her with another man. Even though that other man was the Dominus Noster.

A scuffle between some of the soldiers broke out and Lucian walked over to where they were drinking and fighting.

"What's going on?" Lucian called out angrily and both the fighting Romans stopped and stood up straight.

"Princep, it is a case of honour." The first soldier said, and Lucian looked from him to the other soldier.

"Legionary?" Lucian asked the second brawler.

"He has called question over my bravery."

"Is this true?" Lucian asked but the first legionary hung his head. "We have not seen battle for some time, Milites." Lucian shouted angrily at both soldiers. "No one here is above an admonition, if you wake the General." Lucian turned and walked back the way that he had come.

Lucian knew that it was going to be a long trip back to Rome and already the army was beginning to feel the strain. Some had formed attachments to the Lycians, and this was their way to show their disappointment at having to leave.

He pulled back the curtain and went inside the tent and smiled across at Sabina and held out his hand to her. He would now enjoy the satisfaction that she would give him.

Chapter 27

Nunc Tempus

Luca picked up his sword and put it into its scabbard and fed his belt through the loop. He tied back his long silky black mane. He wore just his long leather coat over his leather trousers. Their patrol would surely lead to a fight as they were going into wolf territory and there was a turf war brewing between the different wolf gangs.

Luca picked up his helmet and left his penthouse. He wished he didn't have to go out on patrol, instead he had wanted to spend the night with Thea. As he thought of her, he smiled. He found a welcome solace in her arms, and in her bed. Thea reminded Luca so much of Porcia.

He started the panigale and tore out of the underground. Luca was driving fast, and the buildings whizzed by in a blur. He enjoyed the power of the bike. The freedom.

Luca drove into the tunnel and overtook several cars, who sounded the horns angrily as he passed them. He didn't care, all that was on his mind was getting to the bottom of who the navar was, and how he would stop its reign of terror amongst the mortals and the dregs.

As he drove into the district where the theatre was that his show was going to be staged, Luca saw the familiar figure of Willis. He recognised the tallish but slouched frame and the unctuous way in which he carried himself as he walked. He was suspicious at best.

Luca brought the panigale to a stop and turned off the engine and observed him from a distance. Luca watched as Willis walked along the street, glancing every now and then into some of the windows, not that there were any trendy shops in the area. It was a little dilapidated and investment was badly needed. Luca got off the bike and removed his helmet. He glanced around briefly and then placed his helmet on the handlebar of the bike.

As he began to walk at a distance behind Willis, he smelt his aroma, he was in hunter mode. Willis was on the prowl, but Luca didn't know for what. Women? A blow job? Or maybe some gear, though he didn't seem the type to use narcotics.

The sound of a bike made Luca turn around, he saw Bjorn, park up his panigale and remove his helmet. Luca raised his arm and in lightning speed slid across to one of the darkened doorways of the shuttered-up shops. Bjorn smiled as he joined him.

"What are you trailing?" Bjorn asked in a hushed tone as he followed Luca's gaze.

"That guy, creeping along the shop fronts." Luca replied almost in a whisper as he pointed across to where the theatre manager was lurking and jerking to the side.

"Who is he?" Bjorn asked as he too kept a watchful eye on Willis now.

"That's George Willis," Luca said in a hushed tone. "He's the theatre manager where I'm directing the play." Bjorn looked at him and smiled.

"You're trailing a fan?" Bjorn said with a hint of teasing to his voice and Luca grinned at him. "How avant-garde, General but shouldn't he be trailing you?" Both the vampires chuckled as they looked back over to where Willis was walking.

"He's no fan of mine." Luca admitted and looked across to where Willis had stopped abruptly. "But he's very eager to stop me from talking to the old janitor, though. He thinks I am a bad influence on him." Bjorn chuckled again as he looked at Luca.

"Are you?" Luca grinned at Bjorn and then shook his head.

"Willis is greedy, and I also think he's doing some dodgy dealings within the theatre." Luca said as they walked on a few paces slowly, the vampires used the doorways as cover. "He's very keen to make sure that I don't speak with old Frankie."

They stopped walking and observed as Willis went into a bar. There was loud music coming from it and the two vampires stopped for a moment.

"What kind of dealings?" Bjorn asked him. "Narcotics?"

"I'm not sure, but he was vocal about his dislike for Greyson." Bjorn stared at him. "I think he may know something about Greyson's death, but I can't be sure."

"Is that a hunch, Luca?" Bjorn asked in a sceptical tone. "Or wishful thinking perhaps?"

"I don't honestly know, Bjorn." Luca replied as he looked at the Viking. "Nothing about this case is what I am used to or making an informed judgement on." They both nodded.

"Do you want to check out the bar?" Bjorn asked him. "Or do you want me to do it, since he won't recognise me." Luca thought about it for a moment and then nodded.

"I'll make my way around the back," Luca told him. "In case he marks that you are following him." Bjorn nodded and walked on and into the bar.

Luca quickly glanced around and then walked carefully down the darkened alley toward the back of the bar. There was a couple standing against the wall, making out. Luca ignored them and walked on, alerted to anything that may jump at him and try catch him off guard. There was no chance of that happening. Luca was far too experienced for that.

As he walked slowly, he had his hand on the hilt of his sword, ready to pull it from its scabbard at any moment. The alley was quiet and besides the couple there was no one else around.

Luca decided to make his way to the other end, his senses were highly aroused, and he sniffed the air. There was nothing unusual in the air, apart from the pheromones coming from the couple as they reached the climax of their foreplay.

A sound! It was a can being kicked. Luca stopped in his tracks. The alley was dark, save for the intermittent light emitted from the lights over the garage door. Carefully Luca removed his sword and walked, using the shadows of the wall, as cover. He looked around, his vision was sharp, as sharp as an eagle. He heard the heavy breathing, and as he looked on, he saw the laboured limp of a shee as she tried to walk. With a great effort on her part, she had remained upright for a few more paces, and then suddenly she fell to the ground.

Luca quickly ran to her aid and turned her onto her back, it was Mercelle, and she was bleeding badly.

"What happened?" Luca asked her as her eyes closed and she kept falling in and out of alertness. "Mercelle." He tapped at her cheek with his left hand to keep her awake.

"The...the..." her breath was laboured as she tried to talk. "The hix...he hurt..." Her eyes closed once more.

"Mercelle, did the hix do this to you?" Luca asked hurriedly but she shook her head and then closed her eyes for good.

Damn! He thought to himself.

Luca stood up straight and put his sword back in its scabbard. He looked around and then he saw Bjorn running quickly toward him. When he saw the lifeless body of the shee on the ground he looked at Luca.

"What happened?" Luca let out a long sigh and stood with his hands on his hips.

"She said something incoherent about the hix." Luca told him as he shook his head and then he hit his hand against the wall in frustration.

"I thought the shees hired the hix to help them," Bjorn said quickly. "Why would he kill her?" Luca agreed and looked at the lifeless body on the ground. Maybe the hix had betrayed the banshees, took their money and then killed them. It wasn't beyond the mercenaries to double cross the ones who hired them. The hix were notorious for their schemes.

"We can't leave her here, Bjorn." Luca said as he glanced at the shee on the ground. "We can't send her to the Eighth either."

"I agree, but what do we do?" Bjorn asked concerned as he glanced at the lifeless body on the ground. They were both uneasy about the situation. Neither of the Militibus knew what to do.

"Get the bike and bring it around here." Luca said after a moment and Bjorn turned and ran hurriedly back to where the bikes were parked up.

It seemed like an age before Bjorn returned with his bike. He parked it up on its stand.

"What are we going to do?" He asked as Luca sighed loudly. "Call the guardians?" Luca shook his head. It was the logical thing to do but yet, he knew if they did, it would release one hell of a storm back in the Sixth with the council of Elders. Luca didn't want that...just yet.

"You can take her back to her nest. I'll follow on my bike." Luca said and he helped Bjorn get the body of the shee, rather unsteadily onto his bike. Bjorn got on behind her. "The nest is near that factory we passed two nights ago." Luca slapped Bjorn on the back and ran down the alley to get his own bike.

It didn't take long for Luca to catch up with Bjorn and side by side they drove to where the shee nest was located.

They carefully took Mercelle's body from the bike and Bjorn carried her lifeless body over his shoulder. Luca walked carefully over to the door and listened for a moment, for signs of life inside the building. Luca vaguely heard movement. He nodded to Bjorn and then Luca opened the door, he went inside, followed by his friend.

There were three shees, sitting on car seats around a small pitiful fire. They wore long white dresses, which resembled Victorian night garments. They were startled by the vampires and jumped to their feet. Then they saw the lifeless body of their leader on Bjorn's shoulder.

"What did you do to Mercelle?" The tall, blonde banshee asked in a wail as Bjorn laid the slain shee onto the ground at her feet.

"My name is Luca, I'm the Militibus commanding officer," Luca said as he came forward. "This is my officer, Bjorn. We were patrolling tonight when Mercelle came down an alley, she collapsed and died in front of me." Luca said as he removed his leather glove and immediately took control of the situation. The three shees looked at each other, as if trying to work out if they believed him or not.

"Who did this to her?" The blonde shee asked.

"I don't know." Luca replied honestly. "She was incoherent, but she did say something about a hix." Luca glanced across at Bjorn. "I will find who did this, but I need you to tell me, who is the hix and where was Mercelle meeting him." The three banshees remained silent. This frustrated Luca further. How the hell was he meant to help them when they wouldn't talk? This was typical behaviour of the dregs though. They clammed up when they really should talk to the Militibus.

"If you know, just tell us," Bjorn pleaded with them, but they still remained quiet, refusing to speak to the Militibus.

"Damn it, why won't you talk?" He yelled as Luca looked at Bjorn, he could feel his exasperation too.

"She told us she was meeting Djano at the back of the carpet shop." The dark haired shee said almost in a whisper. "But he wouldn't do this. Not Djano." She protested and Luca stepped forward and stood up straight. "He wouldn't do this, Djano, he was straight up you know." The shee repeated again as if to convince Luca.

"Why do you think he wouldn't?" Luca demanded from her. "He's a mercenary. Mercenaries usually turn for a higher price."

"They were partners." The blonde shee blurted out. There was an infuriated sigh from the other shees at the admission.

"You mean they were mating?" Bjorn asked in disbelief, and she nodded.

"Mercelle told my officers, she had hired the hix for protection, she never mentioned they were having an affair." Luca said disbelievingly. "But you're saying they were nest mates." The blonde nodded again, and she turned her head to look at the other shees, who were glaring back at her as though she had betrayed the nest by talking to the Militibus.

"Mercelle knew the Militibus would send Djano back to the Seventh or the Eight, so she had to protect him." Luca swore under his breath as he glared at Maisa.

"Was she in pup?" Bjorn asked abruptly. The three shees just looked at the ground.

"She was pregnant?" Luca raised his voice incredulously now. "The shees are breeding?" He roared and then sighed. The blonde nodded. "Were the other shees after mating too?" Bjorn looked at him and then to the blonde shee. This was becoming a serious problem, the shees knew they weren't allowed to breed. The situation had become even more complicated now.

"Yes, we all have." Maisa, the dark haired shee said in a murmur. "We're all in pup."

"With Djano?" They nodded again. Luca let out a long sigh.

"The hix is the closest to our kind that there is here in this dimension." The blonde Risa said, a little more boldly now as she looked at Luca, with a daring expression.

"That's not of interest to us," Luca said and walked over to where Bjorn stood and with his back to the three shees, he said in a hushed tone. "I think we found our reason for the deaths of the shees." Bjorn looked at him. Luca turned around and said to them. "Look, we are sorry you lost your leader. We will find who is doing this, in the meantime, do not venture out alone." They nodded and the two vampires left the building.

Outside Luca let out a long slow breath. He knew it was his duty to report the shees and the hix for blatantly breaking the rules of breeding, but Luca didn't care about that. All he cared about was catching the navar, and quickly before any more deaths took place.

"We have to inform the council." Bjorn said as he stopped pacing and looked at Luca.

"I know." Luca sighed. He didn't relish the idea of telling Aristotle this news. "Just let's not go there until after the navar is caught." He glanced at the Berserker who nodded.

"We'll call a progress meeting first thing." Bjorn nodded and they went over to their bikes.

Chapter 28

Luca sat behind his desk, and he rested his chin on his hands. The events of the previous evening had him perturbed. It had been illegal for the dregs to procreate in this dimension. Most couldn't anyway but for those that could, they knew what the consequences would be if they were caught. But what made Luca uneasy was that all the shees had mated with the hix. That wasn't new in the Seventh but here in the Fourth, it had a new level that they would have to quell before it became the norm amongst the dregs.

The council would now have to be informed about what Luca's theory regarding the navar was. Luca certainly didn't relish the idea that he would have to tell Aristoteles. He wasn't the easiest of the Elders to talk to and Luca couldn't relate to him. He doubted that anyone could.

He looked up as the door opened and one by one his officers came into the office. Luca had sent a message for Demis to call back from the Sixth but he had heard nothing from him so he assumed the philosopher would not be joining them.

Typical!

"Who wants a drink?" Luca asked them and stood up. He certainly could use one. Luca didn't wait for a reply and just poured the four glasses and took them back to his desk. He watched as each of them picked up a glass. "Bjorn has informed you of the patrol we did last night?" Luca asked, and he remained standing with his back to the drink's cabinet.

"Yes," Peo said drily and glanced at Luca. "What happened to the shee?" Luca took a quick gulp from his drink.

"She wasn't fully drained, but enough to kill her." Luca replied morosely and finished his drink in a single gulp, then he turned around and refilled his glass.

"What's all this about her being impregnated?" Lanny asked, he was standing in the centre of the office. He had his left hand in his pocket. "The council does not allow breeding amongst the dregs." Luca nodded. This was giving him another metaphorical headache. "Not in this dimension. So why did the shees decide that it was a good idea?"

"The whole nest was impregnated by the hix, Djano." Bjorn said uneasily and glanced across to where Lanny stood. "It appears this Djano is getting himself a hareem." Bjorn shook his head as he downed the whiskey.

"Is that why they were murdered?" Peo asked and looked from Bjorn to Luca. Luca wasn't sure. He hoped it wasn't, though it was a thought which was lurking in his mind. If it was, then they needed to call in some other Militibus from other districts to find the navar. Quickly and put a stop to her.

"What are you thinking General?" Lanny asked and Luca looked at him. "What's troubling you?" The Jarl was very perceptive, and he had a canny way of reading people.

"This isn't good, Militibus," Luca said and sighed audibly. "We don't know much about this navar, and all the homicides have been mainly in the dreg community. Only what, three or so were mortals?" They all agreed. "Of the dregs who were killed, they were mainly shees, all female apart from Greyson."

"What are you thinking, Luca?" Bjorn asked him. "That the navar is deliberately targeting females?"

"I think the navar is weak and is killing female dregs to suck their energy." Luca replied. "Dreg blood isn't a good source of strength but drain a pregnant dreg and you get a better stream, because of the foetus."

"Like an energy drink." Lanny interjected with a smirk.

"If you like." Luca agreed and half chuckled as he glanced at him. The Jarl sometimes could be uncouth.

"That doesn't explain the three humans or Greyson." Lanny said, almost deflating Luca's theory now. "They were males."

"No, but what if, the pregnant shees were an appetiser, the mortals then were the real source of energy?" Peo asked seriously.

"Except, the mortals were killed first." Luca told him and then exhaled.

"I'll buy Peo's appetisers," Lanny said and with his hands on his hips, he paced up and down for a few moments. They all looked at him. "The mortals were bled first, but that was to restore some strength, right?" They all nodded. "The shees being pregnant gave a little more stability so the navar could continue to revive but not be fully operational just yet as it's not on a complete power charge."

"Then what you are saying, Lanny," Bjorn said with a concerned look on his face. "Is that the navar is only just getting started. The mortals are in grave danger." Lanny nodded. "Great!" Bjorn threw his hands in the air in utter frustration. "Psychotic bitch alert."

"If you are right, Lanny, then one of us has to go to the Sixth." Luca said grimly. "We have to let the council know." There was silence in the room as they grasped the gravity of the situation. "We may just need to call in reinforcements from other Militibus teams."

"Who goes to the Sixth, then?" Peo asked. "How do we explain what we are investigating and what we found?" Peo looked at Luca.

"We just tell them it was a routine investigation into dreg gangland activity." Lanny said as he glanced across at the Praetorian. Luca knew that the Jarl spurned the rules whenever it suited him, and in a way that got them the results that they had sometimes. Their district was one of the cleanest and most lawful of all the Militibus districts.

"I agree with Lanny." Bjorn piped in and Luca agreed too. In the early days when they started out, they had been following orders and rules, strictly obeying everything, but it had gotten them chastised for not making informed decisions so eventually they began to flout the rules, and they still got reprimanded but at least they made their own decisions.

"Question is which one of us goes to the Sixth?" Luca asked with an impish grin. He didn't want to go, and he had a great excuse with the production he was working on. He looked at Lanny who put his hands up and shook his head, this made Luca chuckle, as he understood the Jarl's rebellion.

"I have to oversee the new club." Bjorn said with a wicked grin, and he turned to Peo, who just laughed loudly and said as he put the glass down on the desk.

"Wimps, you lot are afraid of Aristoteles." Peo grinned. "I'll go, but you owe me for this, guys."

"Thank you, Peo," Luca said and walked over to the desk. "When this is over, I think we all need one hell of a vacation." They all agreed. "See you later, oh and be vigilant, this thing is getting nasty." He smiled at them as they left the office.

Luca knew that it was worse than any of them even wanted to admit but he had every faith in his men. They never failed him.

Chapter 29

The theatre was alive with activity when Luca arrived. He glanced around and recognised the two detectives, who were questioning the security guards. He saw the theatre manager and he walked over to him.

"What's going on?" Luca asked him as he glanced around the lobby. Willis looked at Luca, a little disdainfully.

"You don't know?" Willis asked and Luca shook his head. "Old Frankie was found dead early this morning." Luca glared at him. The old janitor. Dead?

The poor old soul, Luca thought.

"How did it happen?" Luca asked him emotionless as he glanced around him.

"He was working here late last night," Willis said bitterly as he glared at Luca now. "He obviously fell down drunk, and at his age it was enough to kill him." Luca scowled at him. The few times that he had conversed with the old guy he certainly didn't come across as an old drunk. Sure, Frankie seemed to like to have a few drinks, but he never struck Luca as being an alcoholic. Luca had seen a lot of people with addictions, at the Cyclades hotel like the ones who Father O'Hara worked with, Frankie never struck him as being as desperate as those misfortunate people.

Luca walked away from Willis and walked over to one of the detectives and asked him what happened. The detective looked up at Luca suspiciously and then said in a caustic tone. "The janitor was killed, probably by a wild animal after he fell in a pile of garbage."

"A wild animal?" Luca queried and the cop nodded. "What kind of wild animal?"

"According to your boss, over there," he said. "The janitor was a known alcoholic, a little too much to drink, fell down outside and some wild animals hungry enough began to feed. The old guy was in the wrong place at the right time." Luca lowered his head a little. That didn't sound plausible. Frankie didn't drink that much. Not that he was aware of, Luca had never seen him drunk. A little confused but that was his age. "You have anything to add...Mister..."

"Meridian, Luca Meridian." Luca replied. "Who is the lead detective?" He asked the cop now and he noticed that Willis was hedging closer to them, to hear what they were saying.

"I am, why?" The detective asked and he was sore at the accusation that there was a superior in charge.

"Do you know Detective Sometti?" Luca asked him. The cop nodded, still looking suspiciously at Luca.

"Sure, I do," The cop replied. "Why?" Again, his scepticism was aroused by Luca's questions, and Luca glanced behind him and saw Willis was standing within earshot.

"Will you ask him to give me a call?" Luca asked cagily. "He has my number." The cop nodded and Luca walked away and into the auditorium.

There was a sombre atmosphere on the stage as Luca joined the cast, who were standing around awaiting direction. He looked at each of them and tried to gauge their emotions. There was shock amongst the cast but nothing beyond that. None of them knew or cared about Frankie.

"We are all sorry to hear about the old man." It was Amos who spoke and broke the silence, and Luca turned to look at him and nodded. "But it's what happens when you abuse drink." There was a hushed murmur of agreement amongst the cast members. Luca glared at Amos.

"Did any of you have a conversation with Frankie?" Luca asked, clearly annoyed at them because they had formed that assumption. He knew that none of them cared about what had happened to the old man. They looked at him blankly. "His name was Frankie, the janitor who died out there this morning." Luca pointed beyond the door of the auditorium. Amos looked almost shame faced at Luca and then he hung his head low. The cast remained silent.

"No, I don't believe any of us did." Amos said in an embarrassed voice now.

"Well, I did," Luca said harshly at all of them, as he looked at each of them in turn. "I talked with him, and I had a few drinks with him. I can tell you that he was far from being a drunkard. Frankie was an old man who loved this theatre." He looked around at those who were standing close to him. "The theatre was his life, and he loved to talk about it. The stars that he met. Actors like you, he spoke fondly of. Star struck by the magic of this place." They all lowered their eyes from his. He felt so helpless and so very angry. "So people, we have our opening night in two weeks, let's dedicate this show to an old man who lived for the stage." There was silence for a moment and as Luca began to walk away there was a loud agreement and an applause.

He took up his usual spot in the third row and placed the clipboard on his lap and watched as the actors enacted their roles in the play. They were giving it their all.

Luca's mind just wasn't focused on the play, he was stressed, and he needed an escape. As he looked up at the stage and saw Thea as she accorded all her might to the role of Medea, Luca decided that he wouldn't go out patrolling later, he would spend the night with Thea, let her soothe away his stress as only she could. Luca knew that he was using her, but he didn't care, she was only too happy to oblige him with her body. That was all that mattered to him at that moment.

As the morning ran into the afternoon, as relentlessly as they tried their best in their respective roles, Luca forced the cast to redo the scenes that he wasn't happy with. His temper was frayed, and he had a short fuse with everyone. Luca knew that he shouldn't be taking his frustration out on the cast, but he couldn't help it. When a murder took place in the Fourth and it involved a dreg, Luca usually took it in his stride, and he knew that there were enough informants within the dreg community to help them, but this case was different. He felt a huge loss in the death of the old man. He was an innocent mortal caught up in a situation where a dreg was killing to become powerful, the navar was taking what it needed and it didn't care where it took the blood from, all that mattered was it fed, and when it fed it gained more energy. The more energy it gained the more dangerous it was. The worst part of this was the Militibus had no visual on what they were dealing with. They were chasing blindly, an entity that if it passed them by on the street, none of them would know because Demis didn't give them any detailed description of what it looked like. Luca supposed only that it had taken a human form.

The more that Luca thought about Frankie, the more haunted he became by it. It was like...

But that was a very long time ago, could he really be held responsible for that now? After all this time? Almost two millennia?

"That's a wrap for now." Amos called out and Luca looked at him and then agreed. "We'll all meet back here for full dress rehearsal at two PM."

Luca left the auditorium and as he walked into the lobby, he saw Sometti. He strode over to him and held out his hand, and the detective shook it.

"Meridian, what are you doing here?" Sometti asked and Luca led him outside the theatre. So that they wouldn't be overheard, least of all by Willis.

"I was hired by a client to investigate a suspected infidelity." Luca said and forced a smile. Sometti laughed. "In the theatre here."

"I bet you get great videos, don't you?" Sometti said chuckling and Luca just nodded. "Roddy said to come down here, so, what did you want to talk to me about?" Luca glanced around him, to make sure that there was no one around to eavesdrop on their delicate conversation.

"The janitor, who was killed last night," Luca spoke in a hushed tone. "Is there any way that I can take a look at the body?" The Militibus had helped Sometti and his partner on some cases and there was a mutual professional admiration and respect from all concerned.

"The coroner has taken him downtown, I'm about to go down there now anyway." Sometti said. "You can bum a ride with me." Luca grinned and thanked him and as they walked down the street to Sometti's car neither bothered with small talk. Luca wasn't in the mood anyway.

The journey was taken in silence. Luca had on his sunglasses and his arms were folded across his chest. He looked bored but he wasn't, he was just pensive. Deep in his own personal reveries. Musings that had lain under the surface, hidden but never far away that they didn't pop up when he didn't want them to.

The car pulled into the coroner's and Sometti parked up in a space near the building. Luca got out of the car and walked ahead of the cop. At the top of the steps, he waited for him, and they went inside together.

The long corridor seemed longer than ever as they opened the door and Sometti walked over to the woman, who was wearing a white lab coat, and she had safety glasses on.

"What do I owe the pleasure, Sometti?" She asked Sometti and looked across at Luca and then she smiled warmly at him.

"A stiff was brought in an hour ago, Rosie." Sometti said and glanced at Luca. "My friend here would like to take a look." His voice was dripping with sarcasm. Rosie looked at Luca a little suspiciously and then back at the cop questioningly. "Meridian is helping me out, on the case." He added sheepishly and she walked away, and they followed her.

"I haven't started the autopsy yet," she said candidly as she opened the steel door and pulled out the slab. Luca looked at the ashen face of the old man. He had once been tanned and though he was old, his skin didn't have the old leathery look that most octogenarians had.

Luca walked to the end of the slab and leaned over and checked Frankie's feet. He bent over and peered closer, but he didn't see any puncture wound. He would have to have a closer look.

"You lookin for something in particular, Meridian?" Sometti asked as he studied Luca's demeanour. Luca looked up and smiled across at the assistant coroner.

"Do you have something I can use, Rosie, to separate his toes?" She nodded and walked back into the other room.

"You want to tell me what you are looking for?" Sometti hissed at him in a distrustful tone.

"I will, when I find it." Luca said when he stood up and looked at the assistant when she came toward them with a pair of blue surgical gloves and a pair of scissors and a tweezers. Rosie handed the gloves to Luca, and he put them on and then he took the pair of surgical scissors from her.

He bent over the corpse once more and with his index finger and thumb he examined the toes, one by one. He separated the two end toes, and he moved his head sideways and as he was about to move the other toe, he spotted the two bite marks, almost hidden. To the untrained eye, it was nothing, just a couple of dots. But to Luca's vampiric sight, he recognised the fang marks.

Luca moved the other toes and saw under the big toe another bite. He moved around to the other side of the slab and examined the feet, in the same toes in exactly the same place as on the left foot, the bite marks were mirrored.

He made a mental note of the shape of the marks and then stood up and removed the gloves and handed the scissors back to the assistant.

"Thank you, Rosie." Luca said and walked over to the bin and threw the gloves into it.

"Did you discover anything?" Rosie asked him as she glanced admiringly at his broad chest. Luca didn't know how much he should tell her, so he just smiled and looked at Sometti and then back to the assistant coroner.

"As I suspected," Luca said dispassionately. "It's a Phoneutria rufibarbis bite that the old man suffered." The woman looked at him suspiciously and half turned her head as she gaped at him.

"A spider bite?" Rosie quizzed and Luca nodded. "There's no poisonous spiders wild in LA." The assistant dismissed adamantly.

"No, you're right, there isn't." Luca agreed with her.

"Then what are you saying, Meridian?" Sometti asked as he too began to shake his head in dismay. "How can a spider kill a person if they ain't here?" Luca knew that he was reaching a little with this excuse, but he had to come up with something quickly to throw off Sometti.

"A case I've worked on previously, nasty divorce," Luca looked at Sometti. "He was an importer of exotic animals, arachnids and reptiles." Luca said in a serious tone. "He claimed someone broke into his shop and what they didn't steal, they let free. Animal rights fanatics." Luca felt inspired now.

"How come I never heard of that?" Sometti asked cautiously as he looked disbelievingly at Luca.

"We didn't believe it either," Luca said. "We were hired by the wife to get dirt on the husband, the rest is nothing to do with us." He grinned at Sometti. "We don't investigate theft of exotic animals. Just divorces, Sometti." Luca smiled widely at the detective. He knew of course that the cop was suspicious and probably didn't buy what Luca said.

"Wait, I think I read something about it." The assistant exclaimed now. "Yes, she took him to the cleaners, didn't she? She claimed spousal abuse and got a substantial settlement." Luca agreed with her and now that he had planted the seed in her mind about a Brazilian wandering spider, he was certain that she would go along with it in her report. Luca felt bad that Frankie wouldn't have the justice he deserved by the cops investigating his case fully. But then how could they? It was a supernatural being from another dimension who murdered the old guy. Luca would see to it though, that Frankie got justice. He would avenge the old man. Make amends for...what happened before.

"Thank you," Luca held out his hand to Rosie and smiled fondly at her.

"Any time." Rosie replied flirtatiously as she smoothed a piece of hair behind her ear and walked with them to the door.

Outside the building, Luca turned to Sometti and shook hands with him. "Thanks, Sometti, if there's anything I can do in return, you only have to ask." The cop nodded and as Luca walked down the steps he called after him.

"Does that BS really get you laid, Meridian?" Luca turned back to him and laughed as he walked over to the pavement and hailed a cab.

At least he had something a little more concrete than he had had the previous day. Luca now, had a visual of the shape of the fang marks.

Chapter 30

Thea was moving rhythmically on Luca as he caressed her thighs. She had been the stress relief that he had craved all day, and for the past week since he discovered that old Frankie had been murdered.

Peo had returned from the Sixth earlier, but Luca hadn't had an opportunity to speak with him.

He heard Thea moan as she was beginning to orgasm, but Luca didn't care, all he could think of was his immediate problem and what he was going to do about it.

Luca rolled her off him and sat up in the bed. She looked at him, but he didn't look at her. He couldn't. Luca was aware that he wasn't good company that night.

"Is something wrong, Luca?" Thea asked him and reached out to touch his arm, but he just got out of the bed and walked over to the window and glanced at the floral material of the window dressing. It was dark outside, and besides he couldn't see anything beyond the closed curtain.

"It's not you, Thea," Luca said after a moment and smiled faintly at her as he turned around. He saw her lick her lips as she glanced at his naked body. "I guess you could call it opening night jitters." She smiled back at him and got out of the bed and walked toward him. She was slender, her body was long and thin, he could make out the shape of her ribs under her skin as she walked over to him.

"But opening night isn't until next week, baby." Her voice was like velvet as her cold hand touched his chest softly. He chuckled at that.

"Am I not allowed a few minutes of doubt, Thea?" Luca teased as he took her hand in his and raised it to his mouth and kissed it and she giggled.

"No, you're not, because you are an incredible director, your vision for the play is amazing" she said as he sucked on her finger, and he heard her gasp as he gazed at her intently. "You are an incredible man," Luca sucked on another of her fingers, and she giggled now. "An incredible lover." He took her ring finger into his mouth and caressed the tip of it with his tongue, he watched as she closed her eyes. "A very beautiful man with the most amazing..." He bit her finger in a gentle teasing way, and she caught her breath as he sucked her fingers again. His fangs were hurting as they descended again.

"Thea, let me start all over again," Luca said as he picked her up in his arms and brought her back over to the bed. "You've convinced me all that I am." He laughed as he covered her body with his, and they made love again. This time, Luca performed but just for his own pleasure. His own needs paramount over Thea's.

Thea was lying in Luca's arms, as he caressed her bare shoulder with his thumb, he was thinking about the night of passion that they had shared. He had been sleeping with her for several weeks now and he had enjoyed every moment of it. Luca had had many lovers over the centuries but none that he could honestly say he felt anything other than the release that they gave him in the bedroom.

A memory of the concubines he had enjoyed before and after battle, flashed before him. The Roman armies, particularly the officers, had enjoyed some desirable delicacies and Luca smiled to himself when he witnessed some of the orgies. He had of course taken part in some, but his favourite concubine had been a slave's daughter, Porcia. She had been the closest to love that Luca had ever come.

Of course, he had been careful not to show the other officers or soldiers his true feelings for her. Porcia had also been the courtesan to the emperor. If Vespasian had discovered that his chief doxy was cavorting with his centurion officer, it would have ended with both Luca and Porcia being executed.

He closed his eyes just briefly as Porcia had invaded his thoughts again. *Why now?* Luca wondered. Though she had occupied his contemplations recently, it wasn't just her, it was...

Damn her for troubling him. Wasn't he disturbed enough?

"Are you OK, Luca?" Thea's soft voice broke into his reverie. He turned to look at her and kissed her on the temple. "You seem so lost in thought, as if you are having a bad memory." Her voice was full of emotion. Luca just looked at her for a moment. She seemed perceptive as to what he was thinking and feeling. As if by chance she knew him intimately, in a way she did. She knew his body, knew what he liked sexually. Did that constitute 'knowing' him? Luca didn't think so.

He was also aware that Thea was looking for something more than just sex, she wanted a relationship, and Luca knew that he wasn't in the market for a relationship but if he was, he certainly wouldn't mind it to be with this woman.

"I just want to tell you how good this evening has been." Luca said and smiled at her. "You are so beautiful, Thea." He kissed her softly on the lips. She was a good kisser, and he could feel himself beginning to enjoy her a little too much. He couldn't stop himself from feeling the way that he did. After two thousand years, was he finally mature enough to love again? He half chuckled at the thought. Of course he wasn't, Luca couldn't afford to fall in love.

"I am so attracted to you." Thea said as she kissed his bare chest. "I can't help myself." Luca wrapped a strand of her hair behind her ear. "I could easily fall in love with you, Luca."

"Thea, don't get too involved with me." Luca warned her carefully, and she looked into his eyes. He knew that his words had hurt her, but he needed to be honest. His life was too complicated regarding involvement with mortal women, and he didn't want to find himself in a situation like the Jarl had. Even though his situation was a lot different to Lanny's, this woman wasn't pure, but Luca knew the complications were the same. The council of Elders would not approve, and they could make life very difficult for him, like restricting his promotional prospects.

"I'm not," Thea replied. "I've never been with a man like you before, that's all." She kissed his chest.

"A man like me?" Luca queried in amusement. She didn't know that he wasn't a mortal man, nor that he was a vampire. The only hint that he was a vampire, and immortal was that he was physically beautiful, a perfect specimen of what a mortal man should be.

"You're a sensitive, handsome man," she said and smiled. "And a plus is you know the classics." Luca laughed heartily and touched her face gently. "You are perfect."

"You think that I'm perfect?" Luca asked her and he chuckled as she nodded. "Thea, darling, I am far from perfect." A brief image of Porcia flashed before him, her hand up to her cheek where he had slapped her hard, the look in her eyes as the words he had used cut to her very soul. He had been hopelessly in love with Porcia. Though their love had been passionate, it was a hopeless thing because they were both slaves. Luca had been a centurion officer, a free man, he was still a slave at Vespasian's beck and call, just like Porcia had been.

"You are, to me." Thea whispered. "That's all that matters." Luca cupped her face in his hands, and they kissed passionately, and he rolled her off him and they began to make love again.

PEO WAS WALKING UP and down in front of the desk as he looked disbelievingly at Luca. "So, the old man was murdered?" Luca nodded gravely. "You still have no idea where the navar is?"

"The only thing that we are certain of is that the monster is getting stronger." Bjorn said and his tone mirrored what they all were feeling. Helplessness.

"What did the council say?" Luca asked Peo, but the Praetorian just shrugged his shoulders and let out a long sigh.

"You know how Aristotle plays matters down." Luca knew only too well, and it was likely to go on for a long time, especially since there was a traitor within the council, and they didn't know who it was. Their hands were pretty much tied. "He wants us to call a meeting with the guardians and have them arrest any dreg engaged in breeding."

"And then do what?" Lanny asked sarcastically. "Depend on the dregs for intel when we get another case? That's going to work in our favour." Luca watched as Lanny shook his head disapprovingly. The Jarl was right, no dreg would volunteer any information if the Militibus imposed a sanction of no sex or breeding.

"Since Frankie was murdered," Luca said sombrely. "There hasn't been a dreg killing. So maybe the navar is reaching full capacity."

"Or maybe it's biding its time for something bigger." Lanny called out from where he stood between the desk and the filing cabinet, Luca had seen the Jarl's predictions before and when he called something out, he was usually right.

"If there is, and another mortal gets it, then there's no way that Sometti will buy that poisonous spider theory of yours again, Luca." Bjorn said and smirked at him. "He's not that dumb."

"Poisonous spider theory?" Peo quizzed as he glanced from one to the other, and Bjorn laughed loudly. "What have I missed here?"

"Another time, Praetorian." Bjorn said between chuckles.

"Is Aristoteles going to pay us a visit or do we have to put up with the old toad?" Lanny asked Peo, who was now grinning from ear to ear.

"He wants us to wrap this up with as little hassle as possible." Peo said gruffly. "The esteemed philosopher is not happy that we went on investigating without making a report to Demis first."

"Of course, the old tadpole denied knowledge of what we were doing." Lanny said and gave out a frustrated moan. "That's just like him."

"He wasn't there, Jarl." Peo defended Demis this time. "He's been giving evidence at his disciplinary hearing." They all turned to look at Peo, who nodded. "The council has relieved him of his duty until we solve this mess and give them a full report."

"Great," Luca moaned loudly. "This is all we need." He shook his head and sighed audibly. Demis had really landed them in it this time. "Demis really has opened a can of worms this time." Luca brushed his hair back from his face now.

"Takes a little heat from us though," Bjorn said a little optimistically, looking on the bright side as usual. "Gives you a chance to focus on your new career." Lanny and Peo laughed now as Luca glared at them and tried to look angry. Though he knew that they were only having a laugh. They had been supportive of the times he hadn't gone on patrol when he said he would. They had assumed he was at the theatre and not in bed with his leading lady.

"It's good to know my friends believe in me." Luca laughed cheerfully as the Militibus left the office.

Chapter 31

It was a couple of days until the opening night of Medea and Luca was feeling a little less stressed than he had been in recent weeks. A lot of the pressure had been taken from him by the Militibus themselves. Lanny had taken over command from Luca, to allow him to focus on the play. For that he had been really grateful. Luca found that he actually enjoyed directing and that he had a flare for it. His interpretation of the play was now seen with his modern vampiric eyes and not his Roman vision, on how he had first seen it performed.

He was relaxing in his penthouse and listening to some of Frederic's later pieces. Some memories had flooded back, mostly good ones about their friendship. Luca leaned back in the sofa and smiled to himself. Frederic had been the only mortal that Luca had trusted enough to tell him that he was a vampire. Chopin had listened to him as he spoke and as he took on board all that Luca had told him, the composer had given him a brilliant smile and said without flinching, in that gentle way of his.

'A fine gift has been bestowed upon you, Lucian, with immortality you will live to see your greatest accomplishments fulfilled. That is something to cherish and to embrace, not to

despise and view as a torment.' Luca had never looked at it like that. He had always seen it as an affliction. Something he had been cursed with. A life he was forced to live without ever having had a say in its creation. Or perhaps it was a punishment for a life that hadn't been without fault. Was he being too hard on himself these days? Wasn't the life he had witnessed when he was a mere mortal a symptom of the time? Or maybe he was just excusing what he had done or hadn't done. Either way, he had played a role, a role which led to this moment.

A bittersweet smile crossed his handsome face as he swirled the old cognac around in the crystal glass and took a sniff. Its aroma was sweet, and its taste had no bitterness, despite it being bottled in eighteen thirty-nine, just ten years before Frederic died. Frederic had brought a case of it to Luca's home, and they had drunk almost two bottles between them. Chopin had announced that he didn't like it, he was a snob when it came to wine and brandy, preferring the French varieties above others. This snobbery had always amused Luca.

Luca took a sip, he enjoyed it, and still had five bottles left in his private collection. He would open a new bottle to drink with his friends after the opening night of the play. It certainly would be an achievement for Luca any way, as it had been a dream that he had harboured since he first saw the play performed in Pompeii, all those centuries ago.

He got up from the sofa and walked over to the stereo and put on a CD, it was Frederic's piano concerto number two. It was Luca's personal favourite, especially since Frederic had played it for Luca first, before he was even due to perform it publicly in Warsaw in March of 1830.

Luca refilled his glass and walked back over to the sofa. He had decided that he was going to stay in and relax. He had told the cast to do whatever would relax them but to take the night off and not worry about the play.

Amos told him that it was a foolish thought and that the cast would surely go out and get roaring drunk. This had amused Luca, and he had told Amos, that it would do him good to go get drunk too.

As he finished the cognac, Luca's phone rang. He picked it up and looked at the number. It was Thea. He just looked at it as it continued to vibrate in his hand. She was a little too insistent about spending time with him. Not that Luca minded, they usually spent their time alone together in bed. It wasn't unpleasant. He just wished that she would understand that he was saving her from getting too involved with him and eventually getting hurt by their inevitable breakup.

The incessant ringing of the phone annoyed him a little as Luca hadn't made any arrangements to meet her, in fact he didn't want to get too close with her because, he had only booked the theatre for two nights and once the production was finished, Luca knew that he wouldn't be seeing Thea again. Luca assumed that she would move on to the next production, either here or perhaps move back East and to Broadway. As far as he was concerned, it was better for both of them if she did, as he didn't see a future in the relationship developing or continuing. Not for Luca and certainly not for Thea, and he wanted to spare her the heartache of leading her on, believing they had something together, something other than sex. In the time since he became immortal, Luca had spared his own feelings, he gave a snide laugh at that. *Feelings!* He was a vampire, he didn't feel, not emotionally. He was void of all that resembled humanity. Yet, deep down hidden within his dark depths, he tried to remain connected to some kind of goodness. Luca knew there was a real possibility of the darkness within him surfacing at any given moment. Just because he was drained of the venomous blood that found its way back into his veins from his dark heart as it pumped relentlessly keeping him alive, ensuring him immortality, he fought it every day, fought so it wouldn't take hold of him. But as hard as he fought the dark side, there was a real possibility that he could lose the battle and succumb to the beast within.

The phone stopped ringing and as he was about to put it on the seat beside him, it burst into life again. Luca picked it up this time and answered it.

"Hello." He said disinterested in his baritone voice.

"Luca?" Thea asked, with a little uncertainty in her tone.

"Hello Thea." Luca said and waited for her to answer.

"Am I disturbing you?" She whispered. Of course she wasn't but he didn't want to spend time with anyone either. He wanted to be alone. At least that's what he told himself. He remained silent for a moment.

"No, not at all." Luca replied presently. "What can I do for you?" He tried to keep his tone businesslike but as her soft voice caressed his ear, it proved difficult for him to remain resolved to his own company. He was getting aroused.

"I just wondered if you were busy?" She spoke softly and he could imagine her smile, with her tongue sliding over her lower lip as she waited for him to respond. It worried him that he knew her mannerisms only too well.

"I'm not busy at all," Luca admitted, but he still remained distant. "I am just having a quiet drink at home."

"Do you want to come over?" Her voice sounded hesitant yet hopeful, and he knew that she wanted to see him, and through the phone with his sharp vampiric ears Luca could hear her heart beating fast, as her blood flowed freely in her veins.

"Do you want me to come over?" Luca teased her now, as his tone softened a little. He knew that if he went over to Thea's apartment, they would end up in bed together and the idea wasn't entirely unpleasant to him, as he gave it some thought, and it was a lot better than staying in his large penthouse on his own, reminiscing about times so long ago, to most people it was a page in history but not to Luca. To Luca it seemed so fresh, it could have been just a month ago.

"Yes, I want you to come over." Thea replied eagerly with a hint of tease in her voice. Luca chuckled and said in a yielding tone.

"I'm on my way." He hung up and put the glass he held onto the coffee table and walked over to the console table and picked up his car keys. He opened the solid mahogany door and left the penthouse.

Chapter 32

Rome 76 AD

The journey from Lycia had taken a little longer than Lucian had anticipated due to Octavius making an unscheduled stop in Creta beforehand and then sailing back to Brundisium and then they rode on horseback to Rome.

It had been a little annoying to Lucian and to the legion as well, but he knew Octavius and he knew that he wouldn't have made the stop if he didn't have to.

The legion marched into Rome and had taken a day's rest before reporting to the emperor. Lucian had hoped that he would be seen now, as worthy of the elusive promotion to General, the promotion that he had craved two years earlier. Perhaps Vespasian was in a more agreeable position and willing to put his appreciation into his Eastern legion by announcing promotions.

He was keen to seek out the company of Porcia too, but first he would have to set his mistress up in a home where he could visit and then he would go to Porcia.

Lucian was keen to see her. It had been far too long. Two years was a long time, even for a lover but he could only admit to himself that what he felt for Porcia was more than a fondness. Anything that he felt for Porcia, was not to be spoken by Lucian, and not in public. He could never whisper openly about his love and affection for her. An affection that perhaps might convince her to leave the emperor as his favoured courtesan. Lucian had saved some money, that would buy Porcia's freedom, but he was unsure of how to broach the subject with the emperor. One simply didn't buy Vespasian's concubine.

It was well into the night when Lucian left the tent where his quarters were. The men were making merry and there were some bawdy conduct coming from the tents where the legionaries were housed.

Lucian wrapped his cloak around him as he walked down the street which led to the offices of the senate.

As he walked, he heard his name being called. Not very loud, barely above a whisper. Lucian turned around but he didn't see anyone there, so he continued walking briskly to the end of the street. His thoughts were on being reunited with his lover.

When he reached the marble steps which led to the building, Lucian stopped, he had his hand on his sword, and he listened intently.

"Lucian Marius Antonius." A voice called out in the darkness, from behind the marble pillar. Lucian stood up straight and waited as he observed the long shadow of the figure who lurked behind the column. "Come." The voice ordered and as he glanced around him, Lucian saw that there was no one else there. He cautiously followed the dark figure down the darkened street and around the back of the building.

The cloaked figure looked at Lucian for a moment and then removed the hood and nodded to Lucian and then he stood aside as another person joined them. Lucian looked on in surprise but he stood perfectly still. Motionless.

Chapter 33

Nunc Tempus

The area where Thea's apartment was located wasn't prime and it lacked the charm and character of the arts district. It was run down and rather derelict.

Luca parked the car and opened the door. He stood for a moment and buttoned his jacket and then crossed the road, observing his surroundings as he did so. Luca opened the small iron gate and walked rapidly along the narrow path and just as he reached the front door it opened widely, and Thea stood there wearing just a tee shirt. Her long shapely legs seemed to go on forever. She smiled broadly at him.

He picked her up in his strong arms and carried her inside and over to the sofa, which had already been pulled out into a bed. Luca gently laid her down on it and covered her body with his and began to kiss her, soft and tenderly at first but then as the passion he was feeling hurriedly took over and his hunger, his lust, surpassed him and within moments, he was making wild passionate love to her. Feasting on her slender body as if his life depended on the meal that her body offered him.

Thea lay in his arms, she was panting and smiling as she traced little circles on his bare chest with her index finger.

Luca let out a contented sigh. It had been what he needed, what he had denied himself for a few days. Though he didn't want to admit it. Thea was good, she was a stress reliever, and he would be sorry that once the production was over, he wouldn't see her again. Just momentarily, Luca wondered if he really had to stop seeing her. But as he looked into her beautiful eyes, he already knew the answer to that. They had no future together.

"I am addicted to the feeling I get when we sleep together." Thea said in a quiet voice. Luca grinned at this, and he kissed her on the cheek.

"You have no idea how much I enjoy fucking you," he said huskily and held her close to him. Luca felt her shiver slightly. "You are so cold, Thea." He said now and rubbed her arm vigorously and she giggled as they kissed passionately.

"I love it when you are rough with me." She replied as her hand slid under the white sheet and found what she wanted to feel inside her again. "I want you to dominate my body and do whatever you want to do to it." Luca glanced at her with a raised eyebrow. She was good in bed, better than he had had in recent months, and yet, it wasn't what he needed, or wanted, not right now.

"You know once Saturday is over, Thea," Luca said as gently as he could muster. "We won't see each other again." He felt her stiffen in his arms. Luca had to be honest with her, no matter how painful it was going to be for her.

"I know, but I wish you didn't say it." Thea said and he could see her eyes gloss over as if she were about to cry. "At least not while we are still in bed together."

"I'm sorry but I can't make promises that I have no intention of keeping." Luca responded truthfully to her. "That's not the way I am." He had always maintained that honesty was best, at least where matters like this was involved. Even if he felt something more than lust for Thea, he wouldn't be able to commit to her. A vampire could only commit to one, and once they did, they were bound together for eternity. Luca had never met any vampiress, hybrid, or human that he felt that way about, and he doubted that he ever would.

"You are an amazing man." Thea said and a tear ran down her cheek, but Luca didn't do anything to wipe it away. "I intend to enjoy more sex with you tonight." Thea tried to sound as though she didn't care. But Luca knew that despite the façade that she did care. She looked at him and then she forced herself to giggle, and Luca smiled seductively and pulled her onto him and closed his eyes momentarily as she sat on him and began to move slowly and purposefully.

"I certainly hope so." He kissed her hard and they began to enjoy each other's bodies once more.

As Thea pressed down on his chest with her right hand, a flash of Porcia's beautiful face, a face that he hadn't seen, in his mind's eye, for millennia, flashed before him.

Porcia!

Chapter 34

The noise backstage was almost as loud as the noise of the audience as they took their seats in the auditorium. Amos had told Luca that he had spoken with Willis and that Willis was pleasantly surprised when both nights were completely sold out.

Luca had been delighted. He also felt a little nervous, and now he knew how Frederic and the other performers felt on opening night. The tension was palpable but yet it was exciting, debilitating and exhilarating all at once. It was an addictive feeling, and one which Luca could easily get used to.

He had seen his friends before Luca came backstage, they were making fun, but he also knew that they too were rooting for him to have a successful show. It was the first time that he had ever done anything like this, and Luca wondered if, the show went well, perhaps he might like to put on another play sometime in the future. Another classic perhaps, or maybe something modern. It was something that he was seriously considering. He had a taste for it now, like the taste of blood, it was addictive.

It certainly had got his creative juices running and he now knew how Frederic felt, that rush just moments before the curtain went back and one stepped out of the darkness and under the spotlight. If he had adrenaline, it would be gushing through him at that moment. Luca smiled to himself now.

To Luca, at that moment, he felt the compulsion, felt the need to be adored. He felt accomplished, whether or not, he ever did another show, this was what Frederic meant when he said to embrace the accomplishment. For Luca felt the achievement of what he had produced. Vindicated, almost...

He walked down the narrow corridor and into the communal area where the cast were assembled while they waited to go on stage. Luca smiled warmly at all of them and said encouragingly to the actors.

"This is it, everyone." Luca looked around at them, he saw Medea and Jason standing slightly away from the cast. "Tonight is what we have worked so hard for, all these weeks." They all agreed. "Now as they say in theatre parlance, break a leg out there tonight." They all clapped, and Luca gave a wave and walked over to Thea and smiled warmly at her and pulled her into his arms and gave her a huge hug. This was a huge moment for her, her big break, as it were.

"Thank you for the beautiful flowers, Luca." Thea whispered and kissed him on the cheek.

"You will be great out there, Medea." Luca said in a low tone and grinned at her. "Go knock them dead." He kissed her full on the mouth, in a passionate embrace, not caring that the entire cast were watching them. It didn't matter now who knew they had had a brief but passionate affair.

When he let her go, Luca walked over to Jason, slapped him on the arm and wished him luck as the stagehand called them to take their positions. Luca smiled as he watched them take their places on stage.

Luca walked over to the side of the stage and watched from the sidelines. As he viewed with pride, he felt someone stand beside him. It was Willis.

"You must be proud, Mister Meridian." Willis said as he watched the plot of the play unfold. "Medea is not an easy drama to stage. Luca turned to look at him and grinned. His dislike for the man was even more evident now as he discovered how he had been getting female actors to call by the theatre disguised with the promise of a part, the women would have to pass his little '*interviews*'. It had taken a few nights of Bjorn following him, for the Militibus to discover the sick and twisted charade that Willis had going for himself at the theatre.

Frankie had found Willis as he interviewed these trusting young actors in Willis's office long after the theatre had closed, it was what the janitor had tried to tell Luca but with his failing memory, the old man's mind wandered back to the good old days that held happier memories for him, a time when the theatre meant something and was Frankie's entire world.

"I know you don't like me very much, Mister Meridian," Willis said and then cleared his throat and smiled a false smile at Luca. "But if you ever feel like you want to put on another play, please feel free to consider me and my humble theatre at your disposal." Luca turned his attention back to the stage. His cast were doing the play justice.

"Willis let's not push it," Luca said acidly, and he turned and glared at him. "Now if you don't mind, I want to watch my play in peace." Luca turned his attention back to the stage, and he sensed the abrupt departure of the manager. Luca grinned to himself now as he enjoyed his production.

During the interval, Luca went out into the lobby to where he saw the Militibus were standing talking to each other as they drank wine. Luca smiled and walked over to them.

"The man of the hour." Peo said with a broad grin and held out his hand to Luca. "I am impressed my Centurion friend, that you actually have a gift." They all laughed heartily, and both Lanny and Bjorn slapped Luca on the back and shook his hand.

"Are you enjoying the performance?" Luca asked them and they all nodded in agreement.

"After the show, we are taking you out to dinner, General." Lanny told him. "Then you can let us know just how much of the play has your actual direction in it." They all laughed jovially, and Luca slapped the Jarl on the arm and beamed at his friend.

"A Viking who is impressed by the arts, now there is something that I must record for posterity." Luca teased him. "I will be delighted to celebrate later. Now take your seats and be blown away by these incredible actors." Luca grinned at his friends and then retreated backstage to observe the rest of the show.

Back on stage, Medea and Jason were fighting, their voices raised as the awful truth emerged of what a jealous Medea had done to their children. The laments from the characters carried out to the stunned audience as Jason's despair and his hatred for the woman who had borne him his children and who he had once loved, stood before him but all he saw now was a vile evil murderess.

The audience in the auditorium were aghast and the gasps of surprise, shock, and horror as despair filled the theatre as Medea and Jason quarrelled on stage.

'No, it was your lustful heart and that new marriage of yours' Medea shouted.

'You decided to kill them...because I loved another...' Jason retorted.

'....But to you it is all that is evil..'

'...Hate me!...'

Thea looked as though she had committed the ultimate betrayal a wife could do, and as Luca watched her mesmerised, he almost forgot it was a play. Luca keenly observed as Jason's grief consumed him as he fell to his knees when he saw the chariot take Medea and the bodies of his dead children away, leaving him to his despair as the cast sang the chorus of Jason's last lament, they were all acting out their respective roles and gave it their all. They were outstanding at their craft, and they had left the audience believing that they had just witnessed the private quarrel between a husband and wife and its tragic outcome.

The curtain closed and there was a loud abrupt, and deafening applause as the audience stood up and cheered as the curtain opened and the cast stepped forward and bowed. The appreciation of the audience blew everyone away.

The curtains closed again and both Jason and Medea beckoned Luca to join them on the stage as they stood together for an encore bow.

Luca was enthralled by the gratitude from the audience as they gave into their enthusiasm as they clapped louder, their appreciation for the classic that had been written thousands of years before, brought to life in the small theatre.

Chapter 35

Luca was the toast of the evening. His friends were singing his praise for his bravery at staging such a play. Peo grinned at Luca and said with a glint in his eye.

"I don't expect the Vikings to appreciate Greek tragedy." Luca laughed and sat back as he observed his two Viking Militibus officers who wore a look of mock horror on their faces.

"Who doesn't enjoy a Greek tragedy, Peo." Lanny said with a wide smile. "I'm just surprised that Romans can appreciate such drama. Remind me again who wrote the tragedies first?" He high fived Bjorn and they laughed as they teased their two Roman friends.

"After tomorrow night," Luca said in a serious tone. "It is back to reality, and we are no closer to finding the navar." It had been playing on his mind, and he did welcome the break that the Militibus gave him so that he could concentrate on producing the play.

"True, we are no closer," Bjorn said morosely. "But then like a Greek tragedy this job of ours rarely runs smoothly, does it?"

"I do have some good news," Lanny said with a grin as he tried to lighten the mood a little. "The elusive key that the old toad lost, I have a strong lead, and I am meeting with the seller tomorrow." They all stared at him, and Peo let out a hearty chuckle.

"Jarl, do you plan on winning this bet too?" Peo said and grinned as Lanny nodded and he raised the glass of red wine to his lips. Peo smirked and said with a chuckle. "Not a chance, my Viking friend."

"You should know by now, Praetorian," Lanny said with a wicked grin. "I deal in the better antiques." Peo's body shook with laughter now as he looked at Lanny.

"At least we agree that Demis will be able to lock the Tenth and prevent any more catastrophises from occurring." Peo said sarcastically, as Lanny and Bjorn chuckled loudly.

"Only until the next one." Luca chimed in. He was enjoying himself and he was about to suggest that they finish the evening at Bjorn's club, when his phone vibrated in his pocket and broke his chain of thought. "Hello," he said as he pushed back his chair and stood up.

"Hello Luca." It was Thea. A slow smile swept across his face. He was surprised to hear from her, he had assumed that the cast had gone out together to celebrate.

"Hey, how are you?" Luca asked cheerfully and wondered why she was calling him.

"I'm home," she whispered in a low tone, and he caught a certain sadness in her voice. "Where are you?"

"I'm having dinner with friends." Luca replied. "Why are you at home? You should be out celebrating with the rest of the cast." There was a pause, and he thought she had hung up. He was about to hang up when he heard her breathe.

"I know, it went really well, didn't it?" Thea asked and he heard the uncertainty in her voice again. He wondered why she didn't go out with the others. The members of the cast were a great bunch of people, and they were all very friendly.

"It was phenomenal, you were superb, Thea." Luca said. "I'll be finished here soon. Do you want me to come over?" He asked. Luca knew that he really shouldn't be encouraging her but what harm was there in spending one last night with his leading lady? Luca knew that his friends wouldn't mind, they would encourage him, especially the Jarl. He grinned to himself now.

"I'd like that." Thea replied softly. "I'll see you soon."

"Sure." Luca said and hung up. He walked back over to the table, but the smile drained from his face when he saw Peo's expression. "What's happened?" Luca asked and sat down as the server brought the bill to their table.

"I just had a call from Dimitri Cartwright," Lanny said sulkily. "He's just spotted a group of suckers in a bar. They're coming into the city."

"Luca, we'll take care of it." Bjorn reassured him when he saw Luca's expression.

"How many suckers?" Luca asked. "Did Dimitri say?"

"There's a gang of about eight." Lanny replied. "The mutt sounded scared, so I told him to stay where he was, and we'd be there shortly." Luca nodded and stood up straight.

"OK, let's get changed and sort these chumps out." Luca grinned at his friends, "I've had enough time off, so let's go." They stood up and left the restaurant together.

Chapter 36

Luca rode in the lead, followed by Lanny and Peo and Bjorn drove side by side. The Militibus were a sight that none of the dregs wanted to see coming toward them. Their reputation was as fierce as the panigales that they rode.

They pulled into the car park of the bar that the werewolf Dimitri Cartwright had informed them that the street vampires were socialising at. They saw four motorbikes parked up. Luca pulled his panigale onto its stand and swished back his long leather coat, his hand was on the hilt of his sword. He was always ready for any eventuality. This time was no exception.

Luca walked with long strides over to the bar, followed by his officers. Inside, they found a group of wolves sitting at a table, drinking beers, seemingly minding their own business. In the darker corner, Luca could see three sluaghs, as was usual for them, they hid in the darkened area, trying to remain unseen.

There were two witches sitting at the bar drinking beer and as Luca glanced across at the pool table, he saw suckers playing. There were six male vampires and two of their females. They were drinking beer and were being loud and obnoxious. Typical street suckers.

He looked at Lanny and nodded as they walked over to the pool table. One of the women hit the male, obviously the leader, on the forearm. He swore as he missed his shot, then he looked up and saw Luca and Lanny standing near the pool table with their legs apart.

"What are you looking at?" The head bloodsucker asked, and the others with him just laughed loudly and glared at the Militibus.

Neither Luca nor Lanny said a word, they just glared back at him.

"I think the cat got their tongue Leo," the sucker who was standing next to one of the females said and laughed hysterically.

"Outside, now." Luca demanded and gripped the handle of his sword, leaving the sucker in no doubt that he meant business. "Just you and your second." Luca insisted and then he began to walk away followed by Lanny.

They waited beside the suckers' motorbikes. Across the carpark there was a couple of oil drums with fires lit and several street dregs were standing around drinking from bottles as they warmed their hands over the barrels.

A few minutes later, the two street vampires came outside, they walked with a swagger which suggested that they were up for a fight. Lanny had drawn his axe and his sword and stood beside the large chopper, anticipating trouble.

"What do you want?" The head sucker asked as he came closer. "We got a right to be here." He stopped in front of Luca, he was much smaller, standing around five foot eleven.

He looked Luca up and down and moved the match he was chewing from side to side.

"Where did you come from?" Luca asked him in a serious tone.

"Who wants to know?" The second sucker asked and chuckled and then spat on the ground. Luca looked at Lanny who had now extended his sword to the sucker's throat.

"The Tempus Militibus." Lanny said and pressed the blade hard against the sucker, and a trickle of blood ran down the vampire's neck. The smile drained from the dregs faces and their expressions changed to one of fear.

"Look man, we don't want no trouble." The second punk said.

"Answer the question then." Lanny said emotionless as he looked at him contemptuously. "Where did you come from?"

"We just got in from Texas, two nights ago." The sucker named Leo said and looked from Lanny to Luca.

"What are you doing in LA?" Luca asked, his pitch and tone didn't change. He was controlled as always.

"We just came to see what the action is like here." Leo said and then looked at Lanny and back to Luca again. "Can you ask him to lower that thing?" He laughed nervously as he looked at Luca, but Luca didn't reply.

"Suckers are not allowed near or in the city limits." Lanny growled and Luca looked across the carpark and saw that the other scumbags were cautiously moving in their direction.

"We didn't know that." Leo said playing dumb and pleading with Luca. "Look we are new in town, OK."

"These rules apply anywhere the Militibus control." Luca said glaring at him. "Are you telling me you came from a place where there are no Militibus?" Lanny pressed the blade a little harder into the second sucker's throat.

"No, no...I'm not." Leo said hurriedly as he looked at his nestmate and grimaced.

"Then why would you think you can just ride into town and do whatever you want here?" Luca asked him, not averting his eyes from the sucker. He didn't trust this slime.

"We heard it was easy here." The second sucker said and then regretted it as soon as he had uttered the words, as he felt the blade pressed harder against his neck.

"Who told you that?" Lanny roared.

"No one." He replied quickly. Lanny looked across and saw the other suckers inching closer to them.

"Tell them to stay back." Lanny ordered and Leo just laughed as they came closer. "So that's how you want to play, is it?" The Jarl asked and swung the axe in his hand in a three sixty.

"Looks like you two are outnumbered, *assholes.*" Leo laughed mockingly now.

"Dormies in inferno." Lanny shouted and swung around decapitating the sucker. His head bounced on the ground and Lanny kicked it next to the body and stood back as the lightning engulfed the head and body until all that remained was a pile of soot.

"Unless you want to join your friend in the Tenth," Luca said in a callous tone. "Tell them to stay where they are."

"Blow me." Leo said and no sooner had he spoken than Luca shouted and raised his sword.

"Requiem in inferno." His sword decapitated the lead sucker and again the lightning engulfed the body, and a mound of soot had formed where the vampire once stood.

Luca turned around and looked at the other suckers and pointed to the two in the front. "Come here." Luca shouted to them, but they were frozen to the spot. Then looking at the females he saw that their fangs were extended, and he strode over to them and grabbed one of them by the arm and dragged her over to where the soot piles were. "You see that," Luca said aggressively as he glared at her. The female vampire nodded. "That will happen to your friends if you don't answer my questions, do you understand me?" She nodded again and retracted her fangs. "I want to know what brought you here, and what you heard about this city?"

"Welte, is getting a gang together." The female said.

"Shut up Lindsey." The male sucker with the eye patch shouted at her. She turned and stared at him, almost faltering as she turned back to look at Luca.

"Your name is Lindsey?" Luca asked and she nodded once more. "Go ahead tell me what Welte is doing?" He looked at her with a softer expression now.

"He said the Militibus are losing their hold on LA, and it was ripe for us..."

"You are dead Lindsey." The sucker called out angrily and then Luca looked over as Peo knocked him to his knees and held the sword to his neck. "I swear you are, bitch!"

"Why does Welte think that?" Luca asked Lindsey, but at first she just shrugged her shoulders, and then she answered him.

"He said the navars are coming and you don't know how to stop them." Lindsey responded sounding frightened and again she glanced over at her boyfriend kneeling on the ground with Peo's sword pressed into his neck.

"What do you know about the navars?" Luca asked her, in a less harsh tone now.

"Shut up, Lindsey or-"

"Putrescet in inferno." Peo shouted and beheaded the male vampire. The female standing beside him screamed and was caught in the lightning as the sucker was reduced to soot, while the female was condensed to salt. Lindsey shrieked violently now as she peered across to where her lover was now just a pile of soot.

"There's one in the city," Lindsey said fearfully as she looked across at the other three suckers, they weren't happy that she was talking to the Militibus, but they were held where they stood by both Lanny and Bjorn's swords.

"Did Welte say where the navar was?" Luca asked her, but she shook her head. "I know that you know something that you are not telling me, Lindsey." Luca said raising his voice a little. "My officers have had their evening interrupted and they aren't too happy about that." Luca nodded over at Lanny who grabbed the sucker with his left hand and dragged him across to where she stood. "Now, tell me what you know, and the Jarl will spare his life." Luca said.

"I don't know," she pleaded and looked at the sucker who was glaring at her. "He knows." She cried out now, and it was evident that she wanted the heat taken away from her.

"Lindsey you stupid bitch." The street vampire shouted at her as Lanny's blade rested against his neck.

"I suggest that you talk, sucker," Lanny said. "Or I will gladly send you to the Tenth."

"I ain't an informer." The sucker said and spat on the ground. "*You asshole.*"

"Is that your final word?" Lanny asked and the sucker just grinned at him. "Putrescet in inferno tibi rubigo." His severed head dropped to the ground and Lanny stood back as the body was consumed with the lightning and seconds later the soot pile was all there was left of the criminal as he joined his friends in the Tenth.

"There's only three of you left," Luca called out to them. "Are you really willing to go to the Tenth because of a lie, that Welte told you?" The two male vampires looked at one another and the dark-haired sucker with the cut off denim jacket came forward and looked at Lindsey. Without warning he drew out and slapped her hard across the face with his fist, she fell to her knees and then he kicked her in the thigh. None of the Militibus intervened to help her.

"Do you want to spend the rest of eternity in the Tenth?" Lanny asked him. The sucker looked at him and then to Luca.

"You sayin it's all a lie, is it?" He sneered. "That Welte isn't ruling LA?" Lanny looked across to Luca and grinned now. "That he didn't do a deal with the navar to take this part of the city?" Lanny shook his head and laughed at this.

"The Tempus Militibus keep this city clean from the dregs." Luca said and glanced over at the other sucker. "When did Welte tell you he was the new ruler?" It pained Luca to even have to say it and maintain a straight face at the same time. When it was all over, he would see to it personally, that Welte was sent to the Tenth.

"He told us at a rally in Nevada, two months ago." The sucker said. "There was a hybrid killed by a navar, he told us he had brought the navar to the city because he and the hybrid had come to a deal about who would rule where." Peo and Bjorn came over to them.

"Go on," Luca encouraged. "Did Welte say who the hybrid was?" The sucker looked at Lindsey and the other vampire and then shook his head. He probably thought that he had said too much already, from the expression on his ugly face.

"Are you sure he didn't give a name?" Peo probed, but the sucker shook his head again. "I don't believe you and I think I should send you to the Tenth to join your scumbag friends." Peo walked over to him and raised his sword. There was fear in the street vampire's eyes, the fear that being sent to the Tenth filled all dregs with. They all knew that there was no return from the Tenth dimension.

"He said the hybrid was called Greyson." The other male sucker called out, and Luca turned around and gaped at him.

"You sure?" The sucker nodded his head. "Get out of here, and don't come back." Luca said angrily. "Not to this city."

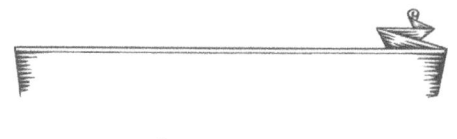

Chapter 37

They drove at speed to the lair which was located outside the city near the hills. It was an old farmhouse which had been abandoned for over two decades and showed considerable signs of decay. The perfect place for a vampire lair.

Luca pulled up nearly two hundred metres from the old gravel and weed covered drive. He turned off the engine and parked the panigale. He took off his helmet and placed it on the handlebar of his motorbike. He smoothed his long silk black hair off his face and looked at the others as they removed their weapons.

"We'll see what he knows first," Luca said. "Any threat from the lair and we send them to the Tenth. No hesitation." The Militibus nodded and Luca strode ahead of them.

When he reached the porch, he looked around. He could hear laughter from within. Luca kicked the door off its hinges and rushed inside.

"Welte!" Luca bellowed and motioned for the Militibus to check out the rooms which led off the hallway.

A tall pale sucker with grey streaked hair appeared from the room at the end of the hall. He glared at Luca but as he tried to make a run for the door, Luca was quicker than him and he lunged at the sucker and brought him down effortlessly.

"Where's Welte?" Luca shouted at him. The sucker groaned and Luca pulled the vampire to his feet and threw him across the room, and he hit the wall hard, face first and then with a heavy thud he fell to the floor. Luca strode over to him and pulled him up. "Don't waste my time." Luca growled. "Where's that little worm?"

"Right here," Lanny replied with a grin as he walked along the hall, and he pushed Welte into the room. "He was quivering behind the door." Lanny teased. "Like the coward that he is."

"Sure, I was." Welte said and glared at Lanny. "Fuck you, I'm not afraid of you psychopaths."

"We're going to have a little talk," Luca said, but he wasn't in the mood for small talk with this sucker. He looked at Lanny. "How many dregs in the house?"

"Six, including those two." Lanny replied.

"Berserker, Praetorian," Luca called out into the hall. "Bring them in here." A few moments later the Militibus came in and shoved the other vampires into the sparsely furnished room.

Luca looked at the street predators and grinned at them. He wasn't in a good mood, but he would enjoy interrogating that little insect, Welte.

"I'm going to ask you some questions," Luca said as he directed his gaze back to Welte. "Every wrong answer, or refusal to answer, will result in the Jarl, or one of the other Militibus sending one of them to the Tenth." He saw the look of fear in the other suckers' eyes.

"I ain't got to answer to you, Meridian." Welte said and spat. Luca glanced over at Peo.

"Requiem in inferno." Peo yelled and he beheaded the vampire to his right.

"What do you know about the navar?" Luca asked him again.

"Blow me." Luca nodded toward Lanny, and the Jarl beheaded the sucker, and grinned at Welte as he did so. The Jarl clearly enjoyed this type of interrogation.

"I am not playing around here, Welte." Luca said aggressively. "Nothing will give me greater pleasure than to send you to the Tenth." With a brazen expression on his face, Welte looked at Luca but said nothing. This incensed Luca even more than he already was. "Berserker, bring that sucker here." Bjorn dragged the vampire over to Luca. He grinned at the punk and asked in a gentler tone. "Tell me what you know about the navar?"

"I know nothing." The vampire said in a snivelling voice with a pleading look in his eyes. He was nervous and Luca could see his pupils were dilated as his eyes had narrowed into hunt mode. His fangs had dropped, and he was ready to bite.

"You want to try and answer that again?" Luca asked him as Bjorn raised his axe to the base of the sucker's neck.

"I don't know nothing." The dreg shouted and Luca nodded toward Bjorn and stepped back as the Berserker duly beheaded the vampire.

"Welte, are you really going to sacrifice your entire lair?" Luca asked him again as he grabbed a chair and pushed the head dreg into it.

"I don't know what you are talking about, Meridian?" Welte said after a few minutes. Lanny began to drag one of the remaining vampires, who began to wriggle and protest, to the centre of the room.

"You do know." Luca said and grinned at him. "I'm a reasonable man, Welte, unlike the Jarl and Praetorian here, they like to send dregs just like you, to the Tenth." Welte looked nervous now as Lanny pressed his sword against the other sucker's throat, a little blood began to trickle from the cut. "Now start talking." Luca demanded. "Or say goodbye to your friend."

"A few months ago, a hybrid came into a bar where the dregs were hanging out." Welte looked at Luca, who was standing up straight with his legs apart, glaring down at him.

"Go on." Luca bellowed.

"First he went over to the wolves, you know that grass, Dimitri Cartwright and his pack." Welte said. "He didn't stay long with them, a few minutes at most." Welte looked around at the other Militibus, they stood motionless as they stared at him.

"Did you hear what they talked about?" Luca asked, but Welte shook his head and then he saw Lanny raise the axe against his lair mate's throat and in an instant, the sucker was reduced to a pile of soot.

"Dimitri told him that it wouldn't be worth it if they got caught." Welte said quickly. Luca could see a trickle of sweat run down his temple. "Pussy!"

"Caught by whom?" Luca persisted in his questions.

"I don't know, you, I guess." Welte said nervously. "The Militibus."

"Who else did he approach?" Luca quizzed.

"No one would talk to him. So, I figured that he might have something worth talking about." Welte said and his red eyes began to lose a little fear but as he looked up at Luca, he grinned momentarily, then changed his mind quickly when he saw the expression on Luca's face, and he became serious once more. "I asked him to meet me outside." Welte continued. "He told me he had immunity because he was connected high up in the Sixth." Luca laughed at this and walked over to Welte and pulled his head backwards, his eyes were bulging, and his fangs were down. "You know real important back in Olympias."

"You stupid sucker, I don't know if I should feel sorry for you or just send you to the Tenth for being that gullible." Luca said sarcastically. "What did the hybrid want?" Luca demanded and the other sucker grunted something. Luca looked angrily across at him. "You have something to add?" The sucker just shook his head. He was perspiring hard.

"Greyson the hybrid, said he needed to get a nest together here, and in a couple of other cities." Welte offered. "Look man I thought he was serious, and we could expand our lair, that's all." Welte whined and Luca lashed out and boxed him across the left jaw. He knocked him off the chair and put his leather booted foot onto Welte's chest.

"Just because you are an idiot, Welte" Luca hollered angrily at him. "Don't be mistaken and think that we are idiots too."

"I don't...I admire the Militibus." Welte grovelled. "I really do."

"We don't care, Welte." Luca kicked him in the kidney. "Why was he getting a nest together?" The sucker sat on the floor and looked at the door, Luca sensed that he was looking for a getaway. "Don't even think about it." Luca warned. "We are a lot faster than you, you little weasel."

"I...wasn't." Welte lied and stood up, a little unsteadily. "The hybrid said he had a score to settle with someone and he wanted a nest so they could train and 'fuck him up' as he put it."

"What happened then?" Luca asked as he picked up the chair and with a strong hand on Welte's shoulder, he forced him back into the chair and glared at the vampire.

"I set up a rally in Nevada, got some suckers to agree to join the new nest." Welte said and looked across at Peo and Bjorn. "He told us to wait until we heard from him, and he would tell us where he had the new nest located."

"How long before you heard from him?" Bjorn asked Welte.

"Three days later," Welte replied. "He told me to get my lair to start moving into the new nest."

"Did he show you the new location?" Peo asked. Welte nodded. "Where was it?"

"It was near an old carpet store, but the stupid bitches, the shees had moved in there." Luca looked at Lanny, with a grave expression.

"Did you know the hybrid was also inviting a navar to join this super nest?" Lanny asked him but Welte just shook his head. "Don't lie to me, sucker." The Jarl shouted.

"Not at first, when I initially went to see the new nest, I saw the navar, but it didn't say anything. It just kept silent and watched." Welte said as he shifted in the chair. The sweat glistened on his forehead as Luca lifted his sword and pointed it to his throat.

"You saw the navar?" Luca asked and Welte nodded.

"She was weak, didn't have any energy, you know, dehydrated and hungry." He said hurriedly. "I didn't think she would be much of a threat to me being ruler here now." Welte snickered now, as his confidence began to grow. "But then she came behind Greyson, pushed him over and drained him, in a matter of seconds." He looked at Luca and Luca saw the fear in the sucker's eyes. "She told me if I wanted the deal to continue, I would have to feed her and I would have the West of the city, there was no negotiation." Welte looked at Luca. "Not with her. She is a mean bitch."

Luca stood up straight and glared at the dreg. Although, Welte was a fool, Luca knew he was telling the truth. He didn't have the wherewithal to make up a tale as elaborate as that.

"When was the last time you saw the navar?" Luca asked him.

"A week ago," Welte said. "I'm meeting with the navar on Wednesday."

"What was the meeting about. The one a week ago?" Lanny asked him and Welte just laughed. "Answer the question." The Jarl roared at him. "Or I will send you to the Tenth." Lanny warned.

"She needed feeding." Welte said and chuckled as he looked at the Jarl. "I got her some old drunk, he worked at some theatre he was falling all over the place couldn't walk straight, so I grabbed him and watched as the navar fed."

Luca turned around and glared at him and then without warning he lunged at him and boxed his face hard and sent his upper and lower left fangs flying out of his mouth.

"General, that won't bring him back." Lanny advised as the Berserker and Peo dragged Luca off the street vampire.

"You better be telling us the truth, Welte," Bjorn hissed at him. "When and where on Wednesday are you meeting with the navar?"

"I ain't telling you, that psycho has blown it." Peo raised his axe and sent the head of the grey streaked vampire flying in the air.

"You want to be next?" Peo growled at him and Welte shook his head. "Then tell us where and when this meeting is to take place."

"Nine, at the carpet shop." Welte said and held his hand up to his mouth. He was bleeding profusely.

"You warn her, and you will be sent to oblivion." Luca roared angrily at the vampire. "You understand?" Welte nodded and the four Militibus left the old farmhouse.

Outside, at their bikes, Luca kicked a stone out of his way. He felt so damn angry and frustrated. Old Frankie died horribly, and there was nothing that Luca really could have done that would have prevented it.

"Well, on an optimistic note." Lanny said as Luca watched him as he picked up his own helmet. "We now know that the navar is female."

"So?" Bjorn asked as he too put on his helmet.

"So, it's more than we knew an hour ago." Lanny said tartly.

"Which is still nothing, Jarl." Peo said but Luca glanced at his officers.

"The Jarl is right," Luca said after a while. "It's a vital piece of intel." He got on his bike and started the engine and tore away back to the city.

Chapter 38

Rome 76 AD

Lucian followed the men into the lavish villa. He glanced around at the opulent surroundings. The divan in the centre of the room surrounded by marbled columns which were decorative and yet functional too. A bowl of red and green grapes was resting on the divan, and a goblet lay on the floor.

The occupant had dismissed the woman who was lying beside him when Lucian and the two other men came inside.

"Lucian Marius Antonius." The young man who was now sitting up called to him and smiled and motioned for Lucian to come closer. Very hesitantly Lucian did as he was told. "I hear you had an uneventful journey from Lycia." Lucian eyed him carefully. The man was known throughout the empire as temperamental at best.

"It was, Caesar." Lucian replied, his tone not giving away how he felt. He didn't like or trust the heir.

"My father is giving a banquet in honour of the returning generals of Lycia." Caesar said and smiled across at Lucian. "I trust you will be there." His smile was as insincere as it was cruel.

"If I am invited, Caesar." Lucian replied carefully. "Though I am not a general." He had no desire to attend any party at the palace, nor to be in any proximity to the emperor. His feelings were not exactly friendly toward Vespasian. But he hid it well.

"I think you may not want to come to the party, Lucian." The Caesar said, still smiling as he reached for the wine goblet, his eyes not leaving Lucian's.

"Why would that be?" Lucian asked and then added. "Caesar." There was silence for a moment and then the young heir gave out a vicious laugh.

"I should think that the entire empire is aware of your...indiscretion." Lucian stiffened now. He knew of course what the heir was referring to, but he didn't want to give credence to the rumour. "I know for certain that my father is aware of it. So, under the circumstances staying out of the Pater Noster's way would be prudent. Don't you think?"

"Caesar, forgive me but I am at a loss as to what you are referencing." Lucian said as he tried to force a smile. He was always on edge around the Caesars and the emperor since his affair with Porcia. Their power was evident, and any perceived treachery would be punished and punished severely.

"Never mind that, Lucian." He replied now and stood up and walked toward Lucian. "It's not important, nor is it why I summoned you here." He eyed Lucian up and down now. Aware that he couldn't look this upstart in the eye, nor look away, all he could do was focus on the brown marble streak on the pillar behind the divan. "Leave us." The Caesar called out to the two men who were still in the room and then he walked over to the bed and picked up a bunch of grapes, he still looked intensely at Lucian, his stare was unnerving. "Now we are alone, Lucian, we can speak...candidly." Caesar looked at him as he bit on a grape. He was a handsome young man, with an intense gaze and a temper that would make the fire mountain of Pompeii growl.

"Caesar." Lucian replied, but he didn't relax. He couldn't, not with the heir so near and in one of his murderous moods, one wrong move or word from Lucian and he knew he would be history.

"I hear talk amongst the army that you are an excellent swordsman. An officer with superb gallantry. Your underlings like you." The Caesar said and smirked now as he continued to pick on the grapes. "Like Julius Caesar, a man of the people." Lucian looked at him but didn't reply. "Are you like our beloved great Caesar, Lucian?" He asked as he put a grape in his mouth. Lucian felt extremely uncomfortable now.

"I would not be presumptuous and liken my military career to the great Caesar." Lucian responded, still he tried hard not to avert his gaze.

"Indeed." The heir replied and took another grape. "I, like the great Julius Caesar, will rule the empire one day, and like Caesar, I have many in my way trying to stop my progression. Many, who wish to use the empire for their own needs, and not for the betterment of what the emperors before us have fought for." He stood up again and began to pace the floor now as he carefully studied Lucian. "Do you believe I will make a good emperor, Lucian or do you think

I will squander the empire's wealth for my own pleasure?" The Caesar stopped pacing and glanced sideways at Lucian. His smile was broad as he waited for Lucian to ply him with praise.

"Emperor Vespasian will be difficult to follow." Lucian said in a careful voice. "But as his son, you will be as great as our beloved emperor." This made the young Caesar laugh out loud.

"Diplomatic just like the great Julius Caesar." He chuckled now and as quickly as he laughed, he stopped and looked almost beseechingly at Lucian. "Then as a loyal subject, I can entrust the problem I, and my brother face...to you, Lucian Marius Antonius." He said as he stood facing Lucian now, with a sardonic grin on his face.

"Of course, Caesar." Lucian replied. But he was getting decidedly uncomfortable with this clandestine meeting as the minutes ticked away. No good was about to be revealed by the young Caesar.

"I hoped you would say that." Caesar said with a self-satisfied expression. "My father's bastard turns sixteen next week. My brother and I are the rightful heirs to the empire, not that suppositious imposter." He studied Lucian once more.

"I don't understand, Caesar." Lucian said as he tried not to flinch in front of the heir.

"It's quite simple, Lucian," he said and placed a hand on Lucian's shoulder. "I want you to rid me of this affliction of my father's." Lucian looked at him for a moment, trying hard to not show the shock on his face at what the Caesar had just suggested. "I don't care how you do it, I just want you to do it."

"Caesar?" Lucian queried, hesitantly now. He knew of course what the legatee meant.

"Kill the bastard, if you refuse, there will of course, be consequences. Do you understand?" The heir said without any emotion in his voice. "Starting with that whore that you call your lover." Lucian felt sick to the pit of his stomach. The right to succession in Rome was a bloody one, assassination was usual. In this case though, the Caesar would surely gain the throne without having to murder a rival, particularly a rival who was not a legitimate successor.

"Caesar." Lucian said trying hard to control his quavering voice. "I cannot do as you request." This made the heir laugh almost hysterically now.

"I wasn't asking you, Lucian." Caesar said and rested his other hand on Lucian's shoulder. "I am ordering you, to kill Rufus Romanus." He said in an aroused voice now. "If you don't, that whore of yours, Porcia will join you in Orcus." Lucian reached for the handle of his sword, and seeing this, the heir laughed and goaded. "Do it, show all of Rome, that you are a betrayer just like your father before you." Lucian glared at him, and he saw the wicked smile on his face. "Think about my request, if you refuse you know the consequences." He turned away from Lucian and walked over to the divan. The meeting was over, and Lucian was dismissed.

OUTSIDE IN THE BALMY night Lucian walked with the weight of what the young Caesar had placed on his shoulders. If he refused to do as he was ordered, the heir would make good on his promise. But Lucian also knew that if he did assassinate the emperor's illegitimate son, Lucian would be captured and stoned to death. Vespasian would also have Lucian's mother, and his father witness his dead body as it was paraded through the streets of Rome.

Vespasian's anger wouldn't stop at Lucian's death. Porcia would also be punished for her role in the assassination of the young Rufus Romanus and she would be tortured and mutilated for her betrayal. Lucian couldn't bear that for Porcia. He loved her.

He wondered how the young Caesar had discovered his affair with Porcia. Lucian had been discreet, hadn't he? Perhaps it was Porcia who had made their dalliance known maybe to her maid or to her aunt.

Lucian just didn't know, but he did know that he would have to make a tough decision, either way, it wouldn't be good. Not for him or Porcia.

Chapter 39

Nunc Tempus

Luca couldn't sleep. He was stressed and he felt a sadness for old Frankie. The way that he had been lured to his death by Welte. Luca had liked the old janitor but he had allowed that to cloud his judgement about him, and that the old man was indeed an alcoholic. If he had been more tuned into his senses, Luca would have seen how vulnerable Frankie had been and not just from the alcohol abuse but from the dregs. He felt guilty and not for the first time in his life.

All those years ago, on that faithful night when that little upstart...

Luca shook his head. What good did it do now anyway? He had been a Centurion officer, his word against the emperor's son.

Porcia! Luca thought. *Sweet innocent, beautiful Porcia!*

He let out a long sigh as he looked out the window and across the shimmering haze of the city. It was early and he would have to go to the theatre in a couple of hours. It was the final showing of Medea.

As Luca thought of the final night, he remembered that he had promised to meet Thea, but he had never called over. He hadn't even called her to tell her he couldn't make it.

He shook his head and ran his fingers through his dark hair. Did it really matter if he didn't? After tonight he wouldn't be seeing her again. He knew that Thea was a beautiful woman, and she would meet a mortal man that would love her the way that she wanted Luca to love her. He certainly wasn't interested in a relationship. Luca mused. Not with Thea, not with anyone. He never was. As a vampire, he was unworthy of love, because of the terrible things that he had done.

Luca turned away from the window and walked back into the bedroom and dressed in casual trousers and a white silk shirt. He put on his beige trench coat and picked up his keys. He decided that he would drive over to Thea's place and explain that he got held up the previous night. He knew that Thea would see it as an excuse, but he owed it to her, at least.

Luca parked his car and glanced across at her tiny single-story apartment. It was so Thea, the bungalow was everything that an up-and-coming stage actor would be attracted to. Luca smiled at this as he crossed the road and went into the tiny front garden and knocked gently on the front door.

The door opened and a sleepy looking Thea stood there in her tee shirt. Luca smiled at her, he couldn't help allowing his eyes to linger on her long legs as she stood aside and let him in.

"I'm sorry I didn't call you last night." Luca apologised as he stood in the centre of the room with his hand on his hip as he looked longingly at her.

"You found something more interesting to do." Thea retorted bitterly. "You don't have to explain to me, Luca. You already told me, that we won't be seeing each other again." She walked over to the sofa bed and sat down and picked up a cushion and placed it on her lap. Luca looked at her long slender legs and her dishevelled hair. She looked stunning first thing. He had to tear his eyes away from leering at her body.

"You're right, Thea, I don't need to explain anything to you, but then again, good manners should have dictated I call you to let you know I wouldn't be over." Luca said with a smile and walked over to the sofa bed and sat down beside her. "I'm sorry Thea, I really am, but I had a good reason for not coming here last night."

"If you say so Luca." She said defiantly and he could see the pained expression on her beautiful elfin face. He reached out and tilted her chin so she would look into his eyes.

"I want to be with you after the show tonight." Luca said. "I want you to leave the theatre with me and let me make you feel special, like a star." He bent his head, and their lips barely touched. She closed her eyes, and he felt her arms go around his neck as their kiss deepened.

"Yes, yes you can spoil me tonight." Thea said as her mood changed now and she smiled warmly at him. "And to make up for leaving me waiting for you last night," she kissed him softly. "You can make love to me now." Luca chuckled and stood up and quickly removed his clothes and then he covered her body with his and took selfishly what she offered him.

LUCA GRINNED AT THEA as they drove to the theatre together. She turned up the sound on the stereo and glanced across at him.

"You have great taste in everything, Luca." Thea said as she turned away and looked out the window. "Particularly music."

"You think so?" Luca teased her with a grin now as he glanced over at her, and she nodded and then rested her hand on his muscular thigh.

"It's a pity you don't see yourself as romantic material." Thea said softly and Luca looked at her briefly. He knew that she was referring to his lack of commitment. But there was no way that he could explain to her why he felt the way that he did.

"Who says I don't?" Luca asked as he glanced across at her and then he grinned at her. "I can do romance." He teased.

"If you do, then why am I not who you see yourself with?" She asked him abruptly. Luca pulled up outside the theatre and turned off the engine. For a brief moment he just looked at her. How could he tell this stunning woman that he was a vampire? That a relationship, like she craved was not something he could have, and he certainly couldn't be sure about spending an eternity with a mortal he had only met a few months earlier. Luca wasn't impetuous. He wasn't the Jarl.

"It may sound like a cliché, Thea," Luca said after a minute or so. "But it isn't you, who is at fault here, it's me." He glanced across at her. "If I were to commit to a woman, it is with someone like you."

"It's OK Luca," she said and opened the door. "I've had a great time with you, after tonight we won't see each other again. I understand that. You told me often enough." Thea got out and banged the door behind her. He swore to himself and then got out and walked down the street and into the theatre.

Luca walked several paces behind her and from her swagger he could see that she was struggling to keep her emotions in check.

Chapter 40

The auditorium was full and as Luca walked down the narrow passageway, he saw George Willis walking toward him. He sniffed the air, and he smelled the corruption from him even at that distance. It was vile and it assaulted Luca's sensitive nose.

"Mister Meridian, another full house. You must be thrilled." Willis said greedily as he smiled at Luca. "Such a pity you won't be staging another successful production any time soon." Luca frowned for a moment and then sneered at him.

"It is men like you, Willis," Luca said sarcastically. "That make me thankful I do the job I do." Luca walked away but he could smell Willis's pheromones emanate through the manager's thick layer of skin. Luca's words were wasted on him.

Luca met the cast as they made their way onto the stage, and he said as he stood before them. "It has been a pleasure working with all of you." Luca smiled at them. "Thank you for all the effort you have put in that made this production the success it has been. Now, all I can say to all of you is have a great show tonight."

"Luca, are you coming out with us after the show?" Jason asked him and Luca flashed all of them a gorgeous smile.

"It will be an honour to go out with you all later." He said to him. "Break a leg." Luca went over to the side of the stage and took up his usual spot and enjoyed the play as his cast gave it their all. The actors had interpreted Euripides just as the great man would have wanted to see his greatest play performed.

After the intermission, when the cast had taken their places again, Luca was standing with his legs apart, completely immersed in the play. His phone vibrated and he took it out of his pocket. It was Peo.

"Hello Peo." Luca said in a hushed tone. "What's up?"

"Sorry to interrupt you, General." Peo said and lowered his own voice. "There's been another murder."

"Who?"

"The werewolf, Dimitri Cartwright." Peo said gravely. "Same as the others. The navar must be stronger now, should we move on Welte again or wait until Wednesday?"

"No, let's see what the sucker gives us." Luca advised. "I'll see you tomorrow." Luca hung up and sensed that he wasn't alone. He turned around and saw the sneaky stance of Willis within the shadows of the lighting stand. "Do you always eavesdrop on other people's conversations, Willis?" Willis gave a smarmy smile as he looked at Luca.

"I assure you, Mister Meridian, it wasn't intentional." Willis answered. "Besides I didn't hear anything important." He chuckled now and Luca walked over to him and stood up to his full height of six foot seven. He cut an impressive and intimidating figure. Willis visually gulped as he looked up at Luca now.

"There was nothing for you to hear." Luca said and looked at him with a disdainful expression. "I think by now you already know what I am." Willis nodded and swallowed more air.

"Look, I have done nothing illegal, those women were all adults, and they consented to sleep with me." Willis rambled on, and it was then that Luca realised, that the theatre manager assumed he was a cop. Luca laughed and slapped him across the face with an open hand. He was spared having to admit to this sleaze bag that he was a vampire.

"If I ever hear of you doing anything like that again, Willis," Luca said in a serious cop like tone. "They will lock you up and throw away the key, do you understand me?" Luca walked away from him and as he took up his spot beside the stage, he heard the applause, and then the curtains closed.

The encore and the applause went on for a very long time as the audience gifted their appreciation for the drama and the players.

Backstage as the final curtain closed, Luca walked over to the cast members and informed them where he was taking them for the celebration. They looked at each other and high fived. Everyone knew of Bjorn's club but they had never stepped inside it, as they could never get a reservation for this exclusive club.

Chapter 41

The wanton moans filled the bedroom of the plush hotel as the lovers devoured each other's bodies.

Thea was bathed in sweat as she moved up and down on Luca. He kissed her passionately as he cupped her face with his hands. Then he rolled her off him. They had been making love all night and yet, neither of them seemed satisfied. Luca wanted more from her.

"You are an incredible woman." Luca whispered as he held her in his arms, and she wrapped her left arm around his broad shoulder. "I had an incredible night, Thea." He looked into her big sad eyes. She smiled at him and kissed him on the mouth. Luca struggled to keep his fangs from descending again. He was so aroused and all he wanted to do was devour Thea's body further.

"Is this how you let down all the women you make love to?" Thea asked him, half serious as she tried to withhold the melancholy from her voice.

"Thea, why do you have so little confidence in yourself?" Luca asked her and she turned onto her back and covered her voluptuous breasts with the crisp white sheet.

"I guess it's because, all I ever did when I was younger, was wait around until I had to move on." She whispered and wiped her eye with the palm of her hand. "I never knew what it would feel like to experience love with a man like you." Luca turned onto his side and cupped her face in his hand. She was so beautiful.

"You'll find someone who is worthy of your love, Thea." Luca said gently and kissed her softly on the mouth. "You just haven't found it with me." He looked into her eyes. "I'm just not that kind of guy, Thea." Her mouth quivered noticeably as he looked intently at her, unable to hide his desire.

"I thought that I had, with you, Luca." She whispered as he felt a tear roll over his thumb. "Oh Luca...I am a blubbering mess." She tried to giggle but he could see that she was struggling with her emotions. "What must you think of me, huh?"

"Thea, I'm not the one for you. Believe me, you don't want a man like me in your life." Luca said gently as she covered his mouth with hers and he felt her tongue probe his mouth. Luca was aroused and he wanted to take her again. "You don't want me."

"I do, tonight." Thea whispered as he raised himself above her and began to thrust long and hard inside her again as he succumbed to the lust of the night.

LUCA DROVE THEA BACK to her small apartment and as she opened the door, she smiled across at him and touched his hand with hers.

"You are one really gorgeous man, Luca Meridian." Thea said and blushed as she leaned over to kiss him full on the mouth. Luca didn't enjoy long drawn-out goodbyes, and he was keen to get rid of Thea. He had called a meeting of the Militibus and already he was running late. He needed to go.

"Be good to yourself, Thea." Luca said and she got out of the car and closed the door, and he drove off at high speed.

Chapter 42

Rome 76 AD

By the time that he had returned to his barracks, Lucian's mood still hadn't improved very much. He stopped at the entrance to his tent and glanced up at the moon. It shone bright and it looked even bigger than usual. With its perfectly round shape and its brightness, it lit up the area around the barracks and the street beyond.

Lucian hadn't believed that the young Caesar had Porcia, so he had called to her villa where she lived with her aunt and her cousin. As he knocked on the door, he was met by the young slave and informed that the mistress was in, but her niece had been away for three days, and no one knew where she was. This had infuriated Lucian as he had only been with her two days after he returned from Lycia.

Porcia and he had discussed Lucian's plans to buy her freedom from the emperor, and she would become his wife. She would be a Centurion officer's wife, and she would accompany him to his next posting, where ever that would be.

Lucian knew that Vespasian wouldn't be happy, but Lucian didn't care. He loved Porcia and she loved him.

Damn that spoilt little upstart!

As he ran his fingers through his hair, Lucian knew that he had to speak with the emperor. Let him know what his heir had asked of him. *But how?*

How the hell did you tell your emperor that his son was so treacherous? Why did it have to be Lucian that had to be the one who was the harbinger of such news?

He strode inside his tent and over to his bed and sat down. Lucian hated being put in this situation. He was a highly regarded Centurion, not a murderer. How could he do what the young Caesar asked of him? Murder another in cold blood so a succession could be diminished by one.

He didn't hear Octavius as he came in and only looked up when he heard him call out.

"Lucian, I have been looking for you." Octavius said in a dower voice. "We are requested by the emperor, at the palace."

"What for?" Lucian asked as he stood up and fixed his tunic and cloak.

"The note only advised us to come at once, and alone." Octavius replied curtly and began to walk over to the opening. "I'll wait outside."

"Coming Domine." Lucian replied and walked behind his commander.

The streets were lively as they made their way through the crowds of revellers. Lucian wondered why they were summoned to the emperor's villa. Vespasian was known throughout for his love of the intrigue but to Octavius, he didn't have a keen sense of humour.

They were given entry to the palace and were escorted to Vespasian's private quarters, away from his advisors and the other courtiers. Both Roman Centurions bowed their heads as the emperor welcomed them and then they stood at ease.

"Octavius, your hastiness as always is admirable." Vespasian said in his charming tone.

"Ave Imperator." Octavius raised his arm and then bowed his head now as did Lucian.

"Lucian Marius Antonius." Vespasian said in a loud and powerful tone. "I understand while you were posted to Lycia you excelled in your duties. I am not surprised. Your father was an exemplary legate." Lucian also raised his arm and then bowed at the compliment. "I have asked my two most loyal officers here because I am in need of assistance." Vespasian said and then stood up. Both Lucian and Octavius retreated backwards as he walked around the divan. "My mistress Porcia has gone, disappeared." Vespasian snapped his fingers as he spoke. "No one has seen her in almost a week." The emperor looked at both his Centurions and Lucian knew that he was studying them carefully for any sign of knowledge that they knew of her whereabouts. Then Vespasian focussed his eyes on Lucian.

Lucian had spent two days with Porcia after his return to Rome and he also knew why she had disappeared but how could he tell the emperor this news?

"Dominus Noster," Octavius said and looked at the emperor. "What can we do?" Lucian felt sick to his stomach as he waited for the emperor to reply.

"Find her, Octavius." Vespasian bellowed at him. "Find her and bring her to me. Where I shall punish her for daring to leave me for another." He then glanced back at Lucian once more. "I want the bitch returned here immediately."

His eyes seemed to bore through Lucian, and Lucian knew then that he would be unable to confide in his emperor the news of the treacherous task entrusted onto him by his son and one of his heirs.

"At once, Dominus Noster." Octavius said and bowed and then he turned to leave, followed by Lucian.

"Lucian Marius Antonius." Vespasian called out and Lucian stopped in his tracks. "A word." Octavius left and Lucian turned around and was face to face with his emperor. He had to remain calm and not let on that he knew anything about Porcia or her whereabouts.

Chapter 43

Nunc Tempus

Luca walked over to the door of his office and turned to his personal assistant and asked her to bring him a strong black coffee. He went inside and saw that his friends were already waiting for him.

"I must be late, or you are eager to get to work for a change." Luca said sarcastically but he wore a grin on his face as the secretary brought in his coffee.

"No, you are definitely late, Luca." Peo said and grinned knowingly back at him. "We are just awaiting your orders." Luca laughed and watched as his assistant left the office.

"So, what happened last night?" Luca asked and Lanny chuckled at that. "Not your sex life, Jarl." Luca retorted and smiled. He could see that they were all in a good mood. "What happened with Dimitri Cartwright?"

"I got a call from him. He said some crap about the suckers in a bar downtown." Lanny said disinterested. "Peo and I drove to the bar, and Dimitri followed us to the restroom."

"He told us Welte was harassing him about being an informant to us." Peo joined in. "There was no one in the stalls so we told him we weren't at his beck and call and as we were there, we had a drink." Lanny grinned now.

"What happened then?" Luca asked. He was concerned that Welte had marked the werewolf. There would be trouble back in the Sixth because Dimitri Cartwright was the son of the highly respected politician, Armistead Cartwright.

"By the time we left, there was a commotion outside," Peo said morosely. "Dimitri and a sucker were going at each other, it was nothing out of the ordinary, so we left them to their fight." Luca nodded. The Militibus usually didn't intervene in minor squabbles between dregs.

"I got a call about an hour or so later from Dimitri's pack mate, Grace." Lanny said in a more professional tone now. "When we got to the address that she gave us, we saw his body shrivelled and drained."

"Do you think it's connected to the navar?" Luca asked both of them. Lanny just shrugged his shoulders.

"It was no secret that Dimitri was an informant for us," Lanny replied. "It could have been a coincidence, and maybe it was a sucker who killed and drained the mutt."

"General, I don't think the brawl and the murder was done by the same sucker." Peo said and Luca stared at him. Peo was always known to weigh things up and not make hurried decisions or rushed opinions.

"The navar?" Luca probed and Peo nodded. "Was the sucker from Welte's lair?"

"We sent most of his lair to the Tenth," Bjorn asserted. "He has only what, eight, maybe nine left in the lair?"

"I don't trust that sucker." Lanny said indignantly. Luca looked at him, Lanny rarely trusted suckers. "He'd sell out his lair if he could get away with it." Luca nodded, he didn't like Welte either and he was unhappy that they had to put their trust in him to catch the navar. But so far, he was the only one who had any contact with the energy vampire.

"OK, Militibus, look, I don't think it was one of Welte's suckers who killed Dimitri Cartwright, I think it was the navar." Luca said and looked at his men. "As Peo said, she's stronger now, maybe as strong as she needs to be to pull off whatever she is planning." They nodded in agreement. "We go all in and send that bitch to the Tenth on Wednesday," Luca said angrily. "Send that sucker Welte with her." He stood up and grinned at them. "Now leave me in some peace, I need to get some sleep." They all laughed and before they left the office, Luca called out. "Jarl, a word." Lanny nodded and came back into the office.

"Something up, General?" He asked and Luca looked at him for a moment. They had been close friends for a very long time. Luca could talk to Lanny about anything. Right now, he needed to talk to his friend.

"Do you have plans tonight, Lanny?" Luca asked him and Lanny shook his head.

"Nothing planned, Luca." He replied. "Why? Do you want to chill and talk?" This made Luca smile. The Jarl was intuitive as always.

"Yes." Luca said with a grin. "Just the two of us, let's go out to dinner." Lanny nodded and then he left the office.

Luca let out a long slow sigh as he rested the palms of his hands flat on his desk.

Chapter 44

Rome 76 AD

The search for the emperor's mistress had gone on for more than a week. She was found hiding in an orange grove several miles from the city. She had been beaten and bruised when Lucian found her. He couldn't be protective, nor could he show his relief that she was safe, if somewhat shaken. All he felt was despair and powerlessness.

What Lucian wanted to do was beat the hell out of the young Caesar for what he had put her through. All the different emotions that were going through Lucian's mind yet, he couldn't show any of them publicly because Porcia was Vespasian's mistress, his slave. Despite having taken her aunt Caenis as his live in lover.

When Porcia was returned to the villa where Vespasian was waiting expectantly for her. She had been first cleaned and bathed in luxurious scented water and then, walked between Lucian and Octavius and presented to the emperor.

He sat on the divan, eating grapes and drinking wine as Porcia was presented to him.

"I owe my Centurions a great debt." Vespasian said with a dry grin as he looked at her and then slyly at Lucian. She had lost weight since her ordeal, and she looked terrified.

Lucian noticed the entrance made by both the young Caesars, Titus and Domitian, as they slipped in unnoticed. "You should be ashamed of yourself, Porcia." Vespasian scolded her in front of the Centurions and then he patted the bed and motioned for her to join him on the divan. This made Lucian's temper rise as he watched his lover meekly join the emperor. "Now, say thank you to Lucian Marius Antonius for bringing you back to me." Vespasian glanced mockingly across to where Lucian stood. He was so angry as he watched Porcia turn and look at him.

"Thank you." Her voice was shaky and barely above a whisper and Lucian could see the tear escape and run down her cheek.

"Come now, is that anyway to thank the Centurion officer for rescuing you from the bandits who stole you, Porcia?" Vespasian goaded, as his eyes were still on Lucian. But Lucian couldn't look away, if he did, he would be killed for the insult. "Thank him properly." The emperor shouted and then slapped her hard across the face. Lucian was incapable of being able to do anything. Anything that he said or did would result in both of their deaths. He gave a side glance to where the two heirs stood, sniggering at the mistreatment of the concubine.

"Thank you, Lucian Marius Antonius." Porcia said loudly now, and Lucian saw that she had regained her composure. She had had enough of his goading. Despite all that she had gone through by her captors and the mistreatment and humiliation that Vespasian metered out to her, Porcia's pride came to the fore and she overcame her shame. Lucian was proud of her.

"That's better." Vespasian said with a chuckle. "Now, come here and show me how sorry you are for disobeying me." Porcia gave a look across to where Lucian and Octavius stood and then glanced at the heirs and finally to the emperor. But he couldn't read her. Lucian didn't know what was going through her mind.

Suddenly Porcia ran toward Octavius and grabbed his dagger and made to run at the emperor, but she was stopped by the legate and in the scuffle, she was mortally wounded in her belly.

Lucian shouted out but as all eyes turned to him, and he quickly corrected himself.

"Is the emperor hurt?" He couldn't care less about the emperor. He was devastated that his lover, his beloved Porcia was dead in a pool of her own blood.

LUCIAN WAS GRIEVING heavily in his quarters at the barracks. He sat with his head in his hands. He was overcome with sorrow. But for him, the worst part was that he was unable to openly mourn the death of his lover.

As Lucian watched the commotion after Porcia was killed, he knew that the emperor knew of their relationship. He also knew that Lucian had planned to buy her freedom. But Vespasian wouldn't have let her go. He would have never allowed Lucian and Porcia to be together, not in life nor in death.

It was as if he had orchestrated the entire tragedy, with the sole intention of killing Porcia.

Lucian stood up and went to pick up his goblet and downed the contents in one gulp. Then he walked out of the tent and out into the night.

As he walked along the crowded streets, Lucian didn't know where he was going, only that he had to get out of his quarters and be amongst people. It was better than being alone. Alone, he harboured plans that involved the demise of Vespasian, because he was emperor, and he had openly claimed Porcia as his property. Vespasian didn't love her, she was a subject, an object that he possessed. He didn't see her as the incredible woman she had been. Lucian knew. He loved her, he wanted her freedom, so he could show her, and anyone else who saw them together that he loved this remarkable woman and that she in turn loved him.

As Lucian walked aimlessly ahead, he quickened his step and as he did, he somehow found himself away from the main thoroughfare and as he tried to get his bearings, Lucian noticed a very tall man flitting in and out of the shadows, his movements fast, almost a blur. Something about his demeanour worried Lucian but it also intrigued him, and he didn't know why.

Without hesitation, Lucian was following the stranger discreetly. As he walked, he kept to the buildings for cover. Then suddenly the tall stranger stopped and was met by two men. The same two men as had accosted Lucian some weeks before.

Lucian watched from a distance as the three of them hurriedly made their way away from the square. With a sixth sense, Lucian knew where they were going and who it was, that they were going to meet. Curiosity set his mind reeling and he felt a terrible compulsion to follow them.

In the shadows of the walled garden, Lucian saw the distinctive figure of the heir as he stood there. His face was twisted into a vile and evil expression as he waited for the stranger to greet him. As Lucian watched the scene from the safety of the shadows, he was surprised when the two men brought out a struggling young man and pushed him into the centre of the path. From the light of the moon, Lucian could see it was Rufus Romanus, Vespasian's illegitimate son.

Lucian knew what was going to happen, but Lucian was too consumed by his grief to intervene and try to prevent it. He watched in the shadows as the tall stranger threw back his cloak and then he heard the laugh from the young Caesar as his stepbrother was set upon by the tall man. The struggle was brief and violent.

Lucian turned and hurriedly retreated back the way that he had come. There was nothing that he could have done, Lucian told himself over and over. He didn't even know if the young man had been slain. All he saw was the stranger pull the boy's head to the side and the stranger bend his own head. Nothing else. Perhaps Rufus Romanus was alive. Lucian didn't see any weapons being used. Nothing which would suggest that the young man was slain. All that Lucian knew was that he refused to believe what he had witnessed.

Chapter 45

Nunc Tempus

Luca ordered a steak, blue and a Midleton whiskey. Lanny closed his menu and grinned and he ordered the same. For several moments neither of the vampires spoke. It wasn't until the server brought them their whiskies that Lanny uttered.

"Iubentium."

"Iubentium." Luca repeated and raised his glass and took a sip of the fine single malt whiskey. Before he replaced it on the table, he glanced at the crystal glass and the fine amber liquid that it contained. It was refined, delicate, and above all, it was needed!

"So, Luca, what cause has you in such a state of pensiveness." Lanny asked with a broad smile on his face.

"Am I pensive, Jarl?" Luca teased him, as if he was biding time, and Lanny just chuckled now and shook his head as he glanced at Luca.

"You sound like a sluagh, Luca." Lanny said through fits of laughter. "Yes, you have been withdrawn and slightly moody of late." Luca stared intently at his friend for a moment now, trying to compose himself. "We have all noticed and we are worried about you."

"I feel as though I have failed on this case, Lanny." Luca spoke after a while. "I let down the mortal, Frankie. Somewhere in my moral stance, I believed the old man wasn't a drunk, when clearly, he needed intervention." He tapped his fingers against the glass as he stared at the amber content. "Intervention that the Padre could have given, if I had approached him."

"That's not failure, Luca," Lanny responded now. "That's not reading the situation clearly, when you are too closely involved. Look at the Padre, does he save all the alcoholics that present to his shelter? I don't believe he does or that he can." Luca glanced across at him. Beyond his fierce reputation, Lanny was quite a philosophical thinker.

"You're right, but that doesn't lessen the fact that I failed the old guy." Luca said as his fingers continued to drum on the glass. The server brought them their starter and the two vampires thanked her. "Do you ever regret the failings of your mortal life, Lanny?" Luca asked suddenly as he looked at the Jarl, who seemed lost in thought momentarily.

"Only for the terrible things I did when I was turned." Lanny said after a moment. "The raids were what we did, what I was born into." Luca glanced at him now. Despite the Jarl's bravado that he was a Viking and all it entailed, Luca knew it was just for show, that it was a brave face for the world. In the coldness of the night when he was alone, the Jarl felt regret. They all felt the regret.

"This wasn't the first time that I failed to save someone vulnerable." Luca said now as he reached for the wine glass and looked at the blood red wine. The memory of Porcia's desperate act filled him with shame once more. "In 76 AD

I was hired, if you like, to assassinate someone." Luca raised the glass to his mouth and took a long sip of the wine. Then Luca replaced the glass on the table and glanced at Lanny. "The illegitimate son of emperor Vespasian." Lanny looked at him, without raising an eyebrow. "Rufus Romanus, he was a sixteen-year-old bastard son to a concubine and the emperor. A kid in today's world." Luca half laughed as he raised the glass again.

"Why was he singled out to be killed?" Lanny asked and Luca took a sip of wine and then held the glass for a moment before placing it back on the table.

"Vespasian had two legitimate heirs, Titus and Domitian. Both privileged, in a time when it was relatively peaceful in the Roman empire." Luca grinned at the memory. "Rome had known little peace but during Vespasian's reign it prospered again. My father prospered and was retired as legate at sixty." Luca grinned at Lanny now who smirked back at him. "Titus became emperor when Vespasian died, he was the more charming of the Caesars. Domitian was demonic. A paranoid despot, with a cruelty any Viking would be proud of." They both laughed at that.

"So why did this Rufus kid have to die?" Lanny asked again and Luca glanced out the window briefly. The street was busy with men and women rushing about, greeting each other and then moving on. A typical night out in LA.

"Domitian wanted to be emperor, so he decided to kill off the competition one by one. Not that Rufus Romanus would have succeeded the throne, he wasn't named as an heir. It was just Domitian showing his power." Luca told Lanny. "He called me to his villa one night, told me to kill his half-brother, and if I didn't..." Luca broke off and reached for his glass but hesitated for a moment as he looked at the wine. He knew that the Jarl wouldn't judge him, not for something like this. For the love of a woman. Then he picked it up and took a long sip before replacing it on the crisp white linen tablecloth.

"Did you kill him, Luca?" Lanny asked him, without a hint of judgement in his voice. Luca looked at his friend and gave a short bitter smile as he shook his head.

"I was involved with a woman. Her name was Porcia." Luca said in a low tone. "She was incredibly beautiful, witty, and intelligent. I was so much in love with her. I was going to marry her." He looked up at Lanny to gauge his response to this information, but his expression hadn't changed. "I was based in the province of Lycia for two years and when I returned to Rome, I was going to buy her freedom from Vespasian."

"Did you?" Lanny asked and Luca shrugged his shoulders. "Why not?"

"It was complicated. Porcia was Vespasian's courtesan." Luca said bitterly. "When I met her, I had no idea." A tainted smile crossed his lips momentarily at the memory of their first meeting. "We were discreet, because we had to be. If the emperor discovered our affair, he would have put us both to death." He picked up his knife and began to cut his steak and the blood pooled on the plate.

"A bit harsh." Lanny admitted. "How did you conceal it?" This made him grin as he shook his head.

"I thought we had," Luca admitted now as he looked at his friend. "But evidently we hadn't." He said bitterly.

"You were discovered?" Lanny asked and Luca nodded.

"Domitian, he told me that he had seen us together in the garden near the bathhouse." Luca told him. "Not only that, but the bastard also told Vespasian, which led to my not being promoted to legate in Lycia."

"Vindictive old toad." Lanny said and Luca had to laugh at that. "So, what happened between you and Porcia?" This pained Luca as he put down his knife and fork.

"She went missing. Porcia was abducted by Domitian, as collateral for me to kill Rufus Romanus." Luca said. "Me and the legate Octavius had to find her, when we did, we brought her back and long story short, she grabbed a dagger to kill Vespasian but ended up stabbing herself." It still hurt to remember the last moments of her life.

"I'm sorry Luca." Lanny said now in a sympathetic voice.

"There was nothing I could do to save her, Lanny." Luca sounded as desperate now as he did at the time it had happened, even though it was two millennia ago. "I failed her."

"How can you say that?" Lanny asked. "What exactly could you have done?" Luca shook his head. He knew Lanny was right. He had been helpless then just as he had been to save old Frankie.

"The crazy thing is, Jarl," Luca said now. "I felt murderous after Porcia died. I walked the streets of Rome, in desperation to banish her death from my mind." He played with the steak on his plate now. The blood made an elaborate pattern on the crisp white plate. "That was when I saw a stranger, he was walking along with the two assassins belonging to Domitian. I followed them, discreetly of course." Luca said and reached for the wine glass and picked it up. Luca rested his elbows on the table as he held the wine glass in both his hands. "To Domitian's villa, where I witnessed the murder of Rufus Romanus." Lanny stared at him. "Only at the time, I wasn't sure a murder had taken place. I wasn't willing to admit to myself that what I saw, actually happened." Lanny looked at him intently now.

"What did you see, Luca?" He asked in a low tone. Luca smiled over at him. There was a silence for a moment between them then Luca said in a hushed tone.

"What I saw was a tall dark stranger, grab the young man and drink his blood." Lanny looked at Luca now.

"Who did you see, who was the stranger?" Lanny asked him as the Jarl reached for his wine glass.

"The same alpha vampire who turned me in Pompeii, in 79AD." Luca admitted bitterly. He took a long gulp from the glass in his hand. He locked eyes with Lanny now, and Luca saw the look of incredulity on his friend's face.

Chapter 46

L anny shrugged his broad shoulders as Luca watched the look of disbelief on his friend's face after he revealed to him who had murdered the son of the emperor.

"Partus?" Lanny asked incredulously as he reached for his own wine glass now as well. "You met him before you were turned? How can that be, Luca?"

"I didn't know it at the time." Luca said as he looked at Lanny's shocked expression. "This is the crazy thing, but when I met him in Pompeii, I didn't recognise him, Lanny."

"Did he recognise you." The Jarl asked.

"I don't believe he saw me that night in Domitian's garden. At least I convinced myself that he hadn't." Luca replied. "But knowing what we know about the alphas, their senses are extremely sensitive, even more so than ours, so I believe now, in hindsight, he knew I was there and knew me again in Pompeii."

"Was Domitian aware of what Partus was?" Lanny asked but Luca shrugged his shoulder. "Luca, if you met Partus prior to being turned, do you think... nah, this is crazy." Lanny broke off.

"What's crazy?" Luca asked.

"Do you think that the alphas had us marked before we were turned?" Luca thought about it for a moment. "That they knew who they wanted to turn?" He looked at Lanny. Luca had given it some thought over the centuries but until now he had formed no opinion. "Sometimes I lay awake and think we were picked for a reason. I don't know why but it just seems too convenient that it was us chosen to be turned into vampires." Luca watched as Lanny took a long sip of the fine merlot.

"Once, my father told me to be wary of a tall dark stranger." Luca admitted to to his friend. "I don't know if he meant Partus or someone else. If he was even referring to vampires. But he was frightened by something he encountered in Noviomagus. He retired after that, and I met him in Rome on his way back to Surrentum." Luca admitted now as he too lifted the wine glass. "Lanny, I really don't know about any of this regarding why we were chosen or turned. But this thing with the navar," Luca said after a moment. "I believe it knows what it wants, the energy that it needs and who it wants to drain." Lanny stared at him now. Incredulously.

"Do you think Demis knows more than he is telling us." Lanny questioned and Luca nodded. "The old toad. Typical."

"What I do know is when this investigation is over, back in the Sixth, we are in for some serious disciplinary action." Luca said and Lanny raised an eyebrow. "Dimitri Cartwright's old man will have something to say about his son's murder." Lanny looked at Luca. They both knew the seriousness of their situation.

Chapter 47

Rome 1760

It was a little stifling, and the heavy navy coat hung on his shoulders almost weighing him down. All he wanted to do was get back to his lodgings and remove the coat and lounge away from the midday sun.

As he walked across the piazza, his destination was predetermined because this was his last day in Rome. Several fine ladies with their handmaids following behind them, passed him and he bowed his head graciously and continued his journey undeterred.

In the distance, he could see the magnificent Colosseum. Its sandstone colour contrasted against the deep blue of the sky. Just for a moment he stopped to look at it. Although he was familiar with this city, he had lived there for a time in his early adult life. The city of Rome held nothing of any great importance for Lucian. Not anymore.

His strides became shorter and slower as he passed by the Forum. Lucian stopped and glanced around. He could see the marbled columns of some of the ancient buildings, as they lay in ruins. This city...*his city*....in its prime was a splendour to behold. Everywhere, there were people, beggars, thieves, soldiers and peasants rubbing shoulders with the rich and the elite of Roman society.

Lucian rested the palm of his hand against the hot surface of the ruined parapet. Quickly he removed it again. Even though he had been given the Militibus blood just weeks earlier, the sun here was much stronger than it was in the city of Vienna, where he and his men were based. It was also easier for his vampiric skin to burn against surfaces like marble.

His eyes cast their eager glance around the Forum. A smile which disguised his inner pain, crossed his lips as he remembered when he had first walked this path. He had been full of dreams, full of ambition for his career. His father had been a legate in the Roman army, it was meant to be Lucian's legacy to follow in his father's footsteps and lead legions, but that had been cruelly taken from him just as Porcia had.

Porcia!

The reason for his walk that morning. He wanted to place a flower near the column where he had promised her that he would buy her freedom. That too, had been swiped from under him when had been sent to Lycia for a posting that lasted two years.

A sigh escaped him as he rested his left foot on the fallen stone and raised the flower to his nose and sniffed it's delicate white petals with the little yellow spikes at the centre.

"Tibi meus flos." Lucian whispered as the flower fell from his hand and landed on the marble stone. Lucian watched as it slipped over the stone and onto the grass. A sudden breeze blew up and lifted the flower and blew it along the grass until it was almost out of sight.

He gave a final longing glance around the fallen columns and then turned and walked back in the direction that he had come. His mind was filled with the reveries of happier times, lovemaking with his lover.

Lucian had lots of time. *Tempus* would always be his, but what he would never have again, was time to be with his lover, Porcia. For she was a memory in a time and place lost to Lucian. Perdidit in caligo temporis.

As he walked back to his lodging, all Lucian could think about was that Porcia was dead, and had been for over a millennium, but he had done his time grieving. It was time to let his dead lover go, and for Lucian, it was Tempus Viveve.

Chapter 48

Nunc Tempus

Luca put on his black leather waistcoat, and left it unbuttoned. He buckled his scabbard around his waist and smoothed his long dark hair off his handsome face. He picked up the sword and glanced at it. Its blade glistened as it caught the glow from the ceiling light. The hues flamed with iridescent colours as the light caught the slight curve of the blade. Luca gave a short smile.

This sword had been given to him when he was made a Centurion officer, and it never left his side. He had depended on it, and it had saved his life many times. He had a substantial armoury in his penthouse, with various swords, daggers and other weapons, all from different centuries. But this sword was the one that he always chose. He loved the feel of the hilt in his hand, how light it felt when he fought, unlike some of the other swords he owned. Heavy and cumbersome.

Luca put on his leather trench coat and walked out of the apartment. He had asked the Militibus to meet him at his office before they went to the carpet store to confront the navar. He wanted to brief the Militibus quickly and see if they had anything new to add to what they already had gathered.

He rode to his office, unhurriedly and without any stress. Luca knew that there were times in the past, when he had faced foes where he wasn't sure what the outcome would be, but for many eras now, he had at his back the cover of three of the best warriors that he had ever served with. The methods that they used, sometimes were questionable but Luca trusted them with his life, and they didn't disappoint. Ever!

He parked up the panigale and walked into the building and went over to the lift and pressed the button for his floor.

Luca opened his office door and removed his helmet and put it down on the desk. When this was over, he would have to report in person to the council of Elders, he would have to tell them how Demis had compromised the Sixth, the council, and the Militibus by allowing his nephew William Greyson through to the Fourth, without the proper assessments being done. He didn't relish it. It felt like he was betraying his old friend. But first and foremost, the security of the Fourth was paramount to the Militibus, anything else was secondary. It was the oath that they had sworn when they were tasked with their commission.

It was up to Luca and his officers to ensure that their district was free from corruption and treachery. Not an easy task at the best of times. It was made a thousand times worse, though, when Demis screwed up. This time, he had bungled up big time.

Luca heard Peo and Bjorn laughing as they walked up the corridor to his office. He turned around and grinned at them.

"On time, perfect." Luca said and was about to ask where the Jarl was when he heard the lift doors open. "Our Jarl, about to make a grand entrance as always." Luca noted and they laughed as Lanny came in and he smirked at them from behind his visor.

"I assume from your laughter that that comment was about me." Lanny said simpering as he removed his helmet.

"Anyone have any new intel besides what we know already?" Luca asked them, without wasting any time on small talk, as he looked at each of them in turn.

"Nothing new from my informants, General." Lanny replied and looked at him with a serious expression.

"Peo?" Luca asked but he shook his head. "Bjorn, anything?"

"No, General, nothing new to add." Bjorn said gravely. Luca nodded. It was just as he had expected, they had no new intel, so they were going in with little knowledge other than the navar was female.

"I've had no contact either from the Sixth," Luca informed them. "As we face this bitch tonight, be careful, Militibus," Luca said in a serious tone. "What we do know is, she is cunning and can move quickly, faster maybe, even than we can, so do not let her get behind you, remain vigilant and don't hesitate to send that parasite to the Tenth." Luca looked at them and then grinned. "Afterwards, the reward will be ecstasy courtesy of the Berserker's club, I'll buy the first round." They all laughed now but Luca knew that when they went out on a mission like this it was always dangerous. Anything could go wrong. "Virtus Militibus."

"Vi et Vitoria." They all chanted and put back on their helmets and left Luca's office.

It was going to be a tense evening ahead, and one Luca wished to be over quickly.

Chapter 49

They drove in single file to where they were going to stake out the carpet shop. Luca had had the shees move out after the murder of their leader. The hix had taken his pack and they had left the city. Luca didn't know where they had gone to, nor did he want to, as it meant he didn't have the nightmare of sending them to the outcast colony of the Seventh.

They parked up their panigales and removed their helmets. The waiting was almost intolerable as they hid in the shadows across from the building. Luca stood with his right side against the stone wall, as he waited for something to happen. It was quiet, too quiet for his liking. It looked completely deserted.

An hour later and there was still no activity in the shop. Luca was beginning to get irritated as he thought of the wild goose chase that the sucker, Welte, had sent them on. It was beginning to feel hopeless once more.

Then he felt a slight bump on his arm as the Jarl motioned to a van, as it pulled up outside the carpet shop. Luca watched from the darkness of the alley as he saw Welte jump out of the passenger seat. The vampire scanned the area and then he looked up and down the alleyway, but when he didn't see anyone, he just hit his hands together obviously relieved that the Militibus were nowhere to be seen. Welte seemed more relaxed now and off guard.

Luca held up his fist and signalled for them to wait. He would let the sucker, and his cronies begin whatever business they were going to conduct before Luca and his warriors broke up their little get-together. He would enjoy sending that leech Welte to the Tenth.

After several long minutes or so of waiting, Luca signalled for them to make their way over to the shop. Quickly and noiselessly, they crossed the road under the security of the shadows, the Militibus backed up against the wall as they moved swiftly.

Luca quickly scanned the cab of the van, it was empty. He motioned for Lanny to open the door, and stealthily they made their way inside the shop. They could hear raised voices coming from the office in the rear. Luca could make out several but he only recognised Welte's voice.

Lanny motioned for Peo and Bjorn to open the door to the office in the back and he would follow them inside. Peo nodded and made his way up to the door and looked backward at Luca, who nodded as he opened the door, both he and Bjorn rushed in with their swords poised followed by Lanny and then Luca.

"What the hell?" A sucker shouted as he was quickly overpowered by Bjorn.

"Hello again Welte," Luca said and grinned at him as Luca moved into the centre of the room. "I almost believed you had given us false intel." The other suckers in the room turned and glared at Welte. They now knew he had betrayed them.

"Where's the navar?" Lanny shouted at them. Welte laughed and shook his head.

"She's here." Welte said and stood aside and the Militibus came face to face with a white ashen faced woman, with white and blue smoke surrounding her in an almost translucent form.

"So, you're the bitch who murdered all those dregs?" Peo raised his voice in her direction, and with a contemptuous expression on his face, as he came forward and scowled at the navar.

"Murder?" The navar asked, as she wore a perplexed look now as the smoke swirled upwards from her upper body. "No vampire, not murder, just necessity." The navar said in a soft voice, almost saddened by the accusation made by Peo.

"Murder is never a necessity, navar." Luca said angrily and stood up straight and looked at the dreg that he had been hunting for months. She had a serene expression and a mesmerising, almost sweet voice.

"My name is Percita." The navar said and as she moved, she seemed to float on air.

"Stop, stay where I can see you," Luca shouted at her. He had no patience with the criminal.

"Such ill manners." Percita said as she closely gazed at him, with her head turned to the side and Luca saw what must have been a smile from her. "Is that what the council teaches its elite these days?" She half turned her head and as the light from the industrial lamp caught her face, she looked almost genteel, like a kindly grandmother. But the reality of what she really was, was far more sinister.

"Remember we have a deal." Welte said, whether he was addressing Percita or Luca, it was unclear to all in the room.

"Berserker, send that sucker to the Tenth." Luca said without taking his eyes from the navar. He didn't want to place himself or his men in danger if she decided to pounce at them and catch them unaware. They were all aware of how cunning the bitch was.

"A wise decision," the navar said. "He was becoming decidedly tiresome." Luca raised his hand and stopped Bjorn before he had beheaded the sucker in front of him.

"What did you promise him?" Luca asked the navar. She laughed and glided backwards this time. "Stay where I can see you." He bellowed at her again, but she just chortled and ignored his demand.

"The light hurts my eyes," Percita said in a soft voice. "I have been sleeping for years, and the light makes me photosensitive." She whimpered as she glanced at Luca. "A vampire should be aware of these things. We are very alike." She simpered.

"I don't care, navar." Luca said as he stared at the dreg. "What did you promise the sucker and the hybrid?" She laughed again, a high-pitched sound that grated on one's nerves like nails on a chalkboard.

"Whatever would have them work for me. Greed is marvellous." Percita said as the smoke from her body swirled around her, almost in a hypnotic dance. "The hybrid wanted to exact revenge on the Elders for banishing his parents, I granted him that. But the sucker," she laughed as she glanced across at Welte. "He's a greedy little monster. He thinks he has leadership potential." Luca glanced across at Welte, he wore a ridiculous grin on his face, as if the navar had praised him.

"He doesn't." Luca said aggressively. "Why did you kill the old man?" He asked and he saw her raise an eyebrow.

"No reason other than I could." Percita said matter of fact. "I can do whatever I want, and you are not able to stop me. None of you are." She spoke proudly emphasising that she had the upper hand.

"You really believe that? If you do, then you are very foolish, and it is that stupidity which has sealed your fate." Luca said as he raised his sword. Suddenly a commotion in the hallway distracted them. "See what that is," he ordered and Peo left the room immediately.

"A wise decision, Militibus." The navar said and smiled across at him.

"Jarl, Berserker, send those two suckers to the Tenth," Luca ordered, his eyes were still on the navar.

A bright light enveloped the two suckers and the navar let out a sound as she saw the light.

"My eyes, my eyes are way too sensitive." She cried out mournfully now. "Give me notice when you do that again." The navar groaned loudly.

"I'll give you notice, alright." Luca said and raised his sword. "Dormies cum diabolo."

"No..." Luca turned as he heard the scream. "Luca...?" He gaped at her, hardly believing what he was seeing.

"Thea, what are you doing here?" Luca asked, his sword still poised, but he was incredulous at seeing her there. She looked at him and then beyond him to the navar floating almost hypnotically. "Thea, you don't want to be here, I'll see you outside, in a few minutes." Luca ordered and as Peo went to take her by the arm, she yanked her arm from him and ran over to the navar. "Thea?" Luca called her name. "Get away from that thing." Thea looked at the navar and smiled warmly at her as she reached out to touch the navar's arm fondly and then she quickly turned to Luca and glared at him for a moment.

"That thing is my mother." Thea cried out. Luca stared disbelievingly at her as a silence descended upon those present in the warehouse office.

Chapter 50

L uca stared at Thea in disbelief, surely, he hadn't heard her right. *She couldn't be serious. Could she?*

"What? The navar is your mother?" Luca demanded as he glared at Thea, his expression full of hatred for the creature floating beside her.

"So," Percita said in a light voice, and a sickening grin. "You're the mortal that Thea is sleeping with." The navar laughed coarsely. "Only you are not mortal are you...Luca?" The dreg wore a cunning look as she touched her daughter's arm gently and caressed it with a long-extended finger.

"What...what do you mean mom?" Thea asked and looked from Luca and then back to her mother.

"Your lover is a vampire, Thea." The navar said and laughed callously now as she glanced back at Luca. "A Tempus Militibus vampire from the Sixth, who works for the organisation who put me to sleep all those years ago. The organisation that left you alone to fend for yourself, dearest daughter." Thea flashed a thunderous look at Luca. All he could do was stare at her with contempt now. He should have known. All the signs were there that she was a dreg. Luca just chose to ignore them. This was to his detriment.

He always advised his officers never to ignore the obvious. Yet he didn't follow his own advice.

"Praetorian, take the girl and Welte outside." Luca said calmly. "Jarl, Berserker, keep guard outside."

"Very well, General." Lanny said and motioned for the others to leave as they charily filed out of the room. Luca saw the Jarl glance back over his shoulder to where Luca and the navar stood. Luca knew that it was unwise to remain alone in the small space with the creature but if anything did go awry, he was bigger than the navar, and he was a trained Roman soldier.

When they were gone, Luca turned to the navar and glared at her for a moment. He hated the dregs, but he despised this one most of all, for what she did to the old janitor, sucking away his life's energy, his blood. He hated her for what she did to her own daughter. There were no depths that the navar wouldn't sink to, or for, her own preservation. She was more contemptable than most dregs that Luca had fought against.

"Thea is a hybrid?" Luca asked her in a detached voice and the navar just laughed at the question.

"Does it matter, General?" Percita mocked, in a malicious voice. "You have dakhanavar DNA all over your body now." Luca glared at her. "Quite the snob, aren't you, Roman? But that didn't matter to you at the time, did it? When you used her body for your own gratification, *Vampire*." Percita began to giggle hysterically as she floated in the air.

"Dormies cum diabolo." Luca yelled as he raised the sword and beheaded the navar.

"Noooo..." Thea screamed from the door as she lunged herself at Luca. "How could you?" Peo ran in and pulled her off Luca. "I hate you. I hate you." She screamed at the top of her voice as she lashed out her arms in front of her.

"General, are you alright?" Peo asked as he tried to hold back Thea. Luca stood up and glanced at the pile of soot on the floor.

"I'm fine." Luca replied. "Take her out of here." He said emotionless as he walked past Thea and went outside. "I'll call the guardians."

He marched over to Welte and grabbed him by the throat. "I should send you to the Tenth for your treachery." Welte tried to extricate himself.

"I delivered the navar to you." Welte bitched at him as he wriggled his legs and tried to wrangle his way out of Luca's grip. "I kept my side of the deal."

"You only did that to save your useless neck." Luca bellowed at him and threw him against the side of the van with a heavy thud. "I promised to spare your worthless life, if you gave me the navar." Luca said angrily. "But if I ever come across your pathetic ass in my district again, Welte. Then so help me but I will send you to the Tenth." Luca walked away from him and looked over to where Peo had Thea's arms firmly gripped behind her back. Luca strode over to her and looked at her. His expression was full of hatred for his former lover. Thea was struggling hard against Peo, and she was enraged. She spat at Luca's handsome face. Peo lashed out and slapped her hard across the face. Thea screamed and turned her head to glare at the Praetorian.

"Let her go, Praetorian." Luca commanded. Peo stared at him. "Let her go," Luca yelled at him. Lanny came over, grabbed Luca's arm and turned Luca to face him.

"General, you can't let her go." Lanny said in a serious tone. "She's a dreg, she has to be sent back." Luca yanked his arm away from the Jarl.

"I give the orders here, Jarl." Luca shouted at him. "Not you, remember that."

"Luca, you can't save her, she will have to stand trial." Peo said in a hushed tone. "Lanny is right, she has to go to the Eight." Luca looked at both his officers, his friends. Then he felt a stinging sensation in his side, again and again. He turned around and he felt the stabbing in his neck. Automatically his hand went to his neck, it felt wet. He looked at Lanny and then he saw him lunge toward him and grab him as Luca fell.

"Quick, Peo, get the bike, take him to the parochial house." Lanny shouted. Luca felt his eyes get heavy as the lukewarm liquid caressed his side, and down his neck.

"Contabescant in inferno." Was the last thing that Luca heard before he lost consciousness.

Luca opened his eyes briefly as he was manhandled. He felt as if he was being pulled in every direction. As if his body was being pulled asunder, but then the pain became too much, and he closed his eyes again.

This was the end. It was all over for him now.
Porcia!

Chapter 51

He felt the sting in his side, and his neck. Then felt the liquid burn his skin and then he heard the voices, but Luca couldn't understand what they said. He tried to sit up but all he could make out was the soft female voice say soothingly.

"There, there, don't move." Her voice was lyrical and comforting, very soothing. Luca opened his eyes and tried to focus on the owner of the voice. She looked like a seraph.

"He's still bleeding, Lanny." The angel said and Luca turned his head and tried to open his eyes. "He is losing a lot of blood. I can't stop the bleeding." Luca could hear the desperation in her voice.

"Ja...Jarl..." He muttered, but it was an effort. Luca closed his eyes once more. He was weak and he knew that he was dying. He would soon be in Orcus.

"General, it's OK." Lanny said, trying to sound reassuring and then he felt the softness of a hand, warm and soft. "Peo is opening the portal. We'll have you fixed soon." He felt tired and his eyes were heavy again. Luca didn't want to go to the portal. He wanted the torment to be over. The torment of what he had done when he was a mortal. What he had done as a vampire. But most of all, Luca wanted to be free. Free of this affliction.

Before he could think again, he felt the hurtling through time, the portal had opened, he saw the lights. Then nothing.

THERE WERE TRICKLES of light peering in through the slit in the blind. Luca groaned as he turned onto his side. He hurt. He couldn't move. Even thinking hurt him.

"Where..."

"You're awake?" The cheerful voice of his friend asked, and Luca turned his head to where the sound was coming from. "Lanny, he's awake." Peo said and Luca focused his gaze on his two friends. Where was he? Why was everything so fast?

"Where am I?" Luca asked as he put his hand over his side. A vague memory of the stabbing came back to him.

"In hospital." Peo said and stood up and his smiling face came into view. "Back in the Sixth, I'm afraid." He added with a gaffe expression.

"How are you feeling?" Lanny asked as he came over to the bed.

"Like I had an argument with a steak knife." Luca said and he tried to smile but it was too much of an effort for him.

"You did, just not a steak knife but a switchblade." Lanny said as he tried to hide his concern with a grin.

"When?" Luca asked and closed his eyes again momentarily. He had lost all concept of time now. "How long have I been here?" He had been stabbed before, in battle when he was mortal. He had forgotten what the pain was like. It was almost amplified tenfold as an immortal.

"Five days." Lanny answered. "Save the questions until you feel better." The Jarl grinned at him, and Luca tried to smile back but he just closed his eyes and fell into a haunted and restless sleep.

Chapter 52

Luca was allowed to leave the hospital two weeks later. He had had a complete transfusion, and his wound had healed without any mark.

He stood up straight and opened the door and walked into the grand room in the office where Aristoteles held council. He looked at the other two elders, Seneca and Zeno.

"Lucian, good to see you have made a complete recovery." Aristotle said as he motioned for Luca to sit down.

"Thank you, Sir." Luca said and sat down. "My care was exceptional." He added.

"Congratulations on capturing the navar." Seneca said and he smiled warmly at Luca as he looked with great concern on his wise face. "I wonder, though it was necessary to send the mother to the Tenth, I would ask you, Lucian, if it was also practical to send the daughter. Could diplomacy have been used regarding the young woman?" The stoic asked and Luca stared at him for a moment. He wondered how much the Elders knew, if they were aware that Luca had had a brief relationship with Thea. He thought that they probably did know, and this was their subtle way of letting him know that they knew all about it.

"Seneca, you are not suggesting leniency for the attempted murder of one of our finest elite Militibus commanders?" Zeno asked him and then chuckled hard as he shook his head in disbelief.

"Of course not, Zeno" Seneca argued. "I'm suggesting talking down a situation before it gets to a position where Lucian was injured." Zeno was still shaking his head and laughing gaily now.

"He could have been killed, Seneca," Aristotle said gravely. "Are you suggesting that Lucian didn't do enough to prevent it?"

"I never said that Ari." Senecca protested vehemently. "I merely asked if there was a better way, through dialogue, perhaps."

"This outdated philosophy is what destroyed the Fourth and led to our demise, Sen." Zeno said in a jovial tone, and the two Elders looked at him.

"Are you able to add to the report compiled by the Jarl?" Aristotle asked as he quickly changed the subject, which was careering to a heated debate between Zeno and Seneca now. Luca looked at the three Elders seated behind the large table. They seemed nervous, unsure. Old.

"No, whatever the Jarl has written, is very comprehensive and precise as to what we investigated and concluded." Luca said in a serious tone. He had no idea what the Jarl had written and whatever it was, Luca would have to take it on the chin. He endangered himself and his men by insisting Peo free Thea. Luca hadn't been thinking straight.

"You have complete faith in the Tempus Militibus that you command, Lucian?" Aristotle asked him with a hint of a smile, and with a slightly incredulous tone. Luca shifted in his chair. Of course, he had every faith in his men. Why wouldn't he?

"Of course, Sir." Luca said confidently but he wondered exactly what Lanny had written.

"You haven't read the report from the Jarl," Seneca said and looked at him. "Yet, you are willing to accept it." Luca nodded. Whatever Lanny wrote in his final report on the navar case, and how Luca handled it. Luca had to accept it. He had compromised all of them by not sending Thea to the Eight when Peo wanted to. Luca knew that he had been snappy with the Jarl when he suggested keeping her restrained, and for no reason other than he was surprised and angry that Thea was the navar's daughter. If the Jarl decided to include Luca's short temper and his dismissal of the Militibus regarding the conversation he had had with the navar and the subsequent argument with Thea, then Luca had no choice but to take his reprimand. Regardless of the consequences.

"The Viking Jarl praises you, your leadership, your command and recommends you receive our highest honour for bravery." Aristotle said and looked at his two council Elders sitting either side of him. Luca stared at them in amazement, he was shocked that Lanny would even suggest that. "We have spoken with the Militibus individually and each of them agree with the Jarl's recommendation." Luca was speechless by this revelation. "We also agree, Lucian." Aristotle informed him with a hint of a smile.

"I couldn't have done it without my Militibus officers." Luca said proudly. "My men are exceptional warriors, and

I am honoured to have them by my side." Luca stood up, paused for a moment and then walked to the door. He turned around and asked. "What news is there of Demis?"

Aristotle cleared his throat and closed the report on his desk and looked at Luca.

"In light of what he has done, using the Tempus Militibus for his own private investigation, and endangering one of its officers." He hesitated for a moment and glanced now at Senecca and then at Zeno. "It was decided amongst the Elders. To...We have given Demis, limited authority whereby he will be unable to cause any more trouble." He said. "For now, at least, he is on a probationary period until his hearing of competency, in twelve weeks." Luca opened the door and left.

Outside the building, Luca could breathe again. The air in the chambers had been stifling. He thought for the briefest of moments that he was going to be reprimanded for endangerment of his men through his carelessness. He deserved nothing less.

As he glanced around the street, Luca thought about the Sixth. It was a paradoxical mystery to him. In its created perfection, the Sixth was flawed, and it was in that fault of its existence that its perfection shone through.

Luca made his way along the pavement, back to his townhouse. He would return to the Fourth in the morning.

Chapter 53

The crisp air though not chilled had the effect of making Luca shiver slightly as he pulled up the collar of his vintage black Hugo Boss trench coat around his neck. He held in his left hand a bunch of cream and light pink oleander flowers wrapped in a paper wrapping.

He walked briskly along the gravel path, with an air of a man who had something important to do. With a vigilant eye he observed his surroundings. Luca was alone.

He had claimed the old janitor's body from the city morgue, so he wouldn't be placed in a pauper's grave, and he had paid for the brief service. Luca felt that it was only a small thing, and it was all that he could do because he had failed in saving the old man from the navar.

The small white marble plaque had only a few words written on it in a calligraphy script:

'Frankie, a man who lived for the theatre. Forever Missed by his friend, LM.'

Luca bent down on his left knee and placed the bouquet of oleander flowers onto the pavement under the dedicative plaque near the theatre, a place where the old man had lived for. He put his hand on the smooth marble and gave a quick smile.

"Rest easy, my friend." Luca stood up and glanced once more at the flowers on the ground and then he turned and began to walk back along the path to where he had parked his car across the street. He got in and for a moment he looked around, but he didn't take in his surroundings.

Then he started the car and pressed play on the stereo and the strains of Frederic's nocturne opus 9 filled the car as Luca drove away.

Chapter 54

Luca ran down the steps into the bar and then walked purposefully over to the booth that his three friends were sitting at. They cheered when they saw him.

"So, when I'm away all that the Tempus Militibus do is hang out in bars." He said teasingly. He held out his hand to each of them. "It's what I would do too." Luca chuckled as he looked at them.

"When did you get back?" Bjorn asked him as he pushed a glass of fine Midleton whiskey toward him. Luca picked it up and took a long sip from the glass and then put it down on the table and sat down. He let out an appreciative sigh.

"Yesterday." Luca said. "I had some paperwork to catch up on in my office."

"Workaholic." Peo jibed jovially as he slapped him on the back. "We kept things ticking over while you were on your extended vacation. We have discussed it and we demand a raise." Luca laughed heartily and then looked across at Lanny.

"Aristoteles sends his regards to you, Jarl." Luca said and grinned as Lanny picked up his glass and took a sip.

"I'm sure he does. Miserable old cad." Lanny joked as he flashed Luca a warm smile. "Did you read the report?" Luca's expression was taut and then he grinned and reached for the glass again and looked at his friend with a serious expression. Lanny looked at him intently and continued. "I tried to be as detailed as you would have been, General."

"You really think I deserve the honour for bravery?" Luca asked him in a serious tone now. Bjorn and Peo looked at Lanny. "I am flattered that you believe that, Lanny, but I am no hero."

"Yes, I do believe you deserve it, General." Lanny replied with an equally intense expression now too. "To remain as reticent and alone with the old bitch like you did, either you were brave or foolish." Lanny grinned at him now. "I know what we all think, but that's up to you to decipher." They raised their glasses. "Fremitus."

"Fremitus." Luca said and grinned at them. "Thank you, all of you. I am sorry for being a dickhead that night."

Bjorn groaned loudly and then they all turned to see the source of his annoyance. Demis was walking toward them.

"What has the old weasel done now?" Lanny asked in a low tone as the old academic waved and sat down at the table beside Bjorn. "Demis, tell us this is a pleasure trip and not something that you have messed up."

"Very funny Jarl," Demis retorted, but he wore a smile and turned to Luca. "Welcome back Lucian, it's good to see you looking so well."

"Thank you, Demis." Luca said with a grin. "What do we owe the pleasure of this visit? It's not a new case, is it?" There was silence at the booth for a moment as the philosopher cleared his throat and then he looked at all of them briefly.

"Have you ever heard of the Belial?" They all looked at him blankly. He smirked as he looked at them. "Well, it's the transcript from the trial of the Devil when he sued Jesus Christ for trespass into Hell?" Demis asked in a deadpan voice now, and they all just continued to look at him. "No? Well, the Latin version has been stolen, and it seems to have made its way here to LA. I need it as it contains a code to lock away a very dangerous dreg in the Tenth for good." The Militibus groaned loudly as Demis helped himself to a glass of fine whiskey and he took a sip. "It's nice to see that I can still make the Tempus Militibus speechless. Iubentium." He raised his glass and took another sip as the vampires just stared at him with frustrated expressions.

The End

Acknowledgements

[i] Excerpts from Medea and other plays by Euripides, & Davie. J (1996) Penguin Classics, Penguin books.

Don't miss out!

Visit the website below and you can sign up to receive emails whenever A D McCabe publishes a new book. There's no charge and no obligation.

https://books2read.com/r/B-A-SEYLB-ORBIF

Connecting independent readers to independent writers.

About the Author

A D McCabe is an Irish fantasy writer specializing in dark, atmospheric storytelling infused with ancient history, gothic themes, and Viking undertones. She is the author of the *Tempus Militibus* series, a gripping blend of supernatural intrigue, deadly secrets, and the weight of history on immortal souls.

A lifelong adventurer and observer, Anna finds inspiration in shadowed alleyways, old bookshops, and the forgotten whispers of the past. Her writing reflects a deep fascination with lost civilizations, the tension between duty and desire, and characters who walk the fine line between darkness and redemption.

When she's not crafting intricate narratives, Anna enjoys gothic rock, a glass of Pinot Grigio, and exploring the world—always with a notebook in hand, ready to capture the next tale waiting in the shadows.

www.ingramcontent.com/pod-product-compliance
Ingram Content Group UK Ltd.
Pitfield, Milton Keynes, MK11 3LW, UK
UKHW020951280325
456847UK00006B/708

9 798230 772774